The Storm Knight I:
Dark Skies

by Zachary Watson

For more information, address: z.watson.author@gmail.com.

Edited by Dana Morck, John Watson, Jordan Perona, & Catherine Hariton

ISBN 979-8-9860285-3-8 (Kindle ebook)
ISBN 979-8-9860285-4-5 (Paperback)

For my family, friends, and everyone who told me I could do this.

Semper Victoria

Other Stories by Zach Watson

The Lost Knight Series
Awakening
Fealty
Ronin
Huntsman
Vengeance
Einherjar

The Storm Knight Series
Dark Skies

Warblades of Saerda Novellas
The Amethyst Blade

Glossary of Terms

Caranat; Literally meaning 'The Language', Caranat is the primary spoken word of the Trahcon people and the Empire in particular.

Humanity; The newest addition to the Empire after Earth was conquered roughly a century in the past. Not particularly well regarded by most others, they are increasingly being forced off of Earth and scattered across various colonial regions. An Imperial Human's term of conscription begins at the age of 15 Imperial (roughly 17 Terran), and lasts until they're 27 (roughly 30 Terran).

Index; The record of an Imperial Citizen's life, used to determine both military promotions as well as to evaluate their progress through the technocratic civilian government.

Delne'lir / Pack of Notables; A uniquely Imperial concept, a Pack of Notables can be anything from a robotics club, to a design bureau, to a multi-world corporation. Each has a very specific focus, and will recruit those whose talent and interests align with that focus.

Naule; A four armed, simian species counted as among the five humanoid races. Universally covered by long strands of hair, their small interstellar nations were overwhelmed and conquered by the Empire several centuries ago.

Sorcery; A range of telekinetic and pyrokinetic abilities focused on manipulating the same sub-reality that allows for FTL travel. Organized as 'spells', the difficulties in learning the more complicated spells ensures few Trahcon learn more than basics in the modern era.

Strike-Wave; The most popular sport in the Empire, featuring two teams of varying size playing on an oval pitch, a single large ball, and a goal at either end.

Trahcon; The founding species of the Empire, and the only Humanoid species naturally capable of manipulating energy without cybernetic enhancement. On average shorter than Humans, they have uniformly gray skin but extremely bright eyes. Unique in possessing a nearly three to one gender imbalance between females to males, and for having a nearly five century long lifespan.

Prologue

Date: Day 18, Month 2, 2156 Imperial
Location: Alzuc, Altair Sector, Empire of the Homeworld

I was pretty terrible at most positions in Strike-Wave. Sure, I was fast enough to be a good sail-runner... but that didn't mean anything when I couldn't interrupt passes. Or make sure my own were fast enough to be accurate.

That tended to happen when you were a useless alien without even basic sorcery.

Goalie though?

Leaping to my right, I snagged the ball before it got anywhere near the net, laughing wildly as I did. "Too slow Ghar!"

"Damned long armed Human!" Ghar laughed as he fell back down the pitch, the rest of the attacking team snapping their heads around as I threw the ball to Yora.

My favorite sister gave me a wild grin, tarah quivering before she raced up field to lead the counter-attack. The rest of the team rolled up in her wake as we tried to break the even score against our rivals.

An introspective girl would see some kind of symbolism in that. Her pack going on ahead of her, leaving her to guard the rear while they did all of the real work.

Me?

I cheered with the rest when Hili made a diving throw that got through, everyone whooping in joy.

"Seven to six!" Yora called mockingly as our pack fell back into a defensive line. "A minute and a half left! Is pack Reath actually going to start trying now?"

Said Pack let out a ragged war cry as they charged forwards, the ball hurtling up and down their line as all fifteen of them came up. Their crashers slammed into ours to create a scrum, all of the sail-runners sweeping to the right.

"Cover!" Hili shouted. "Cover!"

Licking my lips, I moved to the right post just as the ball shot out of the pile. The strong smell of sorcery filled the air as both groups of sail-runners tried to accelerate it... and for once they came out ahead.

Ghar, Pack Reath's best shooter, seized it on the move as he sprinted around our runners. Yora and our other two defenders raced to intercept, locking their arms at full extension to take away as much of the field as they could.

His tarah twitched madly, warning me to what he was up to a single breath before he threw himself forwards. In the instant before he collided with Yora he threw a pass across the field, relying on the collision to stop my packmates from intercepting it.

Little Toln'reath, the tiniest member of either pack, caught the pass in a spinning motion that let him hurl a one-timer at the far post.

Hitting the ground as I dove hurt, a lot, especially on my chest.

But the screaming cheers of my packmates when I came up with the ball in my hands made it worth it. I could barely hear the buzzer when it clanged that time was up, especially when at least five of them all jumped onto me at the same time.

"We won!" Yora screamed into my ear. "We made the Colonial Final, Ashe!"

"We won!" I shouted back, hugging her with one arm and Fea with my other. "Three goals for Fea!"

"Twelve saves for Ashe!" Fea got up on his toes to kiss me on the cheek, both of his tarah quivering madly in excitement. "That's a new record for both of us!"

We celebrated, hollered, and generally bounced up and down for a few more minutes before Yora started ushering us over to embrace our opponents.

"You're too long." Toln complained as he hugged me, his face buried in my stomach. "Stupid Humans, growing up faster than us."

I forced myself to laugh as I hugged him back. His words made it so easy to remember that even the tallest girl in either pack didn't come up to my shoulders. "You can always show me up in the swimming races next week."

"I will!"

Most of the ending ceremony went like that. Some complained that Pack Lori had a Human and meant it bitterly, leaving me to say nothing. Others, like Toln, complained in a teasing way. Ghar laughed it off the loudest, but then he always took defeat well.

"Next year we get to start cross-pack teams." Ghar'reath told me as both groups started to leave the pitch, "You're going to win the goalie position without any trouble for sure."

"I hope so." I replied. "After how much practice I put in."

He grinned and turned to Yora. "She's still making you get up early to help her with that?"

My sister let out a theatrical groan, "Before dawn every day. I keep telling her to relax about it, but you know how she is."

I felt my face heating up. "I'm not that bad!"

They both laughed at me, Ghar stretching up to pat me on the head. "It's all right, Ashe. Your fur is growing back by the way."

"Ugh." I quickly reached up to check, and sure enough I felt prickly stubble along my scalp. "Not again. Yora, why didn't you say something?"

"Because Teacher Jorl found the shaver that we stole on our last trip to the city?" She rolled a shoulder. "She says Humans are furry, and that you have to accept that."

I scowled as we entered the grassy field between the Strike-Wave pitch and the school complex. "I don't *have* to accept anything. I look stupid enough without adding fur to it."

Ghar hummed. "Your little ear-things are pretty ridiculous. Like someone cut off your tarah when you were a baby, but left just enough for you to hear with."

"Ghar!" Yora hissed as I hunched in a bit, fighting the urge to cover the sides of my head. "Fucking rude!"

"What? Honesty is important." He replied defensively. "I like her skin color at least. It's very... uh, brown?"

My sister groaned. "Useless. All of you Reath's are useless."

The young man shrugged before swerving off to the right, his packmates following as they headed for their dorm. That left the rest of mine to swarm up around us, Hili taking my hand with her own.

"He's an idiot." She said at once. "You're a perfect Human, and our packmate."

I smiled a little, "Thanks Hili."

She beamed up at me before skipping ahead to be the first back inside. The rest of us followed, already stripping off sweat soaked shirts and kicking off shoes. My own jersey was up and over my head as I crossed the doorway, which meant I had no idea why Yora had stopped until I ran into her.

"Sorry!" I apologized at once, struggling to get the dark clothing off. "Why did you-"

"Pack form up!" Hili's frantic shout cut me off.

My heart abruptly began a fast beat, my shirt being thrown aside with plenty of others as all sixteen of us frantically raced to form up in two ranks in the entry room.

My alien height worked out for me. Even from the back line I could see the reason for the panic; Teachers Jorl and Illith were both waiting for us, their golden uniforms a sharp contrast to the gray one worn by the woman standing between them.

"Oh no." The whisper came out before I could swallow it.

Just ahead of me, Yora raised her voice. "Lori, salute!"

All of us brought our right arms up, forearms steady while our fists clenched before our throats. Sixteen members of pack Lori spoke in unison, "Honored elders!"

Teacher Illith stepped forwards, crossing his arms high on his chest as he looked over us. "Calm the waves, children."

We all relaxed at once, clasping our arms behind our backs. Everyone but me lowered their tarah in submission, leaving me to duck my head a little. It was the closest I could come, and the teachers said it was how Humans should do it.

Our history instructor, and our pack's personal favorite educator, waited until we settled before speaking again. "Yora'lori. What were today's results?"

"Pack Lori was victorious by a score of seven to six." She replied at once. "Fea'lori scored three goals, bringing his season total to thirty one. Ashe'lori broke her own single-game save record once again, the new total is twelve."

Any other day I would have puffed up in pride... but that day I kept my eyes down.

"Well done, all of you." He sounded like he was smiling. "I expect tonight's celebration to be raucous, but please don't break any windows this time."

Nervous chuckles danced on the surface before being quickly swallowed.

"Do not allow us to interrupt. You're free to clean yourselves and enjoy the rest of your day off." I'd just started to gasp in relief before he hit me with the thunderbolt. "Ashe'lori? Please remain behind."

I bit my lip, hard, fighting against the urge to cry.

Some of my pack shifted their weight, but it was Yora who spoke for us, as always. "Respect, honored elders, but anything you have to say to our packmate is something to say to all of us."

That *did* make me start to tear up, especially when Hili and Reh broke their posture to take each of my hands in theirs.

I heard Illith let out a tired sigh ahead of us. "Please, children. Do not make this harder than it has to be. Your little trick of trying to change her date of birth was clever, but it is time. Yesterday was her fifteenth birthday. We allowed her to remain this extra day as a kindness for her situation."

Yora hissed. "No! She is our sister, we don't care that she's Human!"

The teacher's voice sharpened. "You may not care, but biology cannot be denied! By Imperial Law, on her fifteenth birthday she is a Huntress while you all remain children!"

"But-!"

"Children." The unknown officer cut her off, the woman's voice quiet yet firm. "I am not taking her away at this very moment. You will have some time to say your goodbyes, and she will be free to write and message you as often as she likes."

"...no." Yora whimpered. "Please. She's our sister."

"By blessed Ashahn." Teacher Jorl groaned. "They're too young for this."

"Yes, they are." The nameless woman agreed, "But what's done is done. Go, children. I will send your packmate to you shortly."

"But-"

Her voice sharpened, a strong scent of ozone making my nose scrunch. The effect on my packmates was more severe; they all winced, jerking backwards at the gathering power that everyone but me could hear. "That is an order, child."

They... left me. Slowly, reluctantly. Hili kept my hand in hers until distance forced her to let go. She started sobbing before she left the room, several others doing the same.

A few minutes later only Yora was left, her final defiance leaving her when the two teachers moved up to march her out.

And then I was alone, wearing nothing but sweaty shorts, while an Imperial Officer walked up to me.

"You knew this was coming, didn't you, huntress?"

I swallowed, keeping my eyes on my feet. "Yes, officer."

"I did mean what I said. I don't think I've ever seen a pack going so far as to try hacking the school database to change an age before. For children who shouldn't have even been taught such skills yet, it was quite impressive despite its amateur nature."

"...please don't punish them."

The woman laughed, a gray hand appearing as she reached out to cup my chin. A gentle push made me look up into teal eyes, making me see her smile. "Such loyalty is to be commended, Ashe'lori. I will personally flag your pack for honors."

I tried to speak, choked around the tears I felt running down my cheeks. "Do I have to go?"

Her smile faded quickly. "I am sorry, young one. I am sorry you are in this situation. You should have been placed in a birth-pack with others of your kind. The Empire... failed you in that. The reason I am here at all is because I am tasked with making sure that does not happen again."

"...that's..." I struggled, knowing what I was supposed to say. That what she was doing was good. That I was happy no one else would have to be cut off from their pack like I was.

But I couldn't.

"...it's not fair." I whimpered. "Please. They're my pack."

"I know." She sighed. "Cursed Kahsh. Ashe'lori, I am sorry, but physically you *are* a huntress. You're nearly fully grown, your medical records state you're sexually mature for your species, and you're already becoming more emotionally mature. None of your packmates will reach where you are for another twenty-five years."

I flinched, looking down once again.

"By then," She continued relentlessly, each word driving another strike into my heart. "You will be well into your Guide stage of life. The longer you stay with your birth-pack the harder it's going to be on you. You're going to want levels of maturity and relationships that they will not be able to provide."

I couldn't say anything. I could only feel more tears, feel my breathing start to hiccup.

"You have to be strong, huntress." Her hands grasped my biceps. "It hurts, I know. It is never easy to move on from your birth-pack, but the Empire provides for us all. The pain will heal, in time."

"I..." I choked, shook my head, and just... sobbed.

Those hands pulled me close as I cried, letting me bury my face in her uniformed shoulder.

"It's all right, huntress." She whispered. "I'll watch over your career. It will be all right."

I cried for an hour before she gently brought me to my packmates to say goodbye.

We all cried together then, huddled up in a great pile on our pack's bed.

My tears stained my shirt as I pulled it on.

My shaking hands didn't let me tie my shoes. Yora had to do it, fumbling through the process as she muttered ever more insane plans to try and keep me from leaving.

My arms embraced her one last time before I was led outside.

My feet carried me down the worn trail to the shuttle pad.

My eyes took in the sight of home one last time.

My heart broke as the door shut... and I was carried away to a new life.

Six Years Later

I

"Bay doors secure." The shuttle pilot's voice woke me from my doze, *"Atmosphere stabilized, and we're down. Welcome to Waystation Ah-One-Oh-Seven-Del."*

I was in the middle of yawning so I couldn't roll my eyes at the comment.

It wasn't like there was anyone else on board to hear him. Unless he was talking to the crates of preserved food that I was squeezed in between. Technically speaking I shouldn't have been aboard at all, but my last Dual Commander had been more than happy to get rid of me after I'd gotten my entire Half-Sword reprimanded.

Shoving me onto the first cargo transport headed this way was apparently better than having me linger around for another month.

"Not that my pack wanted me around anymore either." I muttered to myself as I unbuckled and stood up. My back ached from the uncomfortable chair, and I took a moment to stretch out. "Didn't even see me off."

The sound of the hatch sliding open drew my attention to the left, the young pilot poking his head out of the cockpit. "Still talking to yourself, savanna?"

"No one asked you to listen, shark." Finishing my stretch, I grabbed my bag and hauled it up over a shoulder. "Thanks for the ride. Chair could use some cushions though."

He gave me a boyish grin and slapped a nearby panel. The exit ramp promptly began to lower while a quiet chime rang somewhere, the humid air of the station rushing in to meet us.

"No problem. Was nice to have company on the run, and now I get to tell my pack a sad story when I get back home."

I sighed and turned away from him. "I must have been really drunk when you dragged me on board to have told you about what happened."

"Personally I was surprised you were able to walk, never mind complain about how none of them stood up for you."

"...yeah. Need anything before I sail out?"

"Nah, you're not really supposed to be here anyway. May your river be calm, Lori. Sounds like you need some easy days."

I did, and I prayed to the Aspects that I had some coming. "Enjoy your time in safe harbors, Mek."

Leaving him behind, I walked out of the shuttle and into the hangar proper. Cargo automatons were already waiting to take off the crates, their heavy legs letting them stomp around me as I weaved between them.

On the far side I found a bored Naule in the blue uniform of a fellow conscript waiting for me. The black-furred alien watched me approach, grunted, and handed over a data drive before ambling off on all six limbs without a word.

Rude.

Scowling a little at his back, I thumbed the little bit of plastic to boot it up. Its automated scanners picked up my rank badge's signal after a moment, then chirped once before a tiny speaker announced my orders.

"Rifle-Experienced Ashe'lori. Report to Half-Squad Vet for long term assignment. Unit is reserved in Consolidation Area Green. HSL Ruru'vet awaiting you."

Well, at least they were already here so I wouldn't have to find a cabin to bunk in.

Heading out through the same exit as the messenger, I didn't make it far before running into a security station. Another bored conscript, a Naulian woman this time, took my rank chit, scanned it, then waved me through the security door without looking up from the tablet in her lap.

On the other side...

Imperial Waystation Ah-107Del was about the same as every other one that I'd been through. Dull, unadorned, and useless for anything besides acting as a transfer point. The dour surroundings didn't improve my mood as I stepped out of the security station, shifting my bag to my other shoulder before lengthening my strides.

Compared to the bases in the core regions, this one was pretty empty. Just a handful of other transfers, the shades of blue, gray, and black on their uniforms varying depending on their branch and rank. All of them, regardless of species, looked as happy as I was to be here.

I was less than surprised at the glum looks and angled-down tarah. We were off of all the major trading routes. We weren't close to any other nation-states, or even the Airalon Wastes.

No... this was the backwater of backwaters.

The Titan's Colonial Zone.

We were jammed uncomfortably between the well populated Rimward Zone, and the pirate infested Stormshroud. No one sane wanted to get assigned here, which was why I wasn't surprised in the least that this was where I'd ended up.

Where else would they send a stupid Human on her sixth pack in five years?

Closing my eyes, I stepped off to the side and focused on my hearing. On the simple act of listening to the world around me. Officers muttering to one another behind me... complaining about the DataNet connection. Footfalls from boots striking the tiles as men and women moved through the halls. The steady hum of humidifiers and air conditioners.

I let out a final breath and mentally thanked Huvu for teaching me that little act of meditation.

"Should be with you." Another mutter came out as I started walking again, following the signs for the consolidation zones.

"Should be fighting pirates or seeing new worlds. Not stuck on another backwater assignment."

Not that the Empire had cared about my opinion. Well, the bureaucracy probably would have let me go off with my second pack, but *she* would never let that happen. Not with how much effort she had put in to try and make up for what had happened on my very first assignment.

I quickly pushed those thoughts aside. They wouldn't do me any good right now. I had to be focused and prepared to meet my latest squad.

You only had one chance to meet your new pack, and I'd already failed too many of those tests.

A few more minutes of walking brought me to a mess hall, which at least gave me a chance to help myself. While there wasn't anyone cooking in the cafeteria proper, there was someone managing the Waystation's store.

"Rifle." The Trahcon man greeted me, grinning a little as he crossed his arms. "First savanna I've seen through here in months. What are you looking for?"

"Ale, standard box. What do you have that's good?"

He hummed, left tarah rising and falling. "Not the best selection to be honest. You returning to a unit?"

I sighed. "Meeting a new one. Transferred after my last one... let's just say it didn't work out."

"Ah." He got some honor for looking sympathetic rather than judgmental, and got even more for not asking about it. For a Trahcon that was nearly impossible levels of self-control.

"I've got some Yarabu if that's in your price range."

In response I reached up and pulled my rank insignia off, holding it out. "So long as it's their dark."

He shuddered theatrically before taking it. "Of course it's the dark. It's not like we're in the territories where they actually like that pale crap."

The banter made me smile, and helped me relax a little. A quick tap of the small insignia on his console deducted the cost, and then it was back in my hand while he headed back to grab my purchase.

"Here you go." Glass rattled against the plastic box as he settled it. "Good luck."

Getting everything settled in my arms, I thanked him before getting going again.

Walking down more mostly empty hallways let me get to yet another one. The only difference was that it went past 'mostly empty' all the way to 'had only one other person' in it.

Considering that the Trahcon woman was standing right outside of a green-tinged door, it was easy to assume she was a member of my new squad.

From the way she drew herself up on seeing me, letting me see the silver markings on her blue uniform, she was my new Half-Sword Leader. A good one too, from the number of merit honors sewn into both shoulders of her uniform.

Ruru'vet was average height for a Trahcon woman, an inch or two shorter than me. She had a swirling tattoo on the left side of her jaw, colored the same blue as her eyes, and it drew attention to the strength of her gaze.

"So, you're our new savanna." She had a lilting Icar accent that made her sound more attractive than her rather plain features would have suggested. "What's that in your arms?"

"Half-Sword Vet." My arms were full, which stopped me from saluting, but I bowed my head. "Yarabu Dark. A gift for my new pack. I'd have brought more, but we didn't stop anywhere for me to buy proper gifts."

Her tarah lifted in genuine surprise. "...oh."

I felt a weak smile tug at my lips. "Are you out here to put the ignorant alien in her place before she meets the rest of the pack?"

"...maybe." She admitted with an almost wry grin of her own. "Your accent. Altair?"

"One of the colonies. Icar for you?"

"Raised on the world of thunder itself." Vet pursed her gray lips, "I didn't know there were any Human colonies in that sector."

"There aren't. I was raised in a traditional birthing facility."

That earned me a slow blink. "Seriously? How did that happen?"

The old story wasn't one of my favorites, but it was one I'd gotten used to telling. "Bureaucratic error according to the Agent who showed up to conscript me when I aged out of childhood. Someone realized they miscounted the number of people aboard during an emigration. About a dozen Humans got dropped off on the first planet they passed, but I was the only infant."

"Idiots."

"They weren't blessed by Ashahn, that's for sure." I agreed tiredly.

Vet hummed and let her tarah rise and fall. She clearly knew there was a lot more to the story, but evidently decided to leave it there for now. "Well, you're more polite than your Index makes you sound at least. I trust you learned your lesson there?"

My weak smile died. "...if you mean my last assignment, then it depends on what you think the lesson was. If you mean my *other* assignments, I'm pretty sure my Index makes it clear that none of those were my fault."

"It does." Vet tipped her head. "Your first and fourth especially. Aspects know you get some sympathy from me for what happened both of those times, but that doesn't mean I'm going to let you earn my pack a black mark. Understood?"

There was only one response I could give to that. "Understood."

She grunted, flexed her tarah one more time, then motioned towards the door. "As much as I'd like to keep getting to know you, we've got a shuttle to catch. Let's get you inside, introduced, and get your gift delivered before we leave."

"That sounds grand." I shifted the weight in my hands a bit. "May I ask for informality in names?"

"Of course." Another wry smile came and went, "Be rough if we didn't, since we're all from the same birth-pack. Come on then, everyone's been curious since we learned that you were being transferred to us. About half the pack is present right now, everyone else is helping load the ship."

That was good. It was easier to make a good impression on fewer people.

I gave her another nod, and followed her into the staging area when she strode in.

It wasn't a particularly large room, probably sized to fit a full Sword Unit, which meant a Half-Sword would have plenty of space to stretch out in. With only half of even that team present the space felt particularly empty

Besides Ruru, there were three others. Like me they were all in the uniforms of Huntresses and Hunters, the dark blue denoting our status as youthful conscripts. Unlike me most of them had more than a few merits sewn into their shoulders, even if none had quite as many as their leader.

Closest to the door were a pair of men playing a card game on the floor. Both were fairly handsome; slender, with long tarah, and cunning features.

"Hey, our new alien showed up." One of them noted, perking up considerably when he saw what I was carrying. "And she brought ale! I think I'm already falling for her!"

"Shut up, Moriv." Ruru replied. "Ashe? Don't let him take more than one bottle, he's got a problem holding his liquor. The chatty little boy he's stealing money from is Jal."

I gave them my best smile, and shifted the case to offer its contents to them. "It's good to meet you both."

Moriv grinned and bounced up to his feet, drawing a protest from his opponent when he kicked some of the cards around. "You were losing anyway, Jal! Shut up and let me thank the lovely woman who brought us drinks."

A hand reached out to smack his before he could grab a bottle. Ruru followed that up by steering me away to where a woman was double-checking that she had packed her bag. "For that you get yours last. And clean those cards up! We're leaving soon."

He rolled his eyes but lowered his tarah in submission, while the other man chuckled. "Hey, Ashe'lori. Good to meet you."

"And you as well." I replied over my shoulder, trying not to show how happy I was that this was going so well.

Well, it was going well in comparison to my last few introductions. No one was exactly rushing to embrace me or offering to help with what I was carrying, but they were curious and polite instead of cold and dismissive.

It wasn't enough to give me hope, but I'd take it over the alternative.

Ruru kept up her gentle pushing until we reached the only other person present. She was by far the shortest girl I'd seen in a while, not much taller than either of the boys, and her thanks for the ale was an almost embarrassed mutter.

"This is Tolu, our poor little greenfish." Ruru sighed once Tolu had gone back to packing her own bag. "Always hiding in the back. She was really hoping you'd be shorter than she is. Something about Human women being short made her hopeful."

"...most kind of are. Well, at least the few I've met." I admitted, "I'm on the tall side."

A pouting whine from behind us was covered by Ruru snorting. "Heh. Poor girl will find someone she can look down on eventually. Let's get the boys their beer, then we've got to get moving to make our ship."

Seeing a chance to learn something, I quickly spoke up. "My transfer orders didn't say what our assignment was. Where are we going?"

Her expression flattened at once in distaste. "Oshflara."

I blinked. "Never heard of it."

Jal chuckled as he walked over to join us, evidently leaving Moriv to finish cleaning up their mess. "Neither had we. One of the new emigration colonies."

My heart plummeted into the depths of my soul. "...what?"

"Just a few centuries old." He went on, oblivious. "Colonists from Shaidan and Earth both, along with overflow from the Abantia sector. Most of the Humans only came in over the last ten years."

No. Not again.

Ruru took over the narrative. "We're just there to reinforce the standard garrison, assigned to the logistics and support operations. If we're lucky we might get some wildlife patrols or exploration work before they rotate us out again."

Behind us came a groan from Moriv. "It's buried deep in the colonial zone. No chance of pirates or anything fun happening."

"That's no excuse to slack off." Ruru countered. "We've got more than enough merits for a better assignment. If we're on our best behavior, earn a few more marks, we can get transferred to a better theater."

Jal grinned. "Yes *eldest*."

Their banter went on like that as I got lost in my own seas.

An emigre colony. Of the hundreds of colonies within the Empire, the vast majority of which were *not* attempts to make the various species coexist... we'd drawn garrison duty on one.

I trailed behind the others when it came to leave. I should have been trying to integrate. Trying to figure out what my place among them would be, make sure my initial good impression lasted.

But instead... all I could do was dread being surrounded by my own species once again.

II

When you got bounced around between packs as often as I had, you pick up things that I doubted many others in the Empire knew.

For starters; the easiest time to sneak away on your own was in those first couple of days. There was a small window where they hadn't gotten used to having you around yet, where old routines made it easy for everyone to miss that you weren't present.

How long that window lasted depended on how much you screwed up your first impression. For once I thought I'd managed to avoid that, so my window was going to be narrow.

That was fine. It wouldn't take me long to learn more than I should about where we were all going

I followed Ruru at a distance through the ship's dim corridors, doing my best to look casual. Other packs were still getting settled into their cabins all through the ship. That gave me plenty of people to look at, smile at, and occasionally talk to as I stalked my new leader.

Heh. Listen to me. 'Stalking'.

It was hardly some great feat of espionage. She walked the length of the deck we were on, met up with a man I assumed to be our Sword Leader, and then went down one level. Then the two of them walked half the length of that particular deck before ducking into a briefing room.

Considering that the ship had all of three levels that we mere passengers had access to, I wasn't sure I could have lost her if I'd tried.

The only difficult moment was when I realized that everyone at or above the rank of Half-Sword in the entire formation was being called in for the briefing. I had to duck into a restroom to try and remain inconspicuous.

For once luck was with me, and no one came in on their way to the meeting.

Once the last of the footsteps had gone past, I waited an extra couple of minutes before slipping back into the corridor.

After that it was just a matter of lurking outside of the open hatchway and listening.

"...what in the Aspect's holy names is this about?" A woman was complaining. "No one here is under eighty, and we've all got at least ten merits. What the fuck are we doing being assigned to a place like Oshflara?"

A man with a heavy homeworld drawl replied, "Not like there's a war on right now."

Ruru spoke up at that, "No, but we could be in the Shaidan sector hunting down separatists. Or maybe assigned to Trinity to hunt pirates in the Reaches."

"Ha!" Another woman snorted. "I don't think any of us are that lucky."

"Tell me about it." My Half-Sword complained. "I was really hopeful after we finally got off Icar, but honestly I'd rather go back."

"At least you've got a Human in your unit now." A second man with an Icar accent offered. "Maybe she'll be able to help you find places to unwind after hours."

"Doubt it. She was raised on Altair, in a standard birth-pack. Don't think she even speaks any of the Human tongues."

There was a baffled pause before he asked, "What's that story then?"

I was more than happy to hear the hour's chime go off, followed at once by a man speaking. "Attention for the Arsenal Commander."

More than thirty pairs of boots stamped on the decking; it was easy to imagine everyone rising and saluting our commanding officer.

"Calm the waves." A woman whose authoritative tones betrayed her age as a Guide spoke in the silence that followed. "That's enough gossip for now. Arah? Is everyone of the Arsenal Formation present?"

The man who'd called attention replied, "Yes, Arsenal Commander."

I swallowed nervously and took a cautious step back from the doorway. Listening in on the various Sword Leaders gossiping was one thing. Practically expected if you happened to be bored with no duties assigned.

Spying on the entire Arsenal's leader while she gave a briefing was treading in dangerous waters.

"Good." My feet stopped when she resumed, curiosity keeping me there. "I'm not going to disagree with the complaints, I sympathize with all of you. I'd rather be leading a combat command as well. However, that does not change our orders, and I don't want the complaints to turn into something worse among this formation. Understood?"

A unified rumble came back, "Yes, Arsenal Commander."

"Good." She repeated. "Then I will expect to hear nothing more on the subject. Arah, give them the details of our assignment."

Arah, who must have been the Arsenal Second, duly began speaking once again. "Right. This is a standard four year rotation on garrison duty, we'll be attached to a newly formed Squall Formation designated the 711th Colonial. Keep the groaning to a minimum, but we'll be starting the cycle on Del."

Sure enough a chorus of groans came out at once; and I felt my own throat vibrate in quiet agreement.

Cycle Del meant we'd be spending our entire first year on logistical support duty... everyone's least favorite stage of a deployment.

"Quiet." The Second ordered. "That means we get to shift over to Cycle Ah in our second year. Oshflara has very low exploration and mapping rates, so that's something for you and your troops to look forwards to. There's even rumors of smuggling activity, so keep that goal in focus."

That made me perk up a little. Exploring the wilderness looking for smugglers and criminals sounded a whole lot better than supervising loading automatons.

"Now, the local situation. Population is just a few million, a third of which is concentrated in the primary city." I leaned in a bit, listening intently. "Roughly an even split between Trahcon, Naulians, and Humans. Since most of the savannas are forced emigre's, tensions are relatively high. Despite the efforts of the architectural tribunals there's definitive enclaves that have been carved out by the aliens."

I was so focused on what he was saying I didn't hear the footsteps behind me. At least until a hand gently tapped my shoulder.

I had enough self control not to yelp, but I did jump a little.

"Easy." Hands quickly grabbed my arms, the woman's voice low and quiet as she pulled me back. "Quietly now, Rifle. Come on."

A glance over my shoulder made my stomach drop down to my toes. Her black naval uniform had the rank insignia of a Deck Commander, which on a little transport like this probably meant she was...

She grinned at my expression, bright green eyes almost gleaming. "Yes, I'm the Captain. No, I'm not going to get you in trouble with the other grounders. You're not the first Huntress I've caught trying to spy on the officers, and you won't be the last."

"I..."

A finger tapped me on the chin, shutting me up before I could try to give an excuse. "Go on, back to your cabin now."

I swallowed nervously, gave her a shaky salute, and then scampered with whatever dignity I could scrounge up. I made it to the lifts before risking a glance back, just in time to see the ship's captain stride in to the briefing room and close it behind her.

"Stupid." The mutter came out as I jabbed a thumb onto the control panel. "Stupid, stupid, stupid. You stupid idiot savanna."

I was still berating myself by the time I got back to our cabin. Everyone's heads swung around when I walked in, several conversations stopping... which made me feel all kinds of awkward on top of already feeling stupid.

"Hey there." Fyth, at least, perked up a little. She was a well muscled but otherwise plain woman who served as the pack's primary driver, and she'd seemed the most excited to meet me. "Where did you get off to?"

"Exploring." I replied as I stepped over her legs so I could collapse onto the bed that took up most of the limited space. I briefly debated not telling them before deciding to keep up with my policy of making a good first impression.

"I found the briefing room."

That got everyone's attention. I'd hardly collapsed face-first into blue blankets before hands were pulling me over, and I found myself with my head in Hely's muscled lap.

I'd met Hely when we'd arrived on board. She was by far the tallest of the pack, she had at least three inches on me, and was the most heavily tattooed with lightning marks all along her jawline.

"What did you hear?" Strong fingers settled on top of my head, running over the stubble that was my head-fur. "Huh. This is kind of prickly. Isn't it supposed to be soft?"

"Only when it's long, and stop playing with it." I muttered before raising my voice. "Not much. Everyone above us is just as upset as we are about the assignment. And there's worse news."

There was a groan from Jal on the floor. "Please tell me we aren't on Del duty."

"Yup."

More groans from everyone else, Moriv's being the loudest. "Damn. We just finished a Del cycle. Not bloody fair that we're going to be stuck on another one already."

I tried to be positive. "Good news is that we're on Ah cycle right after, and the colony's mostly unexplored. The Arsenal Second said there might be smuggling activity too."

Hely perked up even as she shifted her hands to my shoulders, gently rubbing them. "That's something to look forward to. So long as whoever is already on that cycle doesn't find them first. Did you hear who's already on assignment there?"

"No." I closed my eyes and let myself enjoy the massage. "The ship's captain caught me before they really got into any more. Got distracted listening and didn't hear her coming."

"Oh no." The bed shifted, Tolu's quieter voice coming in from the left.

"You're not getting a reprimand, are you? That'd definitely be some kind of record. The bad kind, I mean."

"She said I'm not the first one she's caught spying, and that she wouldn't." I bit my lip without opening my eyes. "I hope she wasn't just saying that. If I do get us a demerit then I'm sorry."

"Bah." That came from Dahj; from our short introduction she'd clearly come across as Ruru's primary partner. She was also utterly gorgeous, and I'd enjoyed the hug she'd given me as a greeting. "Any one of us would have done the same thing if we'd found the officers. Or did you break open the door or something?"

I huffed. "I like exploring and I'm curious, not stupid. They left it open. Probably waiting for the Captain to show up."

Even with my eyes closed I could feel everyone else relaxing a little. Which was good, but also... also meant that most of them had seriously thought I was capable of doing that.

Wherever I went, my species' reputation struck the shores ahead of me.

"That was all I really heard." I finished. "Species tensions are supposed to be high, but that's pretty normal for an emigration colony. Probably not much fun to be had off base."

Dahj spoke up again, "Really? They're that bad?"

"We've never been to one." Hely supplied. "You sound like you have."

"Twice." Deeply unpleasant memories made me swallow, pushing them back down before I could go on. "They were... rough. I'm not looking forward to another one."

The legs I was resting my head on shifted a little. "Rough because you're raised by us, or just rough in general?"

"Both. If you were hoping I'd be good at finding bars in Human neighborhoods, I'm going to be disappointing."

Hely chuckled. "Only to Moriv."

"Hey!"

Muffled laughter came from Jal. "She's not wrong and you know it."

"Still rude." The other man countered. "Now get your damned deck back out so I can win back what you stole from me this morning."

"Yeah yeah. Any of you girls want to join us?"

Everyone but, Hely, Tolu, and I were interested. I didn't have anything against card games, they were a good way to pass the time, but I just wasn't in the mood.

I'd finally, *finally*, joined a pack where I wasn't immediately ostracized, hated, or ignored. And what had I done? Gotten caught by a high ranking naval officer spying on an officer's briefing.

My morose thoughts were broken when my wrist-comp let out a quiet chime that promised to... well, not help my mood at all.

"Who's that from?" Hely asked, her tarah perked up in interest when I opened my eyes.

I sighed and brought my right arm up, uniform sleeve sliding down a bit to reveal the mesh device wrapped around my forearm. "My sister, Yora'lori."

"Blood or birth-pack?"

"Birth-pack. If I have blood siblings I've got no idea where they are." And they'd probably want nothing to do with me, based on how my interactions with other Humans had gone.

Tolu leaned in from where she was sitting next to me, her quiet voice curious. "You don't look as excited as someone should be."

Another one of my favorite conversations, one I'd also had too many times. "I'm twenty one years old."

She blinked politely. "...so?"

Hely let out a long groan. "Ashahn's blood. They're still kids. That's got to be awkward."

"You have no idea." I hesitated, then flexed my middle and pointing fingers to bring up the new message. The tiny holoprojector promptly displayed it above my wrist, letting us all read the small words.

Ashe,

Another new pack? Is that normal? It seems like you've been in a lot, but I hope they're much nicer than the last group! Send us pictures when you get to another planet so we can all see it! I'm always very jealous that you get to see so many worlds already.

Anyway, Geli is still playing goalie for us, but she's not as good as you. I keep trying to get her to practice every morning like you used to, but she's just too lazy. It's so annoying! We should have won the colonial cup last year if she just tried harder! Could you message her for me and ask her to take it more seriously?

It went on like that for a while longer. Yora complaining some more about the other players, then about classes, and finally her annoyance that her second growth spurt hadn't started yet.

"That's..." To her credit, Hely at least sounded like she tried to think of something to say before giving up. "Definitely a kid's letter."

"This is one of the better ones." I closed it with another gesture. I'd reply later. "The one I got after I tried to tell her about my first assignment was probably the worst, but there've been other ones that... didn't make me feel very good."

Tolu hesitated, then scooted down so she could sprawl out beside me, pressing up against my side. "Tell us about it?"

Hely nodded above me. "You should. I know you're new, but we're supposed to be packmates now. Maybe we can help."

I let out a long breath and let myself be cuddled. "It's not a fun story."

"All the more reason to tell us." Hely replied reasonably. "We can split the waters. I've got plenty of stories to tell too, not all of them are all that great."

"I..." My voice hitched. The memories of the first time I'd been put into a new unit. The first time I'd met other Humans... nothing about that experience had been pleasant. It had come perilously close to being a whole lot worse than that.

"Not... not yet. Maybe later."

Hely pouted, but Tolu pulled me even closer before yawning. "Later is fine. Tell us a good story instead."

Taking in a long breath, I slowly let it out. "My second pack was a Lost Hunter group. People who lost their packs in the Contested Zone. I spent nearly two years with them."

"That sounds fun." Tolu yawned, tucking herself in closer to me. "Tell us about them."

And so I did, losing myself in better memories until it came time for us to sleep.

III

Oshflara was prettier than some of the other worlds I'd been to. The colonial capital was sensibly built around a broad river, and surrounded by the green and golden hues of farm estates.

Even the city itself managed to look appealing despite being built mostly out of prefabricated structures. Everything was laid out in neat, orderly rows, and the dull buildings had all been dressed up as only the Trahcon seemed to know how. Beautiful art covered walls, gardens filled windows, and cloth awnings stretched out to cool the streets.

It was almost homey... and it made it easy to tell which sections were mostly inhabited by my fellow aliens.

Not that we really got to explore in those first couple of weeks. We were too busy with our actual jobs. For Cycle Del that meant logistical support of the general garrison... which was about as much fun as it sounded.

At least when we weren't on supply duty. Then things got a little *too* exciting for my tastes.

"How are you our designated driver!?" I clutched at the truck's door as Fyth slid us around another turn, probably sending a plume of dirt into the farm fields on either side of the road. "I thought this was your thing!"

"It is!" The other woman cackled. "I love driving more than sex or fighting!"

My fingers dug in around the handle as she jammed the accelerator down. "You're going to send the crates flying out of the back if you don't slow down!"

"Relax, we're not going that fast!" Her grin worried me even before she added. "Yet!"

I whimpered and held on as the massive truck picked up even more speed.

We roared down the colonial road at speeds I'd last seen at hovercraft races. From the sounds coming from the truck I didn't think it had ever gone this fast since it had been built, and it wasn't appreciating the abuse.

Not that Fyth seemed to care. She didn't let up on the speed until we got our first glimpses of Outpost Kahkahzi. Even then we didn't exactly slow down so much as we stopped speeding up.

She let the momentum of rolling down a short hill carry us towards the gates, tapping the breaks just enough to make sure we didn't blow through the barricade before it was lowered.

Then she slammed on them to jerk us to a perfect stop in the offloading zone, bouncing me painfully against the restraints.

Yanking them off, I fumbled for the latch, staggering out the moment that I could. My hands fell to my knees as I groaned, trying to will my heart to stop beating quite so quickly. "Ugh.... by the most holy Aspects..."

Muffled laughter came from all around, and I felt a bit of heat in my face.

"Torturing more of your packmates, Vet?" Someone catcalled from the background. "At least this one didn't throw up!"

"Screw all of you!" Fyth shot back with a laugh, her feet appearing in front of me. "She's a lot tougher than Tolu! She's totally fine!"

No. No I wasn't.

Her hard pats on my back didn't really help, but I forced myself not to shove her hand away. Groaning again, I slowly pushed myself back upright and looked around the base we'd pulled into.

It... well, looked like what it was. A small barracks with a supply depot attached, meant to support exploration teams going off to poke around the wilderness. A couple of automatons were already lumbering forwards to unload the supplies we'd brought, while a stack of presumably empty crates waited to be loaded in turn.

Plenty of other conscripts were lingering around to get a good look at the new arrivals. Most were Trahcon, but I caught glimpses of several Naulians in uniform lurking among them. Regardless of species everyone scattered to get back to work when a Dual Commander walked out of a nearby building.

He rolled his eyes and quivered his tarah at the rather blatant behavior before walking over to us.

We both quickly saluted, which he lazily returned before speaking. "Rifleman Fyth'vet. I see you managed to distract the entire base with your entrance. Again."

"Just testing the maintenance on the supply trucks, Commander." She replied innocently. "You'll be happy to know that the brakes are in good condition."

"I'm sure you were, and I'm sure they're a bit worn now." His own voice was dry. "I'm equally sure that you remember what I told you last week."

"I cannot say that I do, sir."

He huffed out a breath, tarah twitching up and then down. "I'd call you out for lying to an officer, but you're going to be suffering soon enough. Sword Leader!"

A nearby woman who'd been supervising the unloading turned at once, saluting. "Commander!"

"Rifleman Vet seems to have forgotten that she would be forced to run laps if she abused another defenseless piece of machinery! Gather up your Sword Formation and make sure her legs don't stop moving until the vehicle has been reloaded!"

Fyth groaned, tarah lowering in submission. "Sir..."

He cocked his head to the right, left tarah flexing out. "What was that, Rifle? Sir, thank you for helping my calisthenic training sir?"

"...thank you for helping my calisthenic training, Commander."

"That's what I thought. Laps around the base. Now."

Still groaning, Fyth pulled out our assignment tablet and handed it to me. I took it, tucking it under one arm. That done she slowly shuffled off, then staggered when the nearby Sword Leader gestured with an arm.

She must have given her a little telekinetic shove to inspire her because Fyth yelped and then actually started running.

I turned back around to see the Dual Commander eyeing me. "You'd be joining her if this wasn't the first time I've seen you along with. Did you try to stop her?"

Pack loyalty told me to lie. Obedience training told me not to.

I tried to split the difference. "I merely requested that she slow down, Commander."

He chuckled, clearly knowing what I was doing. "Close enough. The manifest?"

I handed over the same tablet I'd just been given. He took it, flicked through it for a minute or so, then used a finger to lazily sign the bottom of the report. He handed it back before going on, "Very well. Feel free to take a seat and relax, it'll be a little while."

Blinking, I glanced back to where the unloading was already nearly finished.

The Dual Commander did much the same, laughed again, and then called out to another soldier. "Shut down the automatons as soon as the unloading is complete, and take a break. I want them back online in a half hour to finish the job."

Grins and muffled laughter came along with plenty of amused glances to where Fyth was running along the inside of the base's walls while members of the garrison amused themselves by calling out 'encouragement'.

"Oh." I said before giving him another salute, "Commander."

He gave me another lazy one in return before walking back inside, leaving me to try and find a place to get out of the way.

Lacking any convenient benches, I settled for jumping onto one of the empty cargo crates that we were due to take back to the city. It gave me a pretty good vantage point to watch Fyth suffer.

I felt a little bad for her, but considering how many heart attacks she'd given me on the drive... I didn't feel *that* bad for her.

Settling in, I leaned back and tried to enjoy simply being off of the base for a little while. The sun was out, the air was warm, and I got to avoid helping move supplies around.

I was thinking about writing a letter to Huvu, telling her that I was finally fitting in among a new pack, when the low rumble of hovercraft drew my attention.

A quick look around let me spot two of them coming down the same road we'd used, kicking up even more dust than we probably had. That faded quickly as they slowed to a crawl, sedately making their final approach like professionals rather than maniacs.

They settled onto the ground one at a time beside our truck, forcing me to bring a hand up to shield my eyes before their engines cut out. I lowered it in time to see a Half-Sword emerging from the back of the nearer one...

And all eight of them were Humans.

The Half-Sword Leader was pale skinned, and had dyed his fur a vibrant shade of red. His brown eyes were already locked onto me as he walked over, an easy smile on his lips.

I fought the urge to flinch when he approached, and then again when he said something in a language I didn't know.

"I don't speak that language, Half-Sword." I replied as politely as I could, hoping I at least sounded casual.

His smile flickered. "Ah, my apologies for assuming Hindi was your parent's tongue. English, then? Or Mandarin?"

"I only speak Caranat." My back tightened up as the rest of the pack began to come forward. Six men, two women. Half were pale, half had the same dusky brown skin that I had. All eight had dyed their fur just like their leader, and let it grow out far more than I ever had.

For their part, all of them were staring at me, taking in my uniform, my shaved scalp, and the lack of others of our kind with me.

"Ah." That smile was gone now. "May I ask where you're from?"

I purposefully misunderstood him. "The Seven Hundred and Eleventh Colonial. Newly assigned to the capital, I'm here on a supply drop off."

One of the other pale men, narrowed his eyes. "That's not what the HSL asked, girl. What emigration colony did they dump you on?"

"Or your parents." Another offered. "Were they from one of the early shipments?"

Dammit. They were all so *tall*. I was used to being among the tallest in any group, but I was shorter than any but the women among them. I couldn't see past them to where Fyth was, or if anyone else was coming over.

I tried to buy myself some time by sliding to my feet, stretching out as if I'd gotten stiff from sitting around for too long. That didn't really give me a better view, so I gave them a limited answer.

"Alzuc." I told them. "I never knew my parents. File says I was an orphaned infant, excess cargo on the emigration ship."

A woman snorted and muttered something in a Human tongue that was probably insulting about the Empire. I held my own; I'd learned that painful lesson. Defending the Empire to people who clearly resented it never ended well for me.

"Alzuc?" The HSL hummed. He'd progressed from not-smiling to openly looking annoyed at how I was dragging things out. Behind him one of the women, the one with a darker color than the other, grimaced.

She, at least, had guessed what I was up to. Probably what I was trying to avoid saying too.

"I've never heard of Alzuc." He went on, clearly prodding me to tell him which region it was in.

"I'm not surprised. It's a big Empire, and Alzuc isn't all that industrious." I evaded again. "Where are you all from? Here?"

"I wish." The man shook his head. "This place at least has weather and skies. They dumped us all on Rakichak."

"Never heard of it." I echoed.

He snorted and echoed me in turn. "I'm not surprised. It's a dead world, tidally locked to its star. Got enough water trapped under the surface to make the caverns habitable, but it's a miserable shithole."

Good. They were talking about themselves. Humans loved to do that just as much as Trahcon, I just had to keep them going.

"Is it a-"

He cut me off. "You *were* raised by proper parents, right? Not in one of those facilities?"

A brief spike of anger cut through my nerves. The Lori may still have been children, but they were my *packmates.* My siblings. The ones I would remember fondly for the rest of my life.

Something must have shown in my face because his own began to twist.

I don't know if I was about to snap at them, or about to regain control of my temper, when I was saved by the same Dual Commander who I'd spoken with earlier.

"Rich'matthews." His sharp voice made all nine of us turn to see the officer staring us down.

"...Commander." The Half-Sword and his unit, I sincerely doubted they were a true pack, all saluted. "My apologies for delaying my report, sir. We were not expecting to see another of our species here and became distracted."

"Understandable, but this is not the time." The tone now was cold, crisp. The warmth and banter he'd shown Fyth and I entirely absent. "Inside for debriefing, you and your Half-Sword. Rifle-Experienced Lori, report back to your truck for departure."

"Commander." I saluted again, but I couldn't really go anywhere since I was still mostly surrounded.

Rich'matthews and the others moved off slowly, walking just barely fast enough to avoid giving the Commander an excuse to snap at them.

He followed behind them without sparing me another look. I swallowed, hoping I hadn't made an enemy of the base's officer in addition to eight more Humans.

A sweaty Fyth emerged from behind the truck as I approached, her own expression worried. "Ashe? What was that about?"

"They wanted to say hello."

Her head cocked to one side. "That's a whirlpool of shit. They blocked you in, and I know enough about Human expressions to notice that they didn't look happy."

I grimaced. "...other Humans don't like me, much."

"Why?"

"Can we talk in the truck?" I asked somewhat desperately. "I'd really like to be ready to leave."

She nodded at once, ushering me along. I risked a look over my shoulder as we walked and spotted at least two of the others looking back at me. From a distance I couldn't tell what they were thinking, but I doubted they liked how close the two of us were walking.

It was a sharp relief to climb into the passenger's seat. Spotting the automatons moving to start loading the back was even better.

"Talk." Fyth demanded as soon as the doors closed. "What's going on?"

I let out a ragged breath. "It's because I was raised in a birthing facility, because I don't speak any of their languages. Pretty much all of the ones I've met are emigres who... don't approve of the Empire."

Blue eyes narrowed, shifting to stare hard at the building they'd all vanished into. "Were they saying anything against the Empire?"

"No. Implied maybe, but I think they're the type who are smart enough to not be open about that kind of thing." My lips turned down. "I've met the other kind too. They tend to be... pretty blatant, and not all that smart."

Fyth grunted. "I've only met Naulian versions of people like that, but they sound pretty much the same. Bet they all run off to the Reaches to become pirates as soon as their conscription ends."

They probably would, assuming they didn't try to find the Ark Fleet. Or go all the way to the Far Reaches and join a warlord's army or something.

Still, something in her words made me frown in thought.

"The Naule you met." I shifted in my seat so that I could face her. "On Icar?"

"Ahshan's blood no." She shook her head. "Trip to one of the other bases, two weeks ago. The one Ruru came with me on."

I felt myself frowning. "...huh."

"What?"

"...a blatantly rebellious alien Half-Sword, plus an all-Human Half-Sword? At two exploration outposts on an emigration colony?"

She blinked. "What about them?"

Probably nothing, but... something about it struck me as odd. Ah-Cycle was the favorite part of the four year rotation because it meant a lot of time off base. A lot of time out in the wilderness, or building isolated outposts far away from civilization.

A group of soldiers who didn't like the Empire would have a lot of opportunity to...

I forced my waves to settle, to calm down. "Sorry... it's nothing. Just, rattled and paranoid I guess."

"You sure?"

"Yeah." It was probably just my usual reaction to other Humans, and how they reacted to me. I was jumping to the worst possible conclusion, just like all too many people did to me.

No. I wouldn't stoop to their level.

"Yeah." I said again. "It's nothing."

She eyed me some more, then slowly rolled a shoulder. "All right, if you say so. We've got tonight off, want to grab Hely and sail to the nearest bar?"

My head fell back against the seat, my eyes closed as I started to focus on my hearing. The calming routine slowly washing over me.

"That sounds great. Thank you.... wait. Are you going to drive normally on the way back?"

"Define 'normally' for me."

I could only groan.

IV

I tried to push the incident at Kahkahzi away over the next month. Tried to focus on falling into the local routine, on getting used to actually living and working with my new packmates.

Sadly it seemed like the harder I tried to ignore it all, the more little things I started noticing while we worked.

"Ashe..." Ruru groaned as she walked into the cubicle square we shared for office work. "Why are you still in here? You were supposed to be off duty an hour ago."

I was? The clock on my console told me that she was being kind. It was closer to an hour and a half since Jal had left, leaving me to pour over the same reports I'd spent the day filling out and processing.

"Oh. Sorry." I apologized. "We were going out tonight, right?"

"If we leave right now, yes." She held a hand out for me to take, hauling me out of my seat once I clasped it. "I know you're not behind on the food supplies for the southern sector. The Dual Commander just praised us yesterday for getting those in early, so why in Ashahn's holy name are you still here?"

"I'm... investigating something."

Ruru gave me an flat look as we left the space, her shoulder driving open the nearby doorway to let us get outside. "What could possibly be worth investigating in this place's food deliveries?"

Great. She was already poking holes in it, not a good sign. I thought about the best way to say my thoughts as I followed her out, the setting sun mostly hidden by the tall buildings to the east.

We set off, following the outside of the offices, heading back towards our barracks.

"Not for the locals, for the outposts." I said finally. "I think there's something odd with the assignments."

"That's really not sounding all that interesting either. Why the interest?"

I rolled a shoulder. "Curiosity, and... a feeling. I want to know how many alien units are on the Ah-Cycle right now."

"Why?" She pressed. "Jealous?"

"No. Well... yes." I admitted. "Aren't you?"

"Of course I am." She huffed, pushing her hands into her uniform pockets. "And I'm looking forwards to mocking them when they're all on Ae-Cycle and we get to be the ones sunning ourselves in the wild."

That was a bit much. Ae-Cycle wasn't exactly bad. Patrolling in and around the colony proper was still a huge step up from back-line work.

Still, that wasn't what I wanted to focus on. "It's not about jealousy. It's about things being strange here."

"Aren't all emigration colonies strange? I'm not seeing where you're going with this."

"Probably nowhere. Like I said, it's a feeling. It's just... it *feels* like there's an unusual amount of alien conscripts around. Especially for an emigration colony. I thought it was Imperial policy to minimize that kind of thing."

I bit my lip, a little surprised when she said nothing in response. After a few silent steps I went on, "I just can't get what I heard in the briefing out of my head. The reports about smugglers. Plus all the alien Half-Swords we've seen are on Del-Cycle, or have you seen any around the base?""

Ruru flicked her near tarah. "That's a little odd, true. And the ones you met with Fyth were bastards, just like the ones she and I met the week before."

"That too."

She sucked in a long breath, then blew it out. "Technically speaking it's your time, and you're just going over data we already have. I can't stop you, but I can say that I think you're wasting your time. They're assholes, but that's not exactly a crime. And they probably just got lucky when it came to assignments."

There was every chance that I *was* wasting my time, and that she was right. It was a big Empire, things worked out for less than pleasant people once in a while.

Still, I didn't think that I could leave it alone. Not until I figured out just what had set me off. If I was right that something strange was going on, or if I was just being paranoid and edgy from running into other Humans again.

"Why are you so damned curious about this?" Ruru went on. "Isn't something like this why you got reprimanded on your last assignment?"

My fingers twitched inwards for a moment. "Sort of. I was on Del-Cycle then too, kept getting odd orders for more ammunition from units that didn't seem like they were the type to use the shooting range that much. Did the research and thought I was looking at a smuggling ring."

"Were you?"

"Yup." I sighed. "My old HSL didn't want to hear it. Didn't think I could possibly have come up with anything like that on my own. It got worse when he realized which unit I was accusing. They were friends of most of the pack. So I went above him to the Sword Leader, but she didn't want to hear it either."

Ruru groaned. "I can see where this is going. You went above them too, didn't you?"

I winced. "I... kind of 'borrowed' some remote cameras, set them up, and caught the smugglers in action. Then I took the recordings straight to the Arsenal Commander."

My new HSL shook her head. "Meaning you managed to do the right thing while breaking a whole different set of rules, and then went way above your commander with the evidence."

"Earned three honors, a promotion, a level one demerit, plenty of minor ones, and got really drunk to try and forget the names my last unit called me." I confirmed.

"Did you?"

"I wish."

She huffed. "Bastards. That explains a lot of what's in your index though, and I think I'm getting a feel for you."

I glanced at her, which made her smirk. "You like investigating things, searching the waters for anything that looks odd. Let me guess, you want to apply to join Imperial Intelligence when your term is up, don't you?"

"...I think so." Stepping just ahead of her, I pulled open the barracks door for her. "You?"

"Thanks." She walked in, slowing just enough for me to catch up. "Honestly I'm still thinking on it. The Academy has its appeal, but I don't know if any of the others want to stay in."

"Fyth doesn't." I supplied at once.

Ruru rolled her eyes, our strides matching while we walked down rows of identical doorways. "You don't have to be an Agent to figure that out. Her life goal is to join the Delarah and no one's going to convince her otherwise. Trust me, we've all tried."

Joining the Delarah? The Delne'lir with a near monopoly on hovercraft production? And I thought my little dreams were a bit ambitious. I couldn't imagine how hard it would be to even get the Delarah's attention, never mind actually be invited to take that name.

"Just have to enjoy the next fifteen years with her." Ruru murmured.

It would only be six more for me, but I nodded all the same.

"And don't think I didn't notice your sly little attempt to change the subject." The comment made me hunch in a little guiltily. "You're such a boy, Ashe. Clever, but not half as clever as you think you are."

I pouted a little. "Hey. Don't insult my femininity just because I'm indirect once in a while. I'm plenty feminine."

"Prove it by wearing that outfit that Fyth bought you tonight. She's been very sad that you haven't worn it."

"I..." The look she gave me when we stopped outside of our door was accusatory enough to make me surrender. "All right, all right. I will."

"Good." A hand reached up, one finger poking me in the chin. "You're fitting in well, Ashe. Don't mess it up by going all ice-shark on us. That kind of lone operator stuff is for outsiders, not us."

"I'll try." I promised.

She nodded once, then hauled the door open to reveal the rest of the pack already out of uniform and ready to head out for the evening. They all started complaining that we were late the moment we stepped in, talking over one another to the degree that I could barely pick out the actual words.

At least they all shifted aside to let us scramble to change as well, waiting impatiently while we did.

Our room in the barracks was only slightly larger than the cabin on the ship had been. About the only difference was that there was more space to cram drawers and storage spaces into the walls. Yanking mine open, I pulled out the apology gift that Fyth had bought me after her latest attempt to stop my heart with her driving habits.

Honestly it was a pretty nice outfit. Both the shirt and pants were a dark shade of green that matched the only casual pair of shoes that I owned. She'd even gotten me silver bracelets to wear with it.

I just hadn't seen the need to wear the whole thing if all we were doing was going to the base's lounge to drink with the other conscripts.

A fancy kind of place it was not.

Pulling off my uniform, I threw it into the corner with everyone else's before getting the new outfit on. The complaining didn't let up behind me, spurring me on to redress as quickly as I could.

The pants were tight down to my knees, then flared out around my shins. Showing off my strong thighs while hiding my calves and ankles. Above that the shirt was a bit more... flirty. Sleeveless to best show off my arms, with the back cut down low enough to expose a lot of my spine.

Even better, it had clearly been meant for a Trahcon woman, meaning it was very tight across my chest. Besides showing off my muscles, it flattened out the breasts I'd never liked having.

"How do I look?" I turned around, tugging the bracelets into place. "I think it fits."

Hely and Fyth were in blue versions of what I was wearing, and both gave me grins and gestures of approval. Moriv was a bit more obvious in his appreciation, tugging his bright red coat over an equally bright teal shirt. "Can I be your first in our pack?"

My face heated up at once. "Moriv!"

"What?" His tarah rose, a grin on his lips. "You look hot in that. I keep forgetting you have tattoos since you're always in long sleeves."

I glanced at my left arm, at the storms, tumultuous waves, and broken ships that covered it from wrist to shoulder. If I screwed up again I'd need to expand it to my back, or maybe my chest. "Sorry, Jal. You're cute, but not really my type."

He pouted. "What is your type?"

"Someone with more tattoos than you, and who drinks a lot less."

His fingers snapped. "One of those things can be fixed tonight. There's a good artist who takes commissions. Pack Olik found him when they went out last week."

That made me laugh and pat his head before turning to see if Ruru was finished changing. She was, and she'd gone with the most revealing outfit among us. Her black shirt was more of an open vest, showing off absolutely every muscle she had above the waist.

The blue pants were little better, the same style as the rest of the huntresses in the pack, but hers had steep cuts to show off the silver anklets she was wearing with each step she took.

Fyth snickered. "I think Ruru is more her type."

"You're staring too." I shot back, feeling even warmer. A sensation that didn't improve when I turned to see if everyone else was done, and found Jal settling a necklace on.

He was as handsome as Ruru, though in a more masculine way. A blue vest rode above a tight red shirt, both sleeveless to let him tie alternating ribbons of the same colors around his bare forearms. Blue pants were just as tight all the way down.

"I know, I'm slender and sexy." Jal said modestly. "Everyone ready?"

Everyone nodded, made sure that we had our rank badges in our pockets, and quickly filed out of the room. Since my locker was closest to the door, I found myself walking next to Fyth in the front of the group.

"Where are we going?" I asked, curious. "We didn't all get dressed up just to walk across the base did we?"

The lunatic driver, who was probably becoming my closest friend in the pack, laughed. "Of course not. Our fearless leader got us a table at Storm's Love."

I blinked, then perked up when the wave hit the beach. "How did you manage that?"

Ruru, who was right behind me, chuckled. "By making it two days after we landed, when I realized that it was the best place next to the base."

Another chuckle, this time from Dahj. "So make the most of tonight because it'll be another few months if we like the food."

The prospect of good food and better drinks kept our spirits up on the way to the restaurant. Even the gate sentries slowing us down, making sure we all had our ranks with us didn't damper our enthusiasm.

A short walk to the nearest city corner brought us right to the building itself. It was huge, built of stone and wood instead of prefabs, and absolutely covered in lightning themed art and signage. To one side was a parking lot already filling up, and to the other was a pair of Strike-Wave pitches filled with people picking out teams.

Inside it was already packed even though the sun hadn't finished setting, and Ruru had to shout her name to the gatekeeper before he let us past the entryway. A waitress wearing nothing more than shorts, the better to show off the tattoos that covered every inch of her below the neck, guided us to the bar.

"Your table is outside, be ready in a few minutes!" She shouted, waving for us to wait. "I'll be back to get you! Feel free to get drinks and starters here!"

"Thanks!" Dahj was the closest, so it fell on her to yell back. "We'll be here!"

The bartender, another Trahcon woman wearing very little, came over to take care of us. More shouting and a couple of gestures got us two loaves of dark bread and a variety of strong drinks to enjoy while we waited.

"Fuck this Riverborn is good!" Fyth leaned in so I could hear her, "Try it!"

I took the bright blue drink from her hands and sipped it. Sweet fruit flavors washed over my tongue, with a strong alcoholic kick at the end. "That's great! Try mine!"

"A Void-Star?" When I nodded, she took my much darker glass and sipped it. "Not bad!"

"Better than yours!"

Fyth laughed as we took our own drinks back, "No way! Too strong for me!"

We sipped our drinks, swapped with the others, watched and applauded as the bartender did a few sorcerous tricks with glasses while she refilled the beers of the party next to ours. She gave us a bow, then rose and juggled a few glasses with her mind for fun.

"Show off!" Fyth shouted along with a few others. "Bet she's a priestess during the day!"

"Probably!"Tolu apparently found her voice when she was drinking. "She's got the Aspect Mahkahs on both her shoulders and her biceps! They've got a temple just down the street!"

Hely pounced on that, "Staring much?"

Tolu's yelping denial and furious argument with her closest friend was covered up by the general noise, leaving me to smile and sip my very strong cocktail while turning to watch the crowd.

It was a pretty enjoyable crowd to watch, to be honest. Everyone was dressed up, and practically everyone looked to be of Hunter age. That meant there was a lot of very handsome people of both genders standing at tables, laughing at the bar, or seated in circular booths.

I was enjoying the view, and was trying to pick out my favorite when a bit of motion near the entrance caught my eye.

Another party was coming in... several Trahcon woman in conservative dress, all walking with the slow, deliberate motions of Elders. That wouldn't have really meant much, except a Human man and two Naulians were right behind them.

I only had enough time to realize what I was looking at before one of the staff led them up one of the stairwells.

"Ashe! Ashe!" I nearly spilled my drink when Fyth shouted in my ear, her free hand tugging at my arm. "Drunk already? Come on! Table's ready!"

"Right, sorry!" Casting one more confused look back, I quickly followed everyone else out into the evening air. It was quieter outside, even with two amateur Strike-Wave games being played under lights right next to our seats.

The view was just as good though, considering that nearly all of the players had stripped down to very little.

By the time the main course arrived I'd relaxed again, laughing, teasing, and drinking with my pack.

But come morning... I remembered, and I wondered.

V

The next day was our day of rest for the week. That was good considering how hungover everyone was, myself very much included. Not that the pain in my head stopped me from being the first one to get up, groaning a little as I shuffled over to my locker.

I'd collapsed into sleep as soon as we'd gotten back, but from the bottles on the floor and the smell in the air some of the others must have progressed to drinking and sex after we'd returned.

Since Ruru, Hely, and Fyth were all still in their party clothes I doubted it had been them. A glance at the other side confirmed that Moriv and Tolu were definitely naked and cuddling, while Jal and Dahj were similarly entwined just past them.

I was a little surprised. Tolu hadn't really struck me as being nearly as horny as most Trahcon her age.

"Good for her." I covered a yawn before grabbing a uniform. Shuffling out of the room, I closed the door as quietly as I could before trudging to the baths.

Soaking in hot water for a half hour made me start to feel alive again, and I got the rest of the way when I splashed some cold water onto my face in the sink after. Others on base came and went far more quickly; everyone whose duty shift started in an hour.

During the first couple of weeks I'd gotten stared at a lot. The usual mix of polite curiosity, mild distaste, and the occasional xenophiliac leers.

After two months most of all three had died down, thank the Aspects. That pretty much everyone was in a hurry to get to their stations on time probably helped too.

Once I was done soaking and getting clean, it was time to go through my weekly fur-cut, carefully shaving down the stubble that was getting longer along my scalp.

I left the rest of it as I usually did. It was too annoying to deal with, and my clothing hid the dark strands anyway.

Once I was dressed, I slipped in and out of the room to drop off my things and confirm that everyone else was still asleep. Leaving quietly once again, I took a moment to send a message to Fyth telling everyone I was going out for a while before doing just that.

The morning sentries had just gotten on duty when I arrived at the gate. They, at least, got full body armor and rifles for their job.

"Morning Lori." One of the armed and armored women greeted me when I approached. I recognized her voice even if her helmet hid her features. "Rank chit?"

"Morning Idi." I pulled mine off my uniform, handing it over to be scanned. "Your pack sleep in today? You all rushed through the bath pretty fast."

Her headgear hid her expression, but she threw her head back to make her eye-rolling clear. "We were out even later than your pack was. Rest day?"

"Yeah."

She nodded when her scanner beeped, handing my chit back. "As Rifle-Experienced, you're cleared for twelve hours off base. Don't be late, vague promise of demerits, so on and so forth, you know what I'm supposed to say."

I snorted. "I don't get the full speech today?"

"Nope. Too hungover." Her elbow jammed onto the controls, the gate sliding open enough for me to get out. "Shoo."

I did as ordered, and shortly found myself walking down the colonial streets. This early in the morning there wasn't much traffic on either the streets or the walks, which let me simply stroll along and look around without distractions.

Most of the buildings around the base were about what you'd expect near a base. Lot of bars, lot of restaurants, lots of theaters, lot of saunas and pools.

All good for a bored soldier to relax in, but I had research to do.

The nearest information center was a little over a mile away. It was pretty much the same as I'd seen on similar colonies in the past; just a trio of double-sized prefab blocks stacked on top of one another. The top two levels held the local library, or what passed for one, while the lowest had what I was after.

Consoles with full public information access, and priority links to the DataNet.

"All right." I was the only one in the room this early in the morning, so I didn't feel too awkward talking to myself out loud. "I don't have any proof of anything. Just an odd feeling, odd sightings, and a lot of resentment towards my own species."

That last one did worry me. I mean, I thought I was pretty justified, but I had to acknowledge the prejudice. There was every chance I was seeing things that weren't there.

"But maybe I'm not." Fingers began tapping rapidly across the controls, "Let's see who is running this place, and see if there's actually something to investigate."

The names of the Planetary Council were pretty easy to find. Benefits of a government site with their names, pictures, and short biographies of each one, and the images made me start frowning as soon as I saw them.

They were all Trahcon, which was to be expected. The Technocracy was a lot of things, but rewarding of youth it was not. Positions in Planetary Councils went to the people with the best Indexes and the best connections, and it was really hard for a fifty year old Human to beat a three hundred year old Trahcon in either category.

What was odd was the fact that seven of the nine civilian members were from just two Delne'lir.

Oshflara wasn't exactly a big place, but the notion that only two groups of Notables had members in the planetary council was... unlikely.

I frowned harder as I finished checking the names. "Five from the Noroth, and two form the Keres. Never heard of either one."

Another search led me to their sites, and didn't really clear things up.

The Keres were a pretty typical colonial collection of Notables; less of a corporation and more of a hunting lodge. They apparently liked going after big game down south, and were only active on Oshflara.

The Notable name of Noroth was something else.

"Automation producers and technicians." My fingers tapped a few more times, bringing up the page where they bragged about how many worlds they were active on. "All over this sector. Interesting."

It felt important. I had no idea why, but it definitely felt important.

Returning back to the top level of government didn't clear matters up. The limited biographies didn't tell me much there. They were all middle aged or older Guides, a bit young but not out of place in an isolated colony. None were packmates with each other.

I slumped back in my seat, spinning it a little to the left, then pushing back to the right. "Well that was a waste of an hour. Maybe Ruru was right."

No one was around to answer me, so I handled that part as well. "Maybe, but you haven't checked any of the City Circles yet. Try there before you give up."

I nodded once, leaned forward once again, and got back to work.

Only to let my head fall onto the table a few minutes later.

"Idiot. You idiot."

Oshflara was made up of three species, each of which had clearly divided the primary city into a trio of districts. So *of course* they'd created three different City Circles, each of which was dominated by the species of their respective zone.

Pushing myself up with a groan, I slowly poked around to check for any odd connections that I could find.

There wasn't much to see. The Trahcon Circle's heavy industry representative was a Noroth, not surprising considering the position and that Delne'lir's focus. Since none of the other reps had that name I didn't think it overly suspicious.

Looking at the names of Humans and Naule told me absolutely nothing. The Naule were split evenly between two clans, and the Humans were a complete mismatch as far as I could tell. About the only unusual thing was that the agricultural representative in the Human zone had also taken the Noroth name.

I was about to do a search for his information when my wrist-comp began to chime with an incoming call.

A tap of the mesh brought a video feed up, letting me see Fyth staring at her own device. *"Ashe! Where are you at?"*

"Information center." I idly pushed with my right leg, spinning the chair slowly. "Everyone awake?"

"Eh, mostly. What are you doing at a library on our day off?" She paused, frowned, then groaned. *"This isn't about that research Ruru was complaining about is it?"*

I rolled my eyes. "It is, and you can tell her it's going as well as she thought it would."

"Surf's that deep, huh? Want to take a break and go out with me?"

Two hours ago I'd have said no, but it was pretty clear even to me that I needed to rethink my strategy. Or give up entirely. One or the other.

"Sure. Where are we going?"

"There's supposed to be a track near Fiftieth, I want to check it out."

Logging out of the console with my free hand, I kept the other up as I stood. "That's the opposite direction from me. I'll meet you outside the base."

"I'll be waiting!"

My walk back wasn't any more interesting than my walk over. It was a little warmer with the sun higher in the sky, but the city remained pretty quiet. Here and there I saw other conscripts and a few officers heading out on their own days of relaxation.

A uniformed Fyth was waiting for me just outside of the gates, giving me a quick grin when I came around the last corner. We exchanged a short hug, then I let her pull me along, walking north towards the river.

"So, what did you find out about your alien conspiracy?" She teased once we were moving again. "Ruru told us about your little theory."

I groaned. "Of course she did. Nothing really. Planetary Circle looks legit, except for the fact that they're all from just two Delne'lir."

She blinked a few times, tarah quivering. "Oh. You're taking this seriously, aren't you?"

"You love cars. I love investigating things I find odd." The words were a little defensive, but I couldn't help it. "Does that bother you?"

"No!" Fyth quickly shook her head, "Of course not, Sorry, I just... didn't expect it. What was that about the Notables?"

I told her what I'd found, a little surprised when she listened attentively. When I finished she thought about it for a minute or so before replying.

"I don't know. We've never been on a small colony like this, but it does seem off that only two Notables managed to get packmates at that level. Corruption?"

"Maybe, but I can't think of what that would have to do with smugglers or too many aliens on exploration duty."

She hummed. "Me either to be honest. Did you find anything on other Humans, or the locale Naule?"

I fought the urge to scowl. "Only that this city has three Circles, one for each species' little sector."

Fyth visibly smothered a grin. "Hoping to find people where they shouldn't have been?"

"Kind of." It would have made it very easy to point and say that there was a conspiracy of some sort going on.

A hand gently touched my arm, "You know that not every planet is going to have some kind of grand secret for you to chase down, right?"

"I know. I just..." I shook my head. "...I really feel like something is off. I can't tell *what,* but I know there's something."

She hummed, fingers trailing down to mine. I let her take my hand in hers, the gentle squeeze reassuring. "Well, maybe you need to follow a different current then. I don't know much about conspiracies, but I don't think they'd leave public information that a conscript could find."

I huffed. "Thank you for telling me I was too hopeful so politely."

Teeth appeared as she smiled. "I could be Moriv and call you a silly idiot to your face if you'd rather."

"Ugh, no thanks."

We both chuckled, and I asked, "What did you mean about another current?"

She rolled a shoulder, still holding my hand. "If you think the aliens are up to something, doesn't it make more sense to go and try and talk to them?"

That was as stereotypical advice as could be from a huntress. Possible criminal conspiracy? Don't bother investigating, just go straight into the depths and take them on!

Still...

I blew out a breath as we slowed to a stop at a corner, watching some ground cars roll past. "That's probably the smart thing to do. Go to the Human sector, try and... I don't know. Be Human? Talk about local affairs?"

"Sounds smart." She agreed. "So why not do it?"

"Because I've never met another Human who liked me?" I looked down, scowling at my own chest. At the body that always reminded me I was different. "Because I've never been comfortable *being* Human to begin with?"

Fyth's grip tightened around my hand, her expression turning sad. "Ashe..."

"I..."

She pulled me closer, pulling me into a tight hug. I sagged against her, accepting the comfort.

"It's..." Fyth's breath was warm on my face when she sighed. "I can't say it's all right, because I don't know what you feel. All I can tell you is that your packmates are here for you."

"I..." I fought down a sob, nodded. "Thank you. It's... been a long time since I thought that was true."

Her low growl was so quiet I nearly missed it. I didn't miss her leaning in, gently pressing our lips together before she pulled back. "You have no idea how angry that makes me. Do you want to go back to base?"

It was beyond kind of her to offer, but I didn't want to ruin her day. "No.... no."

We slowly separated. I wiped at my face to make sure I hadn't actually shed any tears, then fixed my uniform. "I'm all right. Just haven't... haven't been able to talk to anyone like that since I left Huvu'ithi's pack. Come on, let's go indulge your hobby since you're helping with mine."

She gave me a tentative grin. "So you'll come with me to watch races if I keep helping you with your little investigation?"

"So long as this isn't some weird xenophilia thing."

That earned me a pout. "Of course not. It's me genuinely liking you. And... maybe having made all of our other packmates sick of hearing me babble about the latest hovercraft models."

I couldn't stop myself from smiling in spite of everything, "You know I won't understand all that much about them."

"And I've got no idea what this odd feeling of yours is, but I like hearing your passion about it." She smiled as well. "And apparently you need someone in your life to make you realize when you're boyishly over-complicating things."

"I am plenty feminine dammit!"

She laughed, and we fell into gentle bickering the rest of the way to the track.

VI

It took me another month to work up the nerve to follow Fyth's advice.

A lot of that month was spent debating what my plan was going to be with the others. Ruru went from being smug that I hadn't found anything to being irritated that I wasn't letting it go. Well, I didn't think she really minded what I did in my spare time so much as she objected to the idea of me going into the Human sector on my own.

Especially because I'd have to be alone if I wanted to have a chance of finding out anything.

Fyth supported me, and so did Hely. Both of the boys were on my side too; I'd barely mentioned the idea of an investigation and they'd both immediately agreed that I should do it, then tell them all about it.

For her part Dahj was siding with Ruru, which she always seemed to, while Tolu was trying to stay out of it.

Thoroughly outvoted, Ruru had been forced to give her blessing, but she'd demanded that at least half of the pack be ready to come and rescue me if something happened. So when the time came, Fythe, Jal, and Moriv found a shopping center to wander around in while I walked across the river.

"Well, this was a good idea." I murmured as I crossed the halfway point, officially entering the Northshore Sector a couple of hours before sunset.

Even though the buildings were the same block style of prefabs, mixed here and there with honest wooden construction, they looked nothing like what I'd left.

Trahcon painted everything with art.

Humans apparently liked solid colors, or no color at all.

Fortunately I didn't have to go very far. The best reviewed bar for conscripts I'd been able to find on the DataNet was right on the river, less than a block from the bridge I'd used to cross.

I felt my feet slow to a stop as the bar itself came into view. It was a pretty nice one. Naturally wooden walls, a huge deck over the water, awnings to shade that porch, and it already looked to be doing a fairly brisk business both inside and out.

It was too easy to notice that there was hardly anyone in conscript uniforms around. Not none, thank the Aspects, but I'd be in a definite minority.

Taking a final few breaths, I told myself that I had to do this. This was my best chance to make progress. I just had to go in, have a drink or two, and see if I could make it one night without inspiring my own species to hate me.

If I did it enough times, maybe they'd talk to me. Reveal something.

Hopefully.

Walking inside, I was struck by the confused rumble of conversations in at least four or five different languages. The lighting was dimmer than in a place like Storm's Love, and the background music was strange.

Oh. And everyone inside was Human. Hard to miss that.

Swallowing, I started forwards, the pale skinned host glancing up at me as I approached. To my relief he greeted me in Caranat. "Good evening, soldier. Bar, table, or booth?"

"Bar, please."

He smiled and waved me on. "Good that you got here early, they'll all be taken soon. Take any seat you like."

"Thank you."

Sliding past him, I weaved between several tables before I got to the square shaped bar in the center of the place. Broad screens above it were split between a Strike-Wave game, and some kind of Human sport involving a ball being kicked around.

About half of the stools were taken, but I found one that had several empty seats on either side. The bartender, a man with skin only slightly lighter than mine, held up one finger while his other kept filling a mug. I nodded to show I understood, and tried to force myself to relax.

Picking up the nearest drink menu, I was pretty relieved to find that I recognized most of them.

"Evening." I looked up to see the bartender lean on an elbow in front of me. Up close he was... handsome, I guessed, but the odd bits of fur around his mouth detracted a lot for me. "What's your poison?"

I blinked a few times, then got what he was asking. "A Dark Nova, please."

"Any food?"

"Uh... bread?"

It was his turn to blink, then glance around. "Damn, sorry. Someone took the food list. I'll get you some naan and a proper menu. Chit or cash?"

"Chit." He took it when I offered it, scanning it before handing the little thing back.

"Thanks, be up soon."

I nodded and found myself sitting quietly.

People watching here was very different from what I was used to. Trahcon bars were riots of noise, filled with people showing off little telekinetic tricks, bar songs would start up at random, and more flirting than I could imagine at times.

Maybe it was just too early, but this place was a lot more... muted.

The company at the bar was mostly older men and women. Their fur was sprinkled with gray and white, and they seemed more interested in their drinks and quiet conversation with their fellow elders than anyone else.

I watched them talk and murmur to one another, lips forming words I couldn't understand.

Motion on my left made me turn back in time to see the bartender settling the dark glass in front of me. His brown eyes moved from mine to the elders, then back again.

"You don't understand a word, do you?"

"That obvious?" I accepted the glass, cupping it in both hands without lifting it.

"You're not the first grayborn who's come through."

"Grayborn?"

He shrugged in the odd way other Humans did; a shoulder going up and down instead of back and forth. "Grayborn, wolf raised, got all kinds of names for it depending on who you talk to. Someone brought up in a facility instead of by their parents."

"Ah." My glass rose slowly, letting me sip it. It was good. Not as well mixed as others I'd had, but far from the worst. "What are they talking about?"

His weight shifted, a hip resting against the bar as he turned sideways on me. "Same thing anyone their age does. Earth."

"Oh. They were...?"

"Born there and forced off?" He nodded grimly. "Yeah. They were all in their teens, I think. Some of the first colonists to land here. The woman on the far right was actually the first owner of this place."

I glanced at her again. "She came back after her conscription then?"

"Her kids were being raised here." A hand rose to tap his own chest, "Plus her grandchildren. Name's Luis Ramos. Yours?"

"Ashe'lori." After a beat I lowered my glass, then held out a hand. He took it without hesitating, shaking it once before letting go.

"Good to meet you. I'll be back with your bread."

With that he slipped off to refill another person's drink on the far side, leaving me to sip my mixed drink in silence once more.

That time I didn't stay alone long; three people came up on my right, taking seats at the stools. The only woman among them ended up next to me, with a pair of men settling in just past her.

To my surprise she made eye contact with me at once, bowing her head slightly. "*Konbanwa.*"

"Good evening." I guessed at the word's meaning.

She gave me a demure smile before turning away. Feeling a little awkward, I did the same, trying to enjoy my drink and ignore the strange situation I found myself in.

It shouldn't have been all that strange. I wasn't unfamiliar with being in bars, even being alone in them.

I was just used to everyone's skin being shades of gray, rather than tan or brown.

"Calm down." I muttered to myself as I took a longer sip of the nearly black liquid. The burn felt better than it should have. "Just calm down Ashe."

I must not have kept my voice down, because the woman to my right leaned over until our shoulders touched. Her accent in Caranat was as unidentifiable as it was thick, but I could understand her just fine.

"Are you all right?"

Heat rushed to my cheeks. "Yes, sorry."

She hummed without lifting her eyes from her menu. "You are too unsettled for that to be the truth. Why so nervous, conscript?"

There was just enough emphasis on the last word to make me even more nervous. My mind immediately dove into the worst possible storm; she could be afraid I was here for some nefarious purpose. Maybe trying to pick a fight, sent in ahead of my pack to give them an excuse to brawl with the locals.

I blurted out part of the truth before I could stop myself. "I'm... I'm not really comfortable with other Humans. Bad experiences."

That seemed to take her aback, but Ramos the Bartender came over before she could reply. He put down a basket filled with thin bread circles, then moved over to take the newcomers orders. All three ordered different beers, but my hopes that they would remain distracted didn't survive long.

"If you are so uncomfortable, why are you here?"

I tore off a bit of the warm bread, shoving it into my mouth to buy myself time to think.

My useless brain mostly told me that the bread was very good while failing to think of a decent excuse.

"My..." I nearly said pack, and only just corrected myself. "...squad thinks I should try to connect. Shouldn't let a few bad waves ruin the entire beach."

She let out a prim little sound. "Gray analogies. Always strange, even if I take their meaning. You speak like one of them."

Ramos spoke before I could. "Ease up on the girl, Akari. She's grayborn, of course she sounds like one of them."

The women flicked her dark eyes to him. "I merely commented on a truth."

"And you sounded insulting about it." He replied easily. "Ease up a little, would ya?"

"I shall... try to 'ease up'." It was almost impressive how she didn't change her tones in the slightest. "Tell us of these... bad waves then. Why you are uncomfortable."

She was short enough I could see that the two men she'd come in with were clearly listening.

I guess it was time for blunt honesty. "The first other Humans I met called me a race traitor, beat me the moment we were alone, and would have raped me if officers hadn't pulled them off of me. I was fifteen and had been conscripted for three days."

Her eyes widened, and one of the men swore under his breath.

"The second time wasn't any better." I went on, quietly but without slowing down. "Pretty much every time I've tried to talk to other members of my own species they hate me for not speaking their language, hate that I cut my fur, and hate me for being raised as I was."

"...that would explain your nervous behavior." She said, voice lowering slightly. "You sound hurt, afraid. You speak the truth, which makes your caution understandable."

"More than that." The man two seats down growled. "Crap like that... shit. We've got enough problems without turning on our own. There's not enough of us in the damned galaxy to hurt each other."

The woman, Akari, nodded. "Yes. You are here to try and embrace your humanity?"

No. I was here to make contacts in the hopes of eventually finding out if anything strange was going on. "No. Well... I don't know. I'm here to try and get over my nerves. Maybe more."

"Good enough for me." Ramos smiled. "Don't you guys think so?"

The black furred man next to Akari tipped his head, while the taller one with brown fur lifted his drink. "It's your family's place, Ramos. So long as there's no singing the praises of the Empire, I don't have any issues."

The bartender gave me a final smile, then was called back to the far side of the square.

"I apologize." Akari spoke again. "I am often called severe. It was not my intention to pressure you."

I quickly shook my head. "It's all right. I'm... just nervous, like I said. I think this is the longest conversation I've ever had with another Human that didn't involve insults or snide comments."

Her nod was slight but grim. "I recall my time as a conscript. I well believe your story."

"Did... that happen to you too?"

"I was not assaulted. My husband would not have stood for it." A slight gesture indicated the man on her right, who was deep in conversation with the other one. "But many other squads despised us. We refused to desert, you see. That was enough."

Taking my drink back into my hands, I sipped some more before replying. "You refused to risk a death sentence and they hated you for it?"

"Indeed." She shook her head. "Fools. Many dream of returning to Earth, or going to the Reaches. The smart ones take the training, the meals the Empire provides before they try. The foolish ones do not. It is usually the latter who rage the most against those who do not gamble their souls alongside them."

"I think I know the type."

Akari sipped her own beer. "Yes. They are sadly common. But this talk is not relaxing, and that is the purpose of this place. I will tell you what it is like to be raised a Human, and then you shall tell me what it is like to be a grayborn."

What followed was one of the strangest conversations of my life.

Knowing generally how other Humans were raised as children was one thing. Hearing her talk about living with her parents and single brother, and no one else, was... incredibly different. Even with her oddly formal and even tones, her words made her fondness for her blood relations clear.

"It sounds nice." I said after she described how her mother cooked for them in the evenings, their father teaching them to mind the farm during the day. "Quiet and peaceful. Maybe a little lonely."

"I was never alone."

I found myself smiling a little. "I had fifteen Trahcon in my birth-pack, and we were one of eight being raised at our facility. Living with just three other people sounds lonely to me."

She pursed her lips as if struggling against a smile of her own. "I cannot imagine how loud that must have been."

"Very." I told her seriously. "Very, very loud. I can't even tell you how many windows got broken on a monthly basis. I think the teachers taught us to play Strike-Wave just to keep us outside for as long as possible."

"I did not think Humans could play that sport."

I lifted my drink. "Only goalie. I still hold the save record on Alzuc. Were there other children for you to play games with?"

"I preferred watching while my brother played football." Her chin rose to nod at one of the screens. "He still does."

Leaning back, I watched men kicking a ball across a field. "...explain the rules to me?"

She tried to, only for Ramos to hear and come over to 'properly' explain things. Their contrasting opinions of how the game should be played made me laugh, something that saw Akari retaliate by telling Ramos that I preferred Strike-Wave.

His theatrical look of betrayal had only made me laugh harder, even if it led to a debate between us over which sport was more interesting.

Two more drinks came and went before a chime on my wrist-comp told me that my packmates were getting impatient.

"Time for me to head out. Early morning duties tomorrow." I made my excuses as I stood up. "Um, will you all be here next week? I'd like to talk some more."

Ramos smiled while Akari bowed.

I had a little investigation to work on, packmates who supported me, and I'd even managed to find a group of fellow Humans I could talk with. For once, the skies looked clear in my life, and the waters calm.

I smiled back at them, and left with lighter steps than I'd entered with.

VII

The Del-Cycle was considered the worst of the four in the rotation for a lot of reasons. One of the largest was the way it made you feel like you weren't really a warrior.

You were rarely issued a weapon, even more rarely issued armor. Every day was spent tracking supplies, moving supplies, fixing equipment, or assisting in constructing infrastructure.

More construction worker than soldier.

Training exercises were as close as we got.

The day after my little excursion, the entire Arsenal Formation, better than four hundred soldiers split between ten Sword Formations, advanced through rolling hills covered in grass nearly as tall as our shorter members. Every hour on the hour we stopped to 'deploy', setting up in the best positions we could given wherever we happened to be.

Drones flitted overhead, feeding data back, grading each Sword. How quickly we dug in, got set up, how good our choice of terrain was, that kind of thing.

Then we got the chime over comms, packed everything up, and got moving again to repeat the process after our next hike.

"Damn this is nice." Ruru groaned when we finally got the clearance to make camp, several hours after the sun had gone down. "I missed this."

Dahj chuckled as she fell onto her ass, pulling her helmet off to reveal her face. "Missed being sore in all the wrong places, with sweat soaked armor clinging to your ass?"

"Oh yeah."

I laughed with everyone else, everything yanking their headgear free. We were allowed to remove those, but the rest of the armor had to stay on until we got back to base tomorrow.

"Half-Sword Vet." A commanding voice saw our laughter cut off, everyone rising to attention when our Sword Leader approached.

Kahs'pak would have been a very unremarkable man if not for his bright green eyes. I'd never had the chance to really talk to him, but he seemed a reasonable leader.

"We're moving to the edge of the forest to camp." He went on. "Bad news is that we're still in training protocol until we get back to base."

There was a collective groan. That meant we would have to post sentries and sleep in shifts.

Jal spoke up at that, "Well, at least we shouldn't get a midnight wake up call then. Or will we?"

"There's always that chance, but I don't think the Arsenal Commander is the type." He shrugged. "Dual-Commander was very happy with how we did, and I haven't heard anything saying the other formations did worse. I think tonight will be calm. If not, drinks will be on me for a while."

Ruru chuckled, "We'll hold you to that, Pak."

"Oh I know you will, Vet. Come on, to the trees."

We joined the general migration out of the long grass and into the small forest laying nearby.

In all honesty I'd rather have stayed in the grasslands. There was enough underbrush and crags to make it hard to find a good place to settle in. We stayed close to the Pak, eventually finding a tiny incline that was mostly clear to claim for ourselves.

Our bedrolls wouldn't do us any real good considering the armor we were wearing, but they made decent pillows.

"Fyth, Ashe." Ruru nodded to the pair of us. "First watch. Dahj and I will be next, then Moriv and Tolu. Hely and Jal get last."

First watch. That was both good and bad. Good in that I wouldn't have my sleep interrupted, bad in that I had to stay awake for the next couple of hours.

Sighing, I dutifully pulled my helmet back on while Fyth did the same. Everyone else got their packs and weapons settled in next to them, then curled up with their heads on their blankets.

For our part Fyth and I checked the nearby area, finding plenty of other Half-Swords doing the exact same thing. One of the other sentries, an older huntress from her voice, realized we hadn't been given an approach signal from the officers. Or a single channel to coordinate sentry activity on.

"Nothing here either." I contributed by confirming the inbox on my wrist-comp was empty. "No transmissions since the call to stop for the night. You think it's a test?"

"Probably."

An HSL from another Sword shrugged. "Easy way to resolve it. Any officers still awake?"

The silence that followed answered her question.

"Wake up a Dual-Commander and find out." The suggestion brought a general chorus of agreement. "That's something an officer should set."

The woman who'd spoken first shook her head. "No. We're in training protocol, that means combat simulation. If the officers forgot, it means they're too tired and need rest. Channel Ten-Fifty. Approach Clear is Blue-Forest. Everyone have that?"

A sarcastic man called back, "Yes, Void-Lord."

"Be serious." She snapped in reply. "I start officer training next year, and I'd rather not get a demerit tonight. Just get the channel open and remember the challenge for your replacements."

The woman who'd suggested waking an officer grunted. "You're Pack Charoi, right?"

"Yeah, I'll take the blame if this is the wrong decision. Now get the channel set and to sentry positions before we get rebuked for standing around talking."

There was a few grumbles from others who didn't like her unilateral decisions, but no one was eager to argue with her and wake up the officers either.

With that out of the way it was mostly a matter of finding good spots. There weren't many that gave us good views, and fewer that didn't involve leaning against trees.

"Hey." I nudged Fyth when she started to do just that. "You'll fall asleep like that."

"Not if you keep me awake." She nudged me back with an elbow. "How did it go last night?"

"Better than it should have."

I quietly relayed the night's events to her. The casual conversations I'd managed to have, and the moderately friendly way I'd been treated. What personal information I'd gotten out of the bartender and Akira.

She hummed when I finished. "See? Plenty of good Humans out there."

I smiled inside my helmet. "Yes, you were right about directly approaching them. Happy?"

"Ecstatic." Her own head shifted back, the armored fan that protected her tarah coming to rest against the tree. "You think you'll find anything about your conspiracy there?"

My smile faded. "No idea to be honest. It's a start at least."

"Probably help if you knew what you were looking for."

"...it would." I admitted. "I think my plan is to go there once a week. Get them used to me. See if I can hear something, or see if anyone approaches me."

Fyth shifted her rifle into her lap, drumming a few fingers on its side. "Sounds boring. Maybe you should talk to one of the boys, they've got good heads for sneaking around."

Maybe I would. The only other plan I'd thought of was one I didn't think I could pull off.

If I pretended to hate the Empire for what I'd gone through, kept my voice loud each time I was there, it would make it a whole lot more likely that I'd be approached by someone. Assuming anyone there was part of... whatever it was might be happening on Oshflara.

Of course Fyth was right about that too. If I was going to figure out the cause for my bad feeling, I needed to know what I was actually looking for.

So far a vague mention of smugglers, an oddly low number of Notables in the planetary government, and two groups of rude aliens on exploration patrols was all I had.

I groaned aloud, which drew a questioning noise.

"Just listing everything I do know in my head." I sighed. "It makes me think Ruru is right, and I'm just paranoid and bored."

Her voice turned dry. "We're on Del-Cycle. Everyone's bored."

"Heh." A quiet chuckle came out of me. "That's true."

"Speaking of, you still going to have time to go with me to the tracks?"

"Of course. Just don't ask me to ride with you unless you want to tell Ruru why I had a heart attack."

"Oh come on." She pouted. "We could go to the lake course where they try out hovercraft. Feel the wind and water spraying over us."

I chuckled, turning away to make sure nothing was going on. "I'd consider it if I didn't know that you'd open the throttle all the way even if you promised to take it easy."

"...probably."

We both laughed quietly.

Fyth slowly stood up as well, though she kept leaning against the tree. "Take a lap around for us? I'll do the next one. Might want to try and keep eyes on the grass too."

"Sure. I'll go watch for thirty, then we swap?"

"Works for me."

Walking a slow patrol around our little incline didn't reveal anything, besides the fact that the Pak had settled in just past us on the same incline. Their own first watch nodded and waved at me, gestures I returned as I picked my way through the brush as quietly as I could.

A couple of the other teams had put sentries out at the edge as well. Some of them shifted until they realized I was one of them, settling back into cover while I found some greenery to hide behind. Some kind of berry bush from the little fruits on it.

Good enough.

Settling on to one knee, I stared out at the hills we'd just spent the day marching through. My helmet's visor turning the night into something nearly clear, letting me watch the wind create waves in the grass.

It was... kind of pretty, especially with the stars above it.

Quiet sounds of someone moving through the forest had me bring my rifle half-up, a challenge ready until I heard Kahs'pak murmur over comms. *"Blue-Forest."*

I eased my gun back, pointing it upwards. "Sword-Leader."

"Lori." He spoke quietly through his helmet, approaching on my left. Falling to a knee beside me, he went on, "I should have thought to have sentries out here. Your idea?"

"Fyth's." I whispered back. "She could use a merit."

"I'll write a recommendation for the Dual-Commander come morning. Anything out there?"

I shook my head. "A nice view. No sign of ships coming and going, or other formations if that's what you're worried about."

"It was." He replied. "Training run back on Icar, they did that to us once. Hoping that the teams on the far side keep their sentries out."

"I'm sure they will."

He tipped his head. "We haven't had a chance to speak since you were assigned to Pack Vet. How are you settling in?"

"Better than I could have hoped." I murmured. "I'm very content with them."

"Good. If anything changes, be sure to come directly to me."

From his tone, I knew what he really meant was 'don't go over my head like you did on your last assignment'. "I will, Sword-Leader."

"Don't be so formal, we're both Hunters here." He groaned a little, changing what knee he was resting on. "Speaking of. Your Index says you used to be a good Strike-Wave player when you were a kid. Interested in diving back into that water?"

I perked up a little. "Is the Arsenal forming a league?"

"Nothing official yet, but the rumor is out there that all of the Arsenals are going to create one. You sound interested."

"...I miss it." I admitted.

"Get any training in on your last assignment?"

"A little. There was an amateur league that was happy to have me, but my HSL liked to give me assignments during their matches. So all I really did was help them practice."

He grunted. "Ruru won't. She's got her faults, but she's got nothing against Humans. You having any issues with that?"

"Only with a Human team who was on Ah-Cycle. Haven't seen them since, and the one time I visited that sector of the city they were polite enough."

"Good." He repeated. "Let me know if that changes too. Empire has enough problems without people dirtying our own rivers."

I nodded, voice lowering further. "Thank you. That means a lot."

Pak rolled a shoulder. "Don't worry about it. On that topic, if anyone in the Sword needs something from the Human sector, would you be willing to pick it up?"

"I could, I'm planning on going back. Why not go as a whole group?"

"Orders." He grumbled. "Supposedly there's a lot of tension between the three City Circles. We're to avoid moving in large groups through either the Human or Naule sectors."

"That... doesn't sound right at all."

"No, it doesn't, but it comes straight from the Storm General herself." Another shrug. "Nothing to do but obey. I'm going to head back, Tira will be over to stand the rest of the watch with you. Keep up the good work."

"Sword Leader." I said distractedly, lost in my thoughts before he even began to move away.

We were supposed to avoid moving in numbers through two thirds of the colonial city? What in Ashahn's holy name was that about? We were the *garrison*. The whole point of us being here was to help keep the world safe and peaceful.

It did explain some of the convoy routes when it came to supplying the other bases around the city, now that I thought about it.

That odd feeling I had, that had seemed to be fading into the depths, rose once again.

Something was going on here, I was sure of it.

I just had to figure out what.

VIII

Once in a while, I could be pretty clever.

I met Luis'ramos on the bridge, smiling in relief that he'd actually showed up. His slacks and long-sleeved shirt looked practical enough, which I hoped meant he was here casually. The last thing I wanted was to make him think I was interested in anything besides having a local friend.

"Thank you for helping me with this."

"No worries." He looked amused when I offered a hand, shaking it once. "Your message said something about a shopping trip?"

"Yeah. And I don't have the faintest idea of what course to set." Tapping my wrist comp, I brought up the list I'd been given to show him. "Half of the Sword Formation wants to try Human drinks."

The fur above his eyes rose. "That's just your Sword?"

"No." I rolled my eyes a little. "Our SL bragged that I agreed to go shopping, and the next thing I knew my inbox was under siege. Even the AC gave me something."

Ramos snorted, "Ah. Well, good news is that I think we can get most of that from one or two stores. Shouldn't take too long. You have a way to carry it all back? That's a lot of bottles."

I waved back the way I'd come, firmly reminding myself to use the right terms. "My squad rented a ground-car, it's parked right over there. You mind riding with?"

"Of course not." His pause was just long enough for me to notice. "Any of your squad coming with?"

"No. We've got orders to avoid moving in numbers through the Northshore." I didn't have to act to frown. "No idea what that's about, but orders are orders."

He grunted. "I think I do. Can tell you about it on the way if you'd like. Probably be good to know, don't want to say the wrong thing at the bar."

"I appreciate it. Come on, car's over here."

The rental wasn't much to look at. A green painted two-seater, with a long section for cargo space in the back. Fyth had nearly retched when I'd picked it out. My comments about the price and economy of it hadn't mattered against the slow speed and 'pathetic handling'.

Honestly I couldn't tell. It went forwards and stopped when I pushed the pedals, and it turned when I wanted it to. That was good enough for me.

Ramos eyed the car, then me as we got in. "Seriously? You rented a L-250?"

I sighed, jamming a thumb on the starter. "You sound like Fyth. It was cheap and it had cargo space all right?"

One of his hands rose to cover his mouth, but his eyes made his grin apparent. "All right, all right."

"Where are we going?"

"Right like we're going to Riverside Cantina. Then go for... five blocks, then turn left. Store will be on the left again just past the intersection."

Nodding, I checked for traffic before slowly pulling out. The quiet hum of the motor was the only sound as we crossed the bridge, my tentative driving skills keeping us well within the limits.

"So..." I tried to think of a clever way to ask, came up with nothing, and went with blunt. "...why is the Army being limited where it can go? I've never heard of that before, even on other emigration colonies."

He shrugged in the odd way other Humans did. "No big secret. There was a big riot five years back, when the last Great Ship dropped off a hundred thousand fresh off of Earth."

"They didn't appreciate coming here?"

"No." Ramos said quietly. "There was also a religious aspect to it all,. Let's just say they didn't appreciate being forced off the homeworld, and were even less happy to find out who they'd have to live with."

"Oh. If it was that bad, why didn't the army move in?"

He shrugged. "I was off world, my own conscription period, so I don't know the full details. According to my grandmother they *did* move in, but a whole bunch of Trahcon advancing across the river just made things worse."

I thought I saw where things were going. "So they sent in alien, I mean, non-Trahcon troops?"

"An all-Naule force, yeah. Their officers managed to negotiate with some of the priests and imams. Got a lot of people to stand down, then corralled the ones who kept throwing bricks." He leaned back in his seat, sighing a little as we rolled past his place of work. "If you'd arrived here just a few months earlier you'd have seen the last of the reconstruction."

"Oh." I said more quietly that time. "It was that bad?"

"Wasn't pretty." A sigh. "Long story short, the Storm General decided that keeping the peace was more important than anything else. So she issued a decree saying only Naulian and Human forces would be stationed in Northshore and West Bend."

"And it worked?"

He nodded. "So far."

I bit my lip. "That explains why I haven't seen other Humans at our base, or at any of the bars around on that side of the river."

"Yeah. Pretty much no one crosses the water if they can help it. But there's a lot of intermingling between us and the Naule now, so the Planetary Circle can send good reports about the species getting along."

The bitterness in his voice was hard to miss. "Are you... all right?"

"Hm?" Brown eyes flicked to me, then he seemed to realize what he'd sounded like. "Oh. Sorry, yeah, I'm fine. And I'm not upset with you or anything. Just... let's talk about something less depressing."

It was hard. It was really hard, there were so many questions I had now. Why hadn't this been in our briefing? Why had we not been told that there'd been violence on that scale here?

I shoved one question down into the depths, then another, and finally drowned my curiosity long enough to say, "Sure... sure. How is the bar doing?"

"Very well." He perked up a little. "We've got the best selection and the best food, and everyone in Northshore knows it. Don't think we've had a slow night in more than a year now."

"Sounds busy. This where we turn?"

"Yeah, this is it." I slid us to a halt, waiting for the turn signal to light. "It is busy, but it's worth it. *Abuela* lives for it, and we've all got a hand in keeping it running."

I nearly asked him if he meant his 'pack', but again just barely managed to correct myself. "You're whole... family?"

He gave me a confused look for a moment before shaking his head. "Right, right, grayborn. Sorry. Yeah, the whole family. *Abuela* runs it, my parents and uncles all help cook, and everyone my age either serves or works the bar. Nearly a dozen of us."

"Sounds like a pack." My foot pressed down on the accelerator when the light turned blue, pulling us onto the next street. "That's not insulting, is it?"

"Not to me, I know what you mean. Might want to avoid the pack word around here though."

"I try." I admitted. "It's really hard sometimes. I didn't even learn the loan word for family until I was a conscript."

"Heh." His laugh didn't have any humor in it. "I could believe it. Pull in here. How many years you have left of service?"

"Six." I feathered the break as a truck rumble past, then pulled into the lot. The store was a fairly large one, the lot was half full. A broad sign above the door was in letters I couldn't read. "What does that mean?"

"Miguel's Grocer. They're good people, friends of my family."

I nodded while I parked, the rental's motor shutting down a moment later. "Thanks. Do you know a good site to learn?"

His smile became warm, "Yeah, I know a few. I'll mail links to you."

The two of us walked inside to find a store that was pretty much the same as any other small-town shop I'd ever been in. Aside from the fact that maybe half of the goods had Caranat labels, forcing me to rely on my new friend to tell what I was buying.

Inside, the store was as busy as the parking lot made it seem. I'd hardly picked out a rolling cart before I started getting the kind of dark looks I was all too familiar with.

"It's the uniform." Ramos stayed close to me, staring back at the locals who'd been eyeing me. They quickly averted their attention, which either spoke to his presence or how popular his pack, dammit, his *family* was.

"And probably your haircut."

"All I have are uniforms and formal clothes." I murmured back. "And my fur isn't going to grow out anytime soon."

"Hair." He corrected absently. "Don't worry about it, just don't wander off."

Considering that he was the only person here that I knew, that wouldn't be an issue. I wasn't quite as nervous as I had been that first night in the Riverside Cantina, but it was hard to throttle the urge to call my packmates. To tell them that going past the edges of Northshore had been too much, and that I needed one of them to come and get me.

"No problem." I said quietly. I didn't want to just cut and run, but I made the mental call to only do one visit today. I'd get the rest of the list some other time. "Hard liquor first?"

"Sounds like a plan."

The looks started to come back after we loaded eight bottles of alcohol into the car, though they were more confused than hostile. And at least Ramos was getting them just as much as I was.

The open staring and shaking of heads came after we fought to get five cases of beer to join them in the cart.

Ramos took it all in good humor, bantering with an older customer who'd been picking out his own drinks before translating for me. "I'm reassuring them that I'm not the one buying all of this."

I glanced between the two grinning men before quickly saying, "It's not all for me either!"

Both of them laughed, the elder moving off while Ramos led me to find the Human style snacks that had been put onto the list.

By the time we finished off most of the list I was very glad that everyone had agreed to pay me back for this. I didn't exactly spend much of my pay, so I had plenty, but this particular trip was anything but cheap.

I could still feel the stares on my back as we packed it all into the car, and tried not to shudder in relief when I got the motor started again.

"You all right?" Ramos asked. "You tightened up like that first night again."

"...I'm fine." Pausing, I amended. "Now that we're out of there. I'm going to head back now. Want me to drop you off at the restaurant?"

"If you could."

I nodded, pulling out of the parking lot as quickly as I could. "Thank you again for coming with. I'd have botched this entirely without you."

"You're welcome." His voice turned wry. "I can't think of another time a woman asked me to help shop because she couldn't read the labels, but at least I got an interesting story out of it."

I tried to give him a quick glare, but couldn't stop my lips from twitching. "That's rude."

"True though."

"Yeah. Still rude." I accelerated a bit to keep up with traffic, feeling myself slowly relax as I made the first turn. "Mind talking to me? It helps when someone else is talking."

"Sure, what about?"

Good question. I still had all of my questions from earlier, but it seemed like a bad idea to push that subject. Something that would let him talk, help me calm down, but that wouldn't ruin this.

"Your conscription." I said after a moment. "What did you do? What colonies did you visit?"

"What any conscript does. I got to spend a lot of time moving boxes from one place to another, wander around exotic alien landscapes, and a whole lot of time complaining about it all."

It turned out he'd spent most of his twelve years in the Stormshroud. He'd hit seven different worlds during his tenure, most of them fairly unpleasant. Despite that he'd managed to avoid seeing even a single pirate raid during that entire period.

"They're not as common as everyone thinks." He confided when I expressed my disappointment. "You only get a couple of raids a year, and the pirates who try it are usually the desperate ones."

"The ones with the worst equipment and chances of pulling it off?"

"Pretty much. We did get one priority alert when I was on Shozuc, but the system fleet drove them off before they could make orbit." He glanced at me. "What about you? Ever seen actual action?"

I shook my head, slowing down as we neared the Riverside Cantina. "No. Only people I know who did were my second pack. They all had Lost Hunter, from a battle in the Contested Zone."

Ramos shook his head. "Can't say I like Trahcon much, no offense, but there's always something sad about seeing them like that. Did they turn out all right?"

"Yeah, they were all pretty close to recovered by the time I was assigned to them. I stayed with them for a while until I was..." I grimaced at the memories, drawing one from him too. He probably remembered what I'd mentioned at the bar, and knew what I was referring to.

"...able to handle what happened with my first assignment. I wanted to stay with them when they got moved back to a combat posting, but I was too green. So instead I started getting bounced from assignment to assignment."

He nodded as the car slowed to a halt out in front of the Riverside Cantina, the signs only just flickering on as they prepared to open. "Well, on the bright side you're on a good one now it seems like. You can reconnect with Humanity, enjoy a colony with clear skies and good weather, and get through your conscription period."

I liked most of that, except for the 'reconnect to Humanity' bit.

I didn't think I'd ever had that connection in the first place, and if I wasn't so interested in figuring out what was going on here, I'd have never walked into his bar.

But that wasn't something you said to someone trying to cheer you up.

"Thanks." I gave him a small smile. "I'll be around the bar on my usual day."

He gave me a grin of his own, then slipped out of the car. "I'll keep your spot open. See you around, Ashe."

His use of my personal name made my fingers twitch slightly, but he was gone before I could ask him to stick to my formal one.

"Ashahn's blood, please don't think I'm interested in you." I muttered, getting the car moving again.

I liked his company, but that was the extent of my interest. "I'll ask Fyth, maybe she'll have good advice."

I'd do that later. First, I had a delivery to make, and other packs to harass about paying me back.

Second... I had a city wide riot to look up.

IX

Despite my newfound research target, I didn't get time to actually work on that project for another week.

Part of that was just the nature of being an Imperial Conscript. When you spent ten hours a day working, two doing physical training, and at least eight sleeping, it didn't leave you with much free time to begin with.

After I'd told everyone about the plans for the Strike-Wave league, what little free time we'd had became dedicated to practicing in advance of the try-outs.

It wasn't until our day of rest that I managed to drag myself back to the Information Center after I woke up, collapsing into one of the comfortable seats with a long groan. I may have loved playing Strike-Wave, even practicing it, but the extra work was leaving me sore literally everywhere.

"...should have just stayed at base and soaked in a pool." I muttered, trying not to move more than I absolutely had to. "Ow. Dammit Ruru, I didn't need to do that many diving saves."

Both of my arms felt like weights as I brought them up to the keyboard, typing slowly.

Oshflara Riots 2157.

My aches and pains faded into the back of my mind when the results popped up. Nearly all of them were news articles of various kinds, and the titles...

The titles weren't flattering to my species.

"Human riots continue into third week." I scrolled slowly, reading aloud as I went. "Alien extremists crash shuttle into starport. Savannas destroy bridge to slow army... why didn't we get any kind of briefing about this?"

Ruru couldn't have known, and Pak would have mentioned it during our conversation. Well, I hoped he would have at least.

Shaking my head, I went back to the search bar and adjusted my query. I needed the start of it. Needed to see if Ramos was telling the truth about what had caused everything. The rest I could look up once I had that foundation secure.

Thirty minutes in and I was pretty sure his story had been mostly accurate. An emigration ship from Earth had arrived, full of very angry Humans not happy about being removed from their homeworld. The first riots had started within a couple of days of their landing.

"He just left out the part where it was less of a riot, and more of a battle." I muttered, frowning as I flicked through more reports.

Returning to the first few I'd found, I flicked through them with a growing sense of unease.

After the third one I brought my wrist-comp up and called Ruru.

"*Ashe.*" The other accepted by voice only. "*I'm sunning myself on the barracks roof. What's going on?*"

"Just a quick question. Did the HSL briefing mention the riots?"

"*Riots? What riots?*"

That answered that question. "Well, less riots and more of a battle between the Humans here and everyone else."

"*They definitely didn't, I'd have remembered that. How far back?*"

"Few years ago. Do me a favor? Ask Pak if the Sword Leaders were told at least?"

She hummed. "*Yeah, I suppose I can help your little project. My meeting with him tomorrow fine?*"

"No rush." I assured her. "I'm just trying to make sense of this."

"*You're too curious for your own good, you know that right?*"

My eyes rolled. "Thank you for being supportive."

A muffled sound, like a tired yawn, came before she replied. *"No problem. I'm going to go back to napping now, don't call again unless there's an invasion or something."*

"Enjoy the sun."

Ruru grunted and hung up, leaving me to arrange my reading list for the rest of the morning. There were several summaries and recaps of what had happened by various journalists, and I wanted to get through each one to really get a feel for what had happened.

Then I could get lunch, maybe get a nap of my own, then see what Fyth was up to.

I was so occupied with my little plan that I missed other people coming in.

One of them scoffed loudly, her voice as loud as it was disdainful. "What is that thing doing south of the river?"

"No idea." Another woman said, "At least it had the courtesy to shave its disgusting fur off."

My fingers twitched inwards, throat going dry. I started to turn around, then grunted in surprised pain when an elbow sharply struck the back of my chair. The impact made the rolling chair slide forwards enough to drive my stomach into the desk, drawing another unhappy sound from my lips.

The two women who'd already spoken were joined by a third, then by a man. Civilian clothing, all adults, which meant they were all Guides. All four made sure to glare at me once I got my head around to see them.

Ashahn's blood. Trahcon supremacists. Of all the times and days to run into a pack like this, it just had to be today. This was bad. This was all kinds of bad.

"Don't you have your own sector to hide in, short-fur?" The first, and tallest of them, growled. "What are you even doing here?"

"...just leaving." I replied quietly, pushing myself back again. "Excuse me, honored elders."

The respect and subservience was enough for one of the women, the one who'd made the comment about my fur. She twitched her tarah before taking a seat... but that still left three of them sneering at me as I got to my feet.

Using the desk to help keep my balance, I carefully slipped past the last pair without incident. That only made me more tense rather than less. When I got to the room's exit I was ready for what I was sure was coming.

The tallest didn't disappoint me.

The moment I was silhouetted in the door she jerked her chin in a sharp nod, a Strike spell lashing invisibly through the air. I couldn't hear it coming like they all could, but I certainly felt it when the telekinetic blow struck me in the lower back.

A younger me would have grabbed at the door to try and stay upright.

A younger me would have opened herself up for a second blow that way.

I let myself be driven forwards, out of the room and onto my knees. It hurt, a lot, but I managed to catch myself on my hands before I could collapse entirely.

"Clumsy alien freak." The only man among them scoffed. "Why the Empire tolerates your barbaric kind I will never understand. Get your fur covered ass back north of the river where it belongs."

"...I am leaving, honored elders." Grabbing the doorway, I got up to one knee, then to both legs.

He glared at me until I stepped out of the doorway, limping down the hall towards the exit.

His spell was crueler than the woman's had been; he hit my right ankle just as I put all of my weight onto it.

The mocking laugh when I fell to the ground faded when he closed the door, leaving me to groan into the floor.

"...ow."

No one was around to watch as I slowly pushed myself up to my hands and knees. Moving from that position to standing again took longer than I'd have liked, and not a second of it felt good.

At least the sunlight outside was warm on my skin.

"Ashahn's blood..." I sighed as I leaned against the building to catch my breath.

It had been a while since I'd run into a group like that. Since my last assignment in fact. Though even the most prejudiced among them hadn't skipped straight to throwing spells the first time I'd met them. Either I was even more unlucky than usual, or the cross-species tensions were even higher than I'd already guessed.

Maybe I wasn't quite as safe to wander around this part of the city as I thought. On my own at least.

Stretching out my legs, I gingerly reached around to rub at my back. It ached enough that I probably had a bruise. Great, I'd have to think of something to say to the others about that.

"Can't tell them what happened." Pushing away from the wall, I started limping back towards the base. "They might try to hunt them down, and the last thing we need is a demerit right after we earned honors for the training exercise."

I got my usual odd looks for talking to myself, but now that I was more aware of it I started to notice the darker ones mixed in.

The lifting of tarah in silent threat displays when I walked past, and the wary expressions when I had to wait next to them for vehicles to roll past.

It made me feel alone and vulnerable among the people I usually felt the most at home with.

I was pretty morose by the time I made it back to the compound. The guards waved me through after the usual scan, letting me make my way to the barracks. Not that I went anywhere near our rooms just yet.

No. I needed another relaxing bath.

At mid morning the base's washrooms were virtually empty. There were just a handful of late risers finishing getting ready for their own days off, or else soaking in the various tubs.

It wasn't until I moved past one of the latter that I realized it was Jal.

"Hey Ashe." He covered a yawn with one hand, the other giving me a tired wave. "You're back early."

"Hey Jal." Fighting down a grimace, I lowered myself to the floor, sitting beside him. "Ran into... unpleasant company."

His tarah flexed out slowly, then jerked back against the sides of his head. "On this side of the river?"

"A pack didn't like a Human working in their center." I shook my head, avoiding the details. "I didn't want to deal with that anymore than I had to, so I came back."

"...damn. Fyth and I will go with next time."

"...thanks." I said quietly. "I think that would be smart."

"What packmates are for. You're a new one, but you're still one of us."

I felt myself smile. "Thanks Jal. That means a lot."

One of his hands waved before he let it fall back into the water. "You come in here looking for us?"

"No, I was going to take another bath to be honest. Everything aches from yesterday's practice. I'm guessing that's why you're still soaking."

"Guessed right." He groaned theatrically. "I thought training for war was tiring, but that's got nothing on Ruru on a Strike-Wave pitch. How many sprints did we even run?"

"A lot, but I ran more drills." Reaching up, I rubbed at my aching breasts. "How many times did I have to throw myself onto the ground to block a shot?"

"Dozens. Water's hot if you want to get in."

"Thanks, I will."

Stripping down, I left my clothing in a neat pile before sliding into the water. There was plenty of room; the tub was big enough to hold five or six people comfortably, and could have probably held our entire pack if all of us tried to get in.

Jal watched with a kind of vague curiosity without looking particularly interested in my body.

"So." He closed his eyes once I was in, content to let his head fall back against the edge. "Did you find anything out?"

Trying not to groan at how good the hot water felt, I mimicked his pose. "I didn't have much time to read, but I don't think my contact was accurate in calling them riots. Sounded more like a full blown insurrection."

"That bad?"

"Several articles mentioned things like the bridges being blown, and suicide shuttles being rammed into things. Entire Arsenal Formations being sent in as full combat teams."

He hummed. "That does sound more exciting than a riot. Does it tell you anything?"

Stretching out my legs, I considered what I'd managed to read, and how it might relate to the few things that I already knew.

"It tells me that things are tenser here than we were told." I said finally. "That there's history I would have thought our briefings should have covered. The restrictions on what army units can go where, the fact that Sword Leaders were only told about that after we landed... it makes me think someone's trying to hide just how bad the cross-species relations are here."

"Only people who could manage that would be the Planetary Circle or the Storm General." Jal's normally jovial tones turned serious. "Those aren't people a conscript can accuse of things like that."

I grimaced, staring up at the ceiling. "I know. Trust me, I know."

"What about your little theory on alien units all being on Ah-Cycle?"

"No idea." I sighed. "Maybe connected to the smuggling, maybe not. I haven't heard or seen anything more on that yet. Still not sure how, or even if, it's all related."

Water splashed a little as he moved around a little, "So what's your next plan?"

"Asked Ruru to see if the SL's were told about the riots. Maybe Pak just didn't feel like telling us. After that, back to reading, maybe see if I can learn anything else from the other Humans."

"Unlikely, but possible." Jal replied. "And that sounds surprisingly patient. Aren't Humans supposed to be anything but?"

A little irritated, I brought a hand near the surface so I could splash some water his way. "Not in the mood for species jokes, Jal."

His wince was almost audible. "Right, sorry. Want me to do anything to help?"

I was about to say no, paused, and reconsidered. "Yeah. If you get a chance, download a reading list on the riots for me? I didn't have time to save what I found this morning."

"Sure, easy enough." He moved some more, waters splashing and dripping. I tilted my head over to see him getting out, sitting on the edge and covering another yawn.

"Done?"

"I've already been in for an hour, and I've got a date with Dahj."

I perked up a little at that. "Good for you! Where are you two going? Fishing?"

"Yup, just outside of the city. She's going to indulge my hobby, then we're off to a tattoo artist so I can watch her learn a bit more about it. What about you? Anything planned with Fyth?"

"Hovercraft race tonight." I confirmed. "If I'm deaf tomorrow, you'll know why."

He laughed and grabbed his towel, starting to dry himself. "I'll warn the rest of the pack. I'll stop by the Information Center on my way to the river, get you your list."

"Thanks Jal."

"No problem Ashe. Enjoy the water!"

"I will."

I let my head fall back, and set about doing exactly that.

X

I set my beer down on the table before admitting, "I'm still not sure how that counts as cheating."

Across the high-top, Fyth groaned. She was my only company that night, after our duties concluded. Ruru had decided to give us the evening before the Strike-Wave tryouts off so that we were in our best shape beforehand.

Which had given Fyth and I time to curl up and watch a recording of a race on Icar before slipping off to the compound's bar to relax and hang out some more.

She explained as patiently as she could. "Because she blocked a legal pass attempt. You can't do that in that section of the course."

"I get that part, I just don't get why it's illegal." I shook my head. "Isn't the point of racing to pass everyone else?"

"It's not about stopping people from passing, it's about stopping them from passing in certain parts of the race. Where the planners think it might be too dangerous."

I stared blankly. "But that was a straightaway, wasn't it?"

"Well, yeah, but that's not the point either. The point is that it *is* a rule and she violated it. She deserved the time penalty that cost her the race."

"So it's a rule... but it's a stupid rule?"

Fyth blinked slowly, "Yeah... I guess you can say that."

"So it's not cheating, it's the violation of a stupid rule." My lips quirked. "Meaning I'm right, and you're wrong."

"...ugh." She groaned, downing more of her own ale before shaking her head. "Yes. Fine. I should have said she pulled an illegal move, I shouldn't have called her a cheater."

"Thank you." I beamed at her. "It's nice to be right."

My packmate rolled her blue eyes, but there was a smile on her face. "Yeah, yeah. All right. You've put up with three hours of me gushing about the race. You can regale me with your investigation now, or did you not figure out anything new?"

"Just a few things. Still trying to make sense of it all."

Fyth nodded seriously. "Where do you want to start?"

"The riots." Leaning back in my seat, I took another sip of my beer before starting. "They definitely weren't riots. It was a full blown battle that lasted close to two months, basically a siege of Northshore until Naulian forces managed to break in and end it."

"So not a negotiated peace like they said then?"

"That apparently came after, in the post-battle riots that got kicked off when the Humans started infighting after they were beaten down."

"Ah." Her tarah lowered, "Were the Sword Leaders told?"

I shook my head. "Only that they were to tell everyone to stay out of the alien sectors. Pak thinks that the Dual-Commanders were at least told more, being officers, but none of them told him. None of the briefing packets had it either."

Her gray lips pursed. "That's weird."

"A bit." I sighed. "More than a bit, really. But I don't know what it means besides the obvious."

"Obvious being that it was horribly humiliating for the government and Storm General, and they're trying to shove it into the deeps?"

I nodded. "Yeah. Which is kind of way above anything I can investigate, so I'm thinking of dropping that entirely."

Fyth tilted her head. "Why haven't you then?"

"Because there hasn't been any riots or problems since then. At least nothing in the local news that matches any of the keywords I could think of."

"So... what? The Humans learned their lesson? The government's been more careful about what laws they pass?" She rolled a shoulder. "Keeping Trahcon units out of their sectors is working to keep them calm?"

"Maybe. I don't know." I thought about it for a few seconds before admitting. "I don't think people get over situations like that so quickly."

"Yeah, probably not. Not sure what else it could be besides their solutions working."

"Me either. That's why I think I am going to drop that line of research for now. If I keep going the only person I can really investigate is the Storm General."

Fyth winced at the very idea. "Please don't."

"I'm curious and determined, not insane." I paused, then added, a little hurt. "You really thought I'd go that far?"

"Well you *are* drinking Bahrishin Dark." She teased. "I've been wondering about your sanity ever since we got here."

I huffed. "Because I have good taste in drinks."

"You certainly have taste, I can't claim that it's good."

"If you're going to keep up with this, I can start dating Moriv or Ruru instead."

Both of her hands rose in surrender. "I yield! I'm sorry!"

Her dramatic reaction made me huff again, but I went back to talking about my investigation without making her apologize further. "So with that one cut adrift, I'm back to just looking up anything I can find on strange unit assignments, smuggling reports, that kind of thing."

"Did you find anything on that?"

"Yes and no." Which was extremely frustrating. "I found one news report a few months back saying that some kind of smuggling operation was broken up in the outskirts, but nothing about who was responsible. Or what was being smuggled. Or who was arrested as a result."

It was Fyth's turn to huff. "That's not very good reporting."

"Tell me about it. It's frustrating." My beer rose and fell as I finished it off. "All I've got left are the unit assignments, which are definitely weird."

She hummed in interest, and I went on. "Did you know the garrison is actually majority Naule?"

Fyth blinked. "Uh, no they aren't. We'd have seen them."

"Oh they definitely are." I shook my head. "Of the three Storm Formations on world, one's entirely Naule, one's half and half with Humans. We're the only Trahcon one, and we've got way more formations assigned to Del-cycle than we should."

"Huh." Tarah worked up and down as she thought about that. "So we're being kept out of sight from the locals, and out of sight of the other units?"

I shrugged. "There's got to be some cooperation, we do have *some* units on the other cycles. It's just way off course compared to what doctrine says."

"Could that be explained by them just avoiding garrisoning us in the other parts of the city?"

"No. Think about it. They could easily assign us to this side of the city, *and* keep our rotations in the Trahcon dominated communities out in the countryside. But they aren't. Even those assignments are mostly being taken by the other formations."

She frowned some more. "Point. What does it mean?"

"I... have no idea." I admitted. "Something, definitely."

My packmate let out a long groan. "Dammit Ashe. Every time I start thinking you're on to something, you admit that you really have no idea what you're even investigating."

"That's the *point* of investigating."

"Can't you at least give me a theory or something?"

I gave her a flat look. "You haven't watched any mystery movies lately, have you? First rule of investigating is that you don't try and pick a course in advance. It ruins everything."

"That makes no sense."

"It makes all the sense. You just don't like thinking about anything that isn't the latest hovercar."

She quickly held up a finger. "Not true. I think about kissing you once in a while."

"Mmhmm. Are cars involved?"

"Sometimes." She admitted shamelessly. "Think you could pin me against the hood of one sometime?"

I felt a little warm when I leaned back in my seat. "Maybe. If you're good."

Fyth grinned, tarah rising in interest, but before we could flirt further one of our packmates called out from the bar's entrance.

"Fyth! Ashe!" I spun my chair to see Moriv jogging over, his expression grim. "Need you both. Fast. Ruru's in deep waters."

Ruru? A glance aside showed Fyth pulling out hard cash to throw onto the table, leaving me free to slide to my feet. "What's going on?"

"Easier for her to explain. Come on."

We followed him outside, then around the building. The outdoor tables were doing a far busier trade with how nice the evening was, the general noise stopping us from speaking until we were a bit farther away.

"Where are we going?" Fyth asked once we were closer to the barracks. "Room?"

"No, training arena."

If she was in trouble and out on the training arena, that was... a bad sign. In my experience, Trahcon in our stage of life tended to react to stress in a handful of pretty predictable ways.

The best case was that they grabbed a few packmates and went off exploring in places they'd never been. Distracting themselves with the new and novel.

The middle case was that they grabbed a few packmates, or whoever was nearby and attractive, and had sex until they forgot their problem.

The worst case...

Jal's yelp of pain as we approached told me that we were in the worst case.

Both of my packmates got up to a quick jog, and I quickly followed suit. Moving around the short wall at the edges of the small arena let us see everyone else in various states of dishevelment.

Ruru was standing in the center of the oval, stripped down to her shorts, revealing shark themed tattoos covering her back. A heavily bruised Jal was being pulled away by an equally battered looking Hely, the two of them collapsing near the wall.

That left Tolu and Dahj, who were slowly circling around our leader.

"Stay out of this Ashe!" Ruru's bark stopped me before I could follow the others closer. "I'm not making an Aspects' damned week worse by seeing you not make the fucking team!"

Clenching my jaw, I held my hands up and stayed back when Moriv and Fyth strode forward to join the threatening circle.

Ruru was apparently in a real mood because she kept swearing. "Fucking come at me already, or I'll start the next bout!"

Four sets of eyes met one another, then Dahj stepped forward as the next opponent. She didn't settle into a stance so much as she simply rushed forwards.

Unseen sorcery lashed out between them, spraying dirt and sand in every direction right before they started swinging fists.

Dahj was pretty good. One of our better fighters in a spar, and she could comfortably take me apart in our training fights.

Ruru beat her down in under a minute, then spun around to attack Moriv. He tried to turn it into more of a sorcerous fight, darting back and away to stay out of her reach. The air positively reeked of ozone, more power flashing and kicking up debris as they fought with their minds and tarah rather than their fists.

His plan worked for a little while, then she caught up to him.

She tossed his moaning body over to where the others were recovering before taking on Fyth.

My usual partner lasted a little longer than Dahj in a fist fight, but mostly because Ruru seemed to be getting worn down. Not that it stopped a nasty one-two combination from knocking the wind out of our driver, leaving her to stagger back.

Little Tolu was the only one left, gamely spreading her hands when it was her turn.

I gave her credit; she was fast and strong despite being the shortest girl among us. She got some good hits in, bruising Ruru's chest and arms, but she couldn't evade forever.

"Fuck." Ruru gasped when Tolu finally surrendered, collapsing at our leader's feat. "Ahshan's... blood. Fuck."

Since everyone else was pretty much out of commission, I took a cautious step forward. "What's this about, Ruru?"

"...our transfer was denied, and thrown back in my face."

I could only blink. "You requested a transfer?"

Her fists clenched while her tarah quivered madly. "*Yes.* After our training exercise, we earned quite a few merits. One each for the Arsenal's performance, then you and Fyth each got one for helping settle the sentry routine. That gave us enough to request a combat assignment."

"Oh." I thought I knew where this was going. "Was it my record that blocked us?"

"No. Well, dammit. Maybe." She shook her head, turning to stalk in my direction. "The assigning officer told me there was no way he would transfer a fifty year garrison team with an alien on it anywhere where they might see combat."

I winced.

"Knock that off! They'd have turned us down even without you."

Probably, but it still stung to hear.

"I was so certain. So was the Dual-Commander. He signed off on the recommendation, told me he was sad to see us go." She finished stomping over, scowling at nothing in particular to our left. "I wanted it to be a surprise for everyone. Then that little bastard was all smug and mocking with his fucking capital accent..."

"Where did you try to transfer us to?" I asked.

"Open ended." Ruru's jaw worked. "Stormshroud, the Contested Territories, or the Earth Garrison. Anywhere that would accept us. I know, I know, it would have sucked for you, I'm sorry. But I wanted to see combat *once* before I have to apply for the academy."

Some part of me was miserably thrilled that we weren't going to Earth.

The rest of me was depressed for Ruru. She was certain to still be accepted by one of the academies, but... her career would definitely be slower.

"I'm sorry." Moving slowly, I carefully put my hands on her shoulders. She tensed up a little, then relaxed when I pulled her into a hug. "Sorry, Ruru. I'd be happy to see combat too, even if it meant Earth."

Ruru inhaled slowly, then her warm breath tickled my neck when she hugged me back. "I'm still pissed. Take me to the bar, get me drunk, and then drag me back to bed."

"What about tomorrow's try-outs?"

"Wake me up anyway, I'm not missing that. Now shut up and find me one of those disgustingly strong drinks you like so much."

I smiled. "As your order, Half-Sword Leader."

XI

"It came down to me and a seriously built huntress from the Second Sword." I recapped for my audience at the Riverside Cantina. "She's taller than me, but I don't think she got enough practice in. Missed three more saves than I did in the final challenge."

Ramos gave me a grin from his side of the bar, "You made the team then?"

"Starting goalie." I hefted my glass up in salute to... well, myself. "Now I get to spend two hours of my downtime every day practicing."

"That's a bit much. Well, you're on Del cycle aren't you? So at least it's something to do, and it'll be good exercise."

I snorted. "That's exactly what Moriv said."

He chuckled. "Good to see that everyone hates that rotation, alien or Human."

Akari shook her head from her seat beside me, her steady voice drier than usual. "What is there not to love about doing paperwork, and moving farmer's produce for them?"

Ramos barked out a laugh. "Sarcasm already? Should I call and warn your husband that you're drunk before sunset?"

The shorter woman rolled her eyes, "Go attend to your other customers, or I shall tell your *abuela* that you are not."

Chuckling, he gave me one more smile before heading off to where a few of the local elders were ready for refills. That left Akari and I alone in our little corner of the bar, my newest drinking partner having the courtesy to have offered me the seat nearest the wall.

"I heard that he accompanied you on a shopping errand in the Northshore." She said once he'd walked away. "Is this true?"

I nodded, setting my drink down. "We only just found out that we're not supposed to move in force up here. That leaves me as the only person in the formation who can easily come to Northshore to pick up more exotic snacks and beer."

Akari hummed. "Why did you ask Ramos to accompany you?"

"Because I knew how to contact him." I told her honestly. "And I needed the help. I couldn't read almost anything in the store, and if he hadn't been there..."

"You were made unwelcome." It was a statement more than a question.

"...yes." I replied quietly. "It wasn't as bad as it could have been, but... yes."

"I see. Next time you wish to do this, you will call me instead."

I blinked. "Why? Ashahn's blood, he didn't think I was interested, did he?"

Her head tilted very slightly. "You understand the problem. I believe he may have. He is already married, and possesses a young boy. Do not seek companionship with him."

"I'm not." One hand rose, "I swear. He was the only one I could think of to call."

"Good. Keep such opinions, and do your best not to encourage him."

"I won't." I promised. "I'm already dating a packmate, I'm not about to go beyond those boundaries anytime soon."

She nodded once more before asking the question I could have expected. "You prefer Trahcon then, like most grayborn?"

I shifted a little in my seat. "Well... yes, I guess? Humans are... weird at the best of times. I've seen one or two that I thought were cute, I guess, but I never had the opportunity to even try."

From her tight breath, I guessed she remembered what I'd told her the first time we'd met.

"Understandable." She murmured. "Well, as you are not sure if you're attracted to Humans, and I am certain that I am not attracted to women, we will cause fewer misunderstandings. May I have your contact information?"

I gave it to her willingly, and she returned the favor. Once we'd both saved it in our wrist-comps, I tried to steer the conversation to safer shores.

"So, what do you do? For work, I mean."

Akari sipped her beer before replying. "Code testing for the Noroth."

I perked up at once. It had been a little while since I'd thought about the group who had so many members on the planetary circle. "The automation producers?"

"Yes." Her sigh was barely audible, but definitely present. "It is not the most engaging work. We verify the latest patches to the controlling software for farming machines. It is exactly as dull as it sounds."

"Can't be worse than Del Cycle." I tried.

For the shortest of moments she smiled, her severity vanishing into something gentle before returning to her normal blank expression. "You would be surprised. Still, the pay is very good. Within a decade we should have enough to purchase a home on a better colony."

"Your..." I nearly said 'bonded', but found the loan-word I was looking for after a moment. "...husband works for them as well?"

"Many in Northshore do. They are the largest employer." She shrugged in the Human way. "He is a staff manager, running internal maintenance. Every day he tells me of the new and interesting ways that people manage to break things."

"How many of them are stupid?"

"Most." That almost smile came and went again. "I allow him to vent over dinner every evening. It calms him, and amuses me."

"Not tonight though." It was easy to tell he wasn't present.

Another shrug. "He is out with Wolfgang, playing football. I did not feel like accompanying them."

"I thought you liked that sport?"

"I enjoy watching professionals play it." She replied. "I love my husband, but that does not make it any less painful to witness his friends attempting to play the game."

I snickered around another sip of my mixed drink. "I think I understand. I'd rather watch a proper league match of Strike Wave than a lot of the flailing I saw at tryouts today."

Akari let out an amused little breath. "I can well imagine. Is that what you hope to do once your term is over?"

"Embarrass myself flailing around?"

That earned me something that was almost a laugh. "No. Strike-Wave, professionally, as a career."

"I..." I paused, then admitted. "I've thought about it sometimes. It would be... fun to be the first real Human player to make it into the sector level teams."

"Are you that good?"

"I don't think so." My head shook once. "Maybe I could make a planetary team or something. It would still be a good life, but... I don't know."

She nodded. "No other talents or desires?"

Yes. I wanted to join Imperial Intelligence, the sooner the better. I wanted to uncover secrets, investigate strange patterns. To work for the one organization in the Empire that might be a fit for who and what I was.

"Not really." I lied, lifting my glass to sip the dark liquid. "Maybe an academy?"

The dryness returned to her voice. "Do not be insulted, but I do not imagine you as an Imperial Officer."

"...me either."

Her near-silent chuckle came along with my more vocal one.

"Why?" I asked when we finished. "Hoping that I'll work with you?"

"Hardly. Merely curious. Most Humans your age..." She shrugged. "Have grander ambitions. Hopes. Wish to travel to those colonies dominated by our kind. I assumed you did not, but that left me curious as to what you might desire instead."

"Oh." That made sense. I was... an outlier. Maybe she was as intrigued by my strange nature as I was by this equally strange colony. "Is that where you want to move? A Human colony?"

"We have yet to decide."

Something in her tone made me test the waters, "Any in particular you're trying to decide on? Maybe I've heard of one."

She shook her head, dark fur shifting with the motion. "There is no point to such thoughts until we have sufficient funding to afford it."

Akari was lying about that. I didn't quite know how I knew, but I felt certain that she already knew exactly where she wanted to go. Where her bonded wanted to go.

True, we didn't really know each other that well yet. We were hardly friends, much less packmates. But there was an obvious world that so many of my fellow Humans were obsessed with.

She wanted to go to Earth... and that was a dangerous thing to admit.

I was trying to think of a way to shift to a safer topic of conversation when I was saved by a new arrival.

A strange arrival.

A Naulian arrival.

"Louis!" The dark furred alien clambered up onto the stool to Akari's right, his lower arms adjusting the vest he wore while his upper pair waved at the bartender. "Beer me you half-furred little boy!"

Instead of being insulted, Ramos barked out a laugh and gave the other man a rude gesture with one hand. "Wait your turn, Korokek, or else you'd be safer not drinking what I bring you!"

Laughter raced up and down the bar, even the elders at the far end snickering along with everyone else.

I felt safe in joining in, guessing this was a common event.

My voice must have been a little louder since he was so close, because he glanced my way, then did a double-take. "Akari! How did a silent soul like you gain the company of such a young female?"

"I spoke to her." Akari replied evenly. "Politely. I know that is beyond your ability to comprehend."

His own deep laugh boomed out. "You haven't changed at all. Introduce me!"

Akari sighed but did so. "Ashe'lori, this is Korokek of Clan Wuqtin."

"An honor." I tipped my head politely.

He beamed at me, showing off his sharp teeth. "Blessings to your clan, Ashe'lori. I see you've earned plenty of merits! Good to see a Human making her way up the technocracy. What brings you out to the Riverside Cantina?"

"She is grayborn." Akari answered before I could. "She wishes to become comfortable around Humans, after poor experiences."

The man's smile faltered at once. "That old story?"

"Not as bad as some, worse than many."

I cleared my throat. "I can tell my own story, Akari. It's all right."

Brown eyes met mine for a moment... then she nodded. "I apologize. It is not my place."

"No, it's all right." Turning back to the Naule, I took him in a bit more critically.

He was as short as most of his kind. Five feet at most, though his double set of arms made him seem larger. Very well dressed in tailored pants and an expensive vest, and the dark fur covering his body was immaculately groomed.

I thought it an easy guess to say he was the wealthiest being in the building.

"Rifleman Experienced Ashe'lori, from Alzuc." I greeted him more formally. "It's good to meet you."

"And you." Reaching around Akari, he offered me a hand. I shook it without hesitation, which seemed to please him. "I would buy you a drink, but sadly I cannot stay for long tonight. Perhaps the next time I come through with a shipment we can converse."

"I would like that." I replied politely... and honestly. What was a rich Naule doing in a place like this?

I meant no offense to Ramos and his family. This was a very pleasant bar, but it was one of dozens in this district alone. I would have expected a man so well dressed to be in a far more upscale area, and in a far more exclusive restaurant.

"Excellent!" He seemed to be one of those people who spoke at full volume at all times. "Then I will see you soon! Louis! Where is my beer!? I need it if I am to properly supervise your brother unloading the shipment!"

Ramos shouted something back in a language I didn't know, but which sounded insulting.

Korokek laughed before sliding back off of his stool, heading around to the doors leading to the kitchen. I watched him amble along on all six limbs before turning a questioning glance to my companion.

"Supplier." She said simply. "Primarily of alcohol."

"Ah."

Akari wasn't finished. "Be careful around him. He has little sense of others, save for what they can amuse him with. I would not meet with him alone if I were you."

"Oh." Lifting my glass, I finished the last of it before setting it back down. "Would you...?"

"I would escort you in this, yes. Tell me those days you will be here, and I will arrange my own visits accordingly."

"Thank you."

And I meant that in many ways. I was truly grateful for her advice, and her offer to replace Ramos as my partner when it came to make further shopping runs. I was less certain as to why she might desire to stay beside me when Korokek came back, but then I knew nothing of the man.

I would probably be grateful for that as well.

More than that... I was grateful for what she had told me about her employment. It had reminded me that I had one avenue of investigation open that I'd practically forgotten about; the Nororth. If they were the largest employer in Northshore, that was... interesting.

Worth investigating for certain, and if I also happened to look up information on Clan Wuqtin...

Of course I wouldn't be doing any research if I didn't get back soon. I was going to be behind on sleep as it was. Plus I had another racetrack date with Fyth later this week, practices, and I needed to help keep an eye on Ruru after what had happened yesterday.

Chopping seas and busy nights lay ahead, which meant I needed to get my rest when and where I could.

Putting my hands on the bar, I slowly pushed myself to my own feet. "I'd better get back to base, on the early shift tomorrow and I'm still exhausted from the tryouts. Thank you for the conversation, and the help. Same time next week?"

"You are quite welcome, and I will be here. One last bit of advice?"

I blinked, then nodded.

"Grow your hair out. You will attract far less attention when you walk among other Humans."

Grow my fur out? I nearly shuddered at the very idea.

But if it meant fewer stares...

"...I'll think about it."

XII

Once I started looking, I started feeling like an idiot pretty quickly.

The Noroth were everywhere on Oshflara. They were the largest employer on the entire planet, completely controlled the automation market, and their largest factories were split between Northshore and West Bend.

I got my chance to really investigate them three weeks later. A huge supply convoy was being sent to one of those factories to pick up new machines, and we were one of the teams ordered to send a driver and partner.

It was more than easy to convince Ruru to send me with Fyth even though the schedule had Dahj going with. For her part Dahj was ecstatic enough to not have to survive Fyth's driving that she'd kissed me full on the mouth, while Fyth was so happy I wanted to go with that she'd done the same right after.

"This is the worst kind of driving." Fyth groaned as we slowly rumbled through the city streets, stuck somewhere in the middle of the convoy. "Might as well have used automatic shuttles or something."

I smiled, "But then we'd have nothing to do, and the Empire can't have that."

"Not true, I could be racing while you watched. Or I could be helping you investigate your little project." She perked up. "Or we could be in bed together."

"All of those do sound a lot better than this." I admitted. "But you missed playing Strike-Wave."

She gave me a quick smile before turning her attention back to the road. "True, or that. I may be terrible at the game, but you look good when you're in goal blocking shots."

My cheeks warmed. "You just like the fact that the uniforms show off my muscles."

"Obviously." Her tarah quivered, "Can you blame me? You've got good ones, and I love the way they flex when you play."

"We're not having sex in the truck while we wait for everything to be loaded. You'll have to wait until we get back."

Fyth tried to pout, but the grin on her lips ruined it rather quickly. "I guess I can hold out that long. Question is can you?"

"I'd rather not get a demerit for being caught in the cab." I smiled. "That's a pretty good incentive."

"Mmm, true." She sighed. "I don't think Ruru could take another demerit right now."

My smile faltered at once, the warmth and excitement draining away in an instant. It left me feeling cold, tired, and more than a little depressed.

I turned my eyes to the city outside of my window. "Yeah."

To her credit, Fyth seemed to realize what I was thinking at once. "It's not your fault, Ashe."

"...doesn't feel like it. This isn't the first time it's happened."

Her growl was low, but the sound of it made me feel a little better. "Shouldn't have happened even once. The whole point of the Empire is to take in other species, isn't it?"

"I guess the sails aren't all down yet."

"Guess not." Turning back let me see Fyth shaking her head. "Right. Tonight, I'm making you forget about all of that. Drinks, bed, that order."

My lips curled a little. "Both of those sound good."

"They'd better." Her right hand left the controls, outstretched towards me. I took it in mine, our fingers squeezing gently for a few long breaths before she pulled it back to help steer.

"Want me to talk?"

"Ashahn's blood, yes please." I groaned, closing my eyes and focusing on nothing but listening. "Just... talk until we get there."

She promptly began to fill the air with her thoughts on the latest model of Delarah hover-bikes, something I knew absolutely nothing about. Not that it stopped the simple sound of her voice from helping to relax me, or stop me from enjoying her incredible enthusiasm for her subject.

That went on for the next twenty minutes until we arrived at one of the factories just outside of the city limits. Following the rest of the convoy, we pulled in through security gates, then Fyth carefully brought us around before backing up towards a loading dock.

"And done." A stab cut the engine, leaving only the sounds of people and machines moving around in the distance. "You want me to handle the manifest?"

"No, it's all right." Grabbing the tablet from the dashboard, I gave the door handle a gentle pull with my other. "I'll be right back. Don't steal the truck!"

"Why would I *want* to?"

Smiling, I waved at her as I got out and closed up after myself. Then it was just a matter of falling in with the others as each truck sent someone off to the right to get our next set of orders and details.

The factory complex itself was massive, looming over us and making even our trucks look fairly small.

It made the tiny office we lined up outside of look even smaller.

"You'd think they could afford a waiting room for us." The man ahead of me complained.

I couldn't help but agree. "No argument. At least it isn't raining."

He glanced back, and then upwards to actually meet my eyes. "True. You're the one that beat out Sili for the Arsenal's Goalie position, right?"

"That's me."

"Impressive. Hope you're up for the first match against the 710th."

I put on a light smirk, "Considering that we're training every day, and

I can't remember seeing them out more than once a week? We'll be pretty prepared at a minimum."

He grinned, "Good. Drown those smug little bastards and I'll buy your pack's drinks at the Storm's Love after."

"Your account might not like that."

"Worth it if I can brag for a month. A pack I know is with them, and they never shut up about how much they love their officers. Be real nice to be able to shove their faces under the water for a while."

My chuckle was joined by several others around us, "I'll do my best in goal."

We chatted a bit more about the team, and our chances in the season that the officers were still planning out. I was confident enough in myself, especially with all of the practice, but I *was* a little worried about our Crashers.

"Arsenal 841 has some big girls in the position." The woman behind me confirmed when I'd ventured the worry. "They'll control the center push, that's for sure. How do our Sail-Runners look?"

"Pretty good. Not the fastest, but they're very good shots." I stretched out my arms, groaning a little as the line moved forward, leaving me up next. "Our defense is solid too. Nice and tall, good teamwork."

She nodded, "They're all from pack Shok aren't they?"

"All but two, they're from Fol. They're fitting in very well though."

"Good to hear." An arm rose, letting us gently bump forearms when the door opened ahead of me. The man we'd been chatting with gave us a quick nod before walking past, leaving me free to move inside.

A Human man was sitting behind a desk just inside, which made me blink a few times in surprise.

From the startled look on his own features, the feeling was mutual.

"...huh, didn't know any of us were in that unit." He managed after a moment. "Transfer?"

115

"Yes, to Pack Vet." I paused, then asked, "I thought all the Human workers for Noroth stayed in Northshore?"

He smiled slightly, "Mostly. I'm here as a temp, covering for someone. Truck number?"

"Twenty-Four." I replied at once, holding my tablet out over his desk. This wasn't the perfect opportunity, but maybe I could learn a little. "How's the work?"

"It's work. Better than being stuck in that uniform." He took it, but wasn't in a hurry to use his security key to unlock it. "The Noroth at least treat us pretty well. Gives us plenty of ways to move up through the technocracy."

I nodded, "Always hard when there's three hundred year old Trahcon around."

He grunted darkly. "Tell me about it. You looking for a place to settle once you're out?"

"Just seeing how things are here for our species." I replied, mostly honest. "It was pretty easy to tell the Noroth were the biggest employers, was curious as to why."

The man relaxed further, smiling as he unlocked the device. "They're good across the board when it comes to treatment, which is pretty hard to find from a Pack of Notables. No comparing us to Trahcon when it comes to advancement tests, understanding about families, that kind of thing."

I nodded again. That would certainly explain their popularity among the Humans.

It was also a violation of Imperial Law, unless Oshflara had an exception. Sure, the technocracy wasn't kind to people shorter lived than Trahcon, but the Empire wasn't about to put someone less qualified in a position of power just to satisfy other species.

If he was freely admitting that they did that... either he'd misspoken, Oshflara had an exception, or it was just publicly known.

"Exception?" I guessed.

"Think so." He shrugged, not looking particularly bothered. "Not like anyone in government is going to call them out since they pretty much own it, and the Storm General knows to keep her mouth shut."

Yeah. I was definitely going to splash myself with cold water for not remembering to look deeper into the Noroth. There was a lot of local context that I felt like I was missing.

"That's good." I said for a lack of anything more profound to say. "No one gives you problems?"

"Me? Not really, I've got contacts and I'm owed favors. Why I'm here today." He paused, chuckled, and then admitted, "Well, that and I wanted a bit of a bonus."

I forced a chuckle as well. "Understandable. Other workers though?"

"Some have problems." He admitted, tapping away on the device a few times, "But most of the grays know to keep their mouths shut so long as no one starts anything. No one wants a repeat of the riots."

"Yeah, they sounded bad."

"You have no idea. You're stuck out at Base Green-Two then?"

I nodded, "I've been in Northshore a few times though. Made a couple of friends, and found a good bar."

"Good on you. Us Humans have to stick together." A final flourish of a finger signed off on the bottom of the report. "Well, I'd be happy to chat with an attractive woman all afternoon, but I've got to keep the line moving."

"I understand." And was rather glad for the line behind me. "Destination and cargo?"

"Four replacement cargo automation. Outpost outside of Vidah."

That was well outside of the city, so at least we'd get to see something new. "Thanks."

"No problem. See you around."

I nodded one last time, took the tablet back, and then headed out. No one outside seemed upset that I'd taken a bit longer than most inside, which I was grateful for. A few minutes of walking got me back to where Fyth was sitting on our truck's hood, legs swinging idly as she waited.

"Where we going?"

"Vidah."

Her tarah perked up. "That's one of the villages, right?"

"I'm already bracing myself for your driving." It was enough of an answer to make her smirk. "Just remember to slow down before we arrive this time."

"Oh? Permission?" Fyth tilted her head. "What's got you in a good mood?"

"Clerk was Human, and he gave me some information on the Noroth." I paused. "Well, that and everyone's really hoping the team does well in our first match."

She grinned, sliding down to the ground. "Get any good offers?"

"Beer for the whole pack at Storm's Love if we win the first match. Definitely more if we win the matches after."

"Excellent." Fyth leaned up, kissing my cheek. "I think we're loaded up, should be good to go. Ready?"

I held up the manifest. "Signed off, ready to go."

"And you're sure I can see how fast we can get this fat barge going?"

"If you crash us, or get us a demerit, I'm *definitely* not going to sleep with you."

She grinned, tarah quivering in more than one kind of excitement. "I'll be careful."

I snorted. "Liar."

"Probably." Another quick peck of my cheek came before she backed off, "Get in! Let's go have some fun!"

XIII

The morning of our first match started off extremely well.

I woke up sore in all of the most pleasant ways thanks to Fyth's attentions the night before, took a long bath before everyone else woke up, and then did a final morning planning session with the Strike-Wave team.

After that I had a light breakfast with my pack, and then went off on my own to do some final stretches before having to report to the pitch just outside of the base.

There wasn't any hint of something wrong until the security guard stopped me from leaving.

"Ashe'lori?" The man on duty asked after he'd scanned by rank badge. "Sorry. You're wanted by an Arsenal Leader for a debriefing."

I blinked, completely baffled. Of all of the things that had been on my mind that morning, an officer looking for me wasn't on the list.

"My Arsenal Leader?" Maybe she was going to give everyone a final speech before the game?

He dashed the idea on the rocks. "No, the 250th's."

That only made confusion worse. I'd never even heard of that designation; it didn't sound like one in our Squall Formation. "Uh. For what?"

"Doesn't say." He jerked his head to the right. "Wait over here, please. We've got a waiting area inside."

His tone was polite, which I appreciated. It cut down on the fact that I had zero choice about this.

I let him lead me inside without any resistance. Walking past the other sentries on duty left me sitting inside of a small room, my only company a few comfortable looking chairs and a wall fountain bubbling away to one side.

Taking the seat nearest, I nodded to the sentry as he waited near the door. He returned the gesture before speaking, "It's not marked as a severe offense, so you're free to call your pack or anyone else you like. If they're not here within the hour we'll get you something to eat."

"Thank you." I replied politely. "Do you think it will take that long? I'm in today's game as a starter."

His tarah twitched. "I'll try to expedite it. If they're not on base at all I think we can swing getting you there, so long as two of us accompany you."

That was both relieving and yet not. As much as I didn't want to miss the game, the notion of showing up with two sentries as an escort would draw the worst kind of attention.

"Thank you." I said all the same.

Giving me a final nod, he closed the door, leaving me with only myself for company.

I managed about a minute or two of paranoid worries before I tapped my wrist-comp, bringing up my contact list. Hesitating over Fyth's name, I scrolled up to select Ruru instead.

She'd be a bit more rational about this.

"*Ashe?*" My Half-Sword accepted the visual request, blinking in surprise when her face appeared above my arm. "*You need a talk or something before the game?*"

"I'm not at the pitch." Turning around and lifting my arm, I let her see the tiny room I was stuck in. "The Arsenal Leader of the 250th ordered me stopped and debriefed."

"*What!? Why?*"

"I don't know." I admitted. "There wasn't a reason given to the sentries, just the order to stop me for a debrief."

Her blue eyes narrowed. "*Severity? It can't be a high level or you wouldn't be calling.*"

"None given, besides it not being severe." I considered it for a moment before going on, "He called it a debriefing, so I don't think there's a demerit warning attached at all."

Ruru twitched her right tarah out, then in. *"Have you been investigating anything you shouldn't have been?"*

I glowered at her, a little insulted. "I'm not stupid, Ruru."

"I know you're not, but I have to ask the damned question and you know it."

Exhaling sharply through my nose, I tipped my head and answered. "No. I've got a new lead that I worked out from talking with locals in Northshore, and from chatting with someone at the Noroth factory on the last run. At most I spent an extra two or three minutes talking with an employee there."

"Nothing else while on duty?"

"No, of course not."

She grunted. *"Maybe they're a packmate to the leader of the 710th, trying to give them an advantage in the match today."*

"You think they'd be that petty?"

"It's that or he's a supremacist bastard looking in to why there's one Human in the entire base."

I was silent for a moment, considering those options before admitting. "I like the petty idea a lot more now."

"Me too. Should I alert our Dual-Commander, or the Arsenal Second?"

"I... don't want to draw that kind of attention just yet." I bit my lip, "If I'm not there by the time the warm-ups start, or if I haven't called you again, then probably tell her."

"There won't be a probably. I'll tell the rest of the team anyway, so they know what's going on. Stay safe, stay smart, Ashe."

"I will, Ruru."

We ended the call, leaving me sitting in a chair with nothing but a quiet fountain for company.

Over the hour that followed, I ran through everything I might have done to end up in this situation.

It wasn't a very long list. I spent one evening a week at the Riverside Cantina, which was during my personal time. Hardly anything an officer at the Arsenal level would care about since I was going alone. All of my research at the information center came on my days off as well.

That just left my early efforts to figure out which garrison units were assigned to which cycle... which I'd also done after my duty hours.

"Fyth's driving?" I muttered, leaning back as much as I could. "She hasn't crashed anything, or damaged a truck. And I'd just get a demerit by message, not a debriefing. She'd be the one stuck in here in that case."

I couldn't think of anything else anyone in the pack may have done. Their hobbies didn't draw as much attention as ours. Jal fished, Dahj did art, Tolu and Ruru read novels, Hely tinkered with machines, and Moriv gardened.

"Nothing that would cause problems. Unless Moriv got drunk without us."

Ashahn's blood. It was definitely sounding like this was going to be about my species more than anything I had done.

Great. Exactly what I wanted to deal with today.

Closing my eyes, I settled in as best as I could to wait, trying to stay relaxed.

In the end it took most of the hour before a single sharp knock preceded an officer in a dark uniform striding into the room. The rank badge of an Arsenal Commander rode on a slim shoulder, his plain features complimented by long tarah.

His dark green eyes took me in when I rose, falling into a salute that left me more than a head taller than him.

"At ease, Rifle-Experienced." He returned the gesture formally. "Sit."

"Sir." I sat at once, my posture rigid and formal.

He remained standing, using the difference to make himself seem taller. "Do you know why you're here, rifle?"

"No sir."

"Do not lie to a superior officer." The instant snap made my back tighten up further. "You have been spending time on duty conducting personal affairs."

Oh. This was about my investigations. That was... unexpected. But why?

I swallowed, "I have conducted no research during my duty hours."

"If you lie to me again you will receive a demerit."

Some little spark of anger rolled around in my chest, but I kept my voice even. "I have not lied, sir. My HSL can confirm that my hour reports are accurate, and that I have not shirked my duties. All of my research has been done on my personal time."

He narrowed his gaze at me. "What do you even think you're doing, conscript?"

"I do not understand the question, sir."

"Your... *research*." He stressed the word. "You claimed you have done all of it during your personal hours. What exactly do you think that you're researching?"

"I am learning about the local situation, sir. Our briefing packets were entirely deficient." When his mouth promptly opened I gambled and rushed out more words, "In my strictly personal opinion, sir."

His glower told me that I'd guessed he'd been about to reprimand me for judging something that far above my level.

When he spoke again some of that irritation bled out all the same. "I also have reports of you going into the Northshore after being told that units assigned to this base are to do no such thing."

"Sir, my Sword Leader only indicated that we were not to move in force." I placed my hands in my lap, trying to keep my voice even in contrast to his. "As I have only gone alone, I did not consider that a problem. Neither did Arsenal Commander Vahl'owri."

"You speak for her now?"

"I have conducted shopping visits on behalf of the Formation, sir. Including orders from Commander Owri about a specific kind of plant she wished to purchase."

"Another lie."

"Sir, I have the verified messages from her military account." My left arm shifted. "I can bring them up if you like, complete with her blessings to travel into Northshore so long as I felt safe going alone."

His left tarah twitched sharply up and out, then retracted against the side of his head. "I see. Then perhaps the Storm General's orders to this Arsenal were not clear enough."

That was so far above my level that anything I would have said would have just set him off again.

I kept my mouth shut.

He gave me a minute of silence to make a mistake, and only once he was sure I wasn't going to did he go on. "Cross species-tensions on this world are particularly high. Your constant back and forth is not something that should be occurring. This activity will cease."

Another little spark. "Sir, I am not in your Arsenal, sir."

Both tarah rose. "You will further receive two demerits. One for insubordination, and another for conducting personal affairs during duty hours."

"Sir..." I inhaled slowly, then brought my left arm up to indicate my wrist-comp. "I request immediate judgment from Commander Vahl'owri."

"She is occupied at a local event."

"Yes sir, I know. I am supposed to be there as well." I lifted my chin. "You have issued two demerits and given me direct orders as an officer outside of my chain of command. As a member of her Arsenal, it is my right to demand judgment from the commander of *my* Arsenal."

The heavy stress on the word didn't go unnoticed from the way his jaw clenched.

"If she is not available, then Squall Commander Gahro should be overseeing cross-unit discipline." I kept my voice even, despite naming an officer who would likely be irate to have to deal with something as petty as two demerits. "I cannot recall if your Arsenal is within our Squall Formation, which may require us to ask yours to sit in judgment as well."

"I know the regulations, *conscript*."

Then why are you here?

I didn't speak the words, but I kept my chin raised to make them clear all the same.

"...I will not disrespect Vahl'owri by dragging her out of her event." He said through gritted teeth. "I will make my formal recommendation all the same, and present my evidence at that time."

"Sir."

"Dismissed, Rifle."

My fingers twitched when he left off the second half of my rank; another deliberate insult. I rose, saluting again, and was a little surprised when he returned it.

I was halfway to the door when I paused, realizing something. "Sir. You did not identify yourself, sir."

He turned, tilting his head to glare up at me. "Cura'tin'keres, Commander of the 250th Titan Arsenal."

"Sir." I tipped my head, and departed as quickly as I could.

I didn't breathe easily until the sentries confirmed I was free to depart, doing my best not to rush through the doors when they opened. The increasingly warm air embraced me when I lengthened my strides, walking as quickly as possible away.

"What in the Aspects' holy names..."

I'd been reamed out by officers before. Both because I'd legitimately done something stupid, and because they'd simply been looking to make a point to a Human with a poor Index.

None of those times had been as... blatantly focused on intimidating me as that had been.

And what was an officer from a completely different Squall Formation doing tracking me down to begin with?

I recognized the Notable Name of Keres, but they'd looked like a bunch of hunting enthusiasts. Nothing worth even a token bit of research.

Had I made a mistake there?

"I guess I'll find out." Swallowing, I accelerated up into a light jog once I was a block away from the base.

I got to the Strike-Wave pitch just as Ruru came striding out, accompanied by a man I vaguely recognized as our Arsenal Second.

"Ah." He drawled. "Just barely in time, Rifle-Experienced. Your team is quite desperate."

"I'm sorry, sir." I sucked in a breath, then took a chance. "The Arsenal Commander of the 250th was attempting to order me to stop visiting Northshore, as well as trying to give me two demerits."

The bored expression on his face vanished at once. "What?"

"What!?" Ruru squawked more loudly a second later, shrinking a little when he gave her a look with one tarah lifted. "Sorry, sir."

He shook his head, already frowning. "Did he give a reason?"

"He claimed I was conducting personal affairs during my assigned hours, and that I was insubordinate when I dared contradict him."

"I see." His head shook. "The 250th's Commander...one of the Keres?"

"Yes sir."

"What seas does he think he's swimming in..." The Arsenal Second huffed. "I will relay this incident to Commander Owri, rest assured that she'll handle it. Try and relax, focus on the game."

I nodded gratefully. "Sir."

He waved for me to go on, and I wasted no time in following Ruru

"Ashe..."

"Later. Please?"

Ruru grimaced, but nodded. "All right. Good luck today, we'll deal with this after."

Exchanging one quick hug didn't really help me find that calm excitement I'd had just an hour and a half prior. I waved off the team's questions when I darted into the locker room, changing as quickly as I could.

I kept shaking through the warm ups, missing at least two easy shots I should have handled.

It wasn't until the first whistle blew, and my feet settled onto my line, that I managed to focus on nothing but the team in front of me... and the ball as it was flung into the air.

XIV

Short version; we won the game by a tidal wave.

Long version; I didn't play anywhere near my best, but I didn't really have to. Our constant practicing had simply left our team far better prepared, more ready to take it seriously. Our opponents simply hadn't been willing to spend that much of their limited free time, and it showed on the pitch.

We'd outplayed them in every part of the game, winning by a total of fifteen to one by the time the final whistle blew.

There were a few grumbles about the differences in the score and in how seriously we'd taken the game, but since our officers were cheering wildly along with the others in our unit, the complaints stayed pretty quiet.

Well, that and the fact that both teams were offered a free round of drinks for putting on a show. That probably helped the most if I was being honest. Not that I was paying much attention to what the other team was feeling after being humiliated.

I was too busy with my own problems. Doing my best to relax and enjoy the trip to the Storm's Love in the aftermath went... well, it went poorly. I was still wallowing in my emotions when we arrived.

It would have been easier to escape from those doldrums if the Arsenal Commander herself hadn't pulled me and Ruru away from our packmates to interrogate us about what had happened.

"What is that tides-damned fool playing at." Commander Owri growled when I'd finished telling her the entire story of what had happened. She'd drawn us into a corner of the place, her Second keeping an empty space between us and the crowd.

"Half-Sword Vet, you can confirm she hasn't wasted time on her hobby?"

Ruru shook her head at once, "Yes, Commander. It's entirely off hours. She's extremely professional. The closest she's come to violating that is a five minute conversation with another Human on our last convoy assignment."

Our superior huffed out an angry little breath. "I'd have to give everyone in the formation a thousand demerits if that warranted a reprimand. Ashe'lori, your investigations. You've kept them limited?"

I nodded at once. "Only public knowledge and light questioning of the locals, sir. I have avoided doing any focused research on anyone above my own ranking."

Her tarah twitched in anger, chin falling and rising in a nod. "Good, then that can't be an issue. I don't know what river he thinks he's swimming in, but I'll handle this storm moving forward."

I let out a quiet sound of relief, "Thank you, sir."

"Did you expect me not to, Rifle-Experienced?"

"With respect, sir." I swallowed, "I, uh, don't have the best experience with officers believing me over other people. Especially when it comes to things that I'm trying to research."

"You mean your last assignment, and the complete and total mess that resulted." And somehow it made me feel worse to know that she knew about it, despite me being one of two hundred or so soldiers under her command.

"Yes, sir."

She huffed. "I could care less about that, or about the other incidents in your Index. You've been in my formation for four months, and you've already earned two merits and shown no signs of problems."

"...thank you, sir."

"You're welcome, Rifle-Experienced. Now, this should have been a good, relaxing way to break up this damned Del-Cycle." There was a frustrated breath, a tight shake of her head. "I know it won't be easy, but I want you to put all of this out of your mind. Focus on today's win, your upcoming games, and your duties. This will be something for the officers to deal with. I'll handle it all."

"Yes sir. Thank you sir."

A strong hand clapped me hard on the shoulder, she gave me a quick nod, then walked back into the crowd with her Second following.

Which left me slumping against Ruru in relief, my packmate sliding an arm around me at once.

"Now that," Ruru murmured into my ear, "Is a good officer. Come on, let's get you another drink. Think you need it. Or maybe five."

"Let's start with an extra strength one and go from there."

She chuckled, pulling me along to where the others were waiting at our table. Someone had already gotten me a Homeworld Hurricane, the tall glass practically calling to me considering how the day had gone.

The bright orange color and fruity smell concealed the sheer amount of alcohol until the half-frozen liquid hit my tongue.

After that I struggled a bit to breathe, covering my lips as I set the glass down.

"Too strong?" Fyth's worried tone told me who'd ordered it for me. "You looked like you needed something heavy."

"No, it's perfect." I reassured her. "Just needed to take a smaller sip to start with."

She nodded, looking relieved before scooting her chair a bit closer to mine. "What did the Commander say?"

Ruru spared me from having to once again relay everything, speaking up. "She's handling it, she believes Ashe, and she's pretty angry."

Jal made an interested sound, "That's good, but can we get the details? All either one of you said was that some bastard from another formation was trying to cause trouble for Ashe."

Our leader recapped what had happened to me before the game had started. From being stopped on my way out of the base, and then on to the other Arsenal Commander trying to give me both orders and demerits in equal measure.

I offered a few comments, confirming bits of the story around deep pulls from my glass.

By the end Fyth and Hely were both growling in anger, and even little Tolu was scowling up a storm.

"Bastard." The shortest woman among us apparently spoke for everyone. "Sounds like he was just looking for an excuse to drown a Human who'd earned too many merits for his liking."

Moriv grunted. "Definitely."

I waited for the chorus of agreement to go all the way around the table before saying, "I... don't think so."

Blinking, Tolu leaned forwards to properly look around Dahj's tall wineglass. "Why not? It seems pretty obvious to me."

"If it had just been giving me demerits, I'd agree." One finger tapped against my cold glass, the condensation leaving my skin wet. "But the order he tried to give me. Telling me I couldn't go into Northshore anymore. That doesn't fit."

Tolu pursed her lips, both tarah working in and out slowly. "...yeah. That's odd. It doesn't make much sense, considering that you *are* Human. The whole point of the order as Pak told us was to stop us from stomping around up there."

"Maybe." Hely shook her head, "But Ashe is the least Human-like Human I've ever met. No offense, Ashe."

"None taken." I replied.

She smiled and then went on, "From what you've said you kind of stick out when you go up there. Maybe he's just trying to avoid an incident."

That earned a huff from Jal. "That current isn't right either, Hely. If the Commander was Human, or Naule, responding to a complaint? Sure, that could be it. But he's Trahcon, and apparently assigned to our base."

"...yeah, concede the point." Hely brought her glass up, sipping once before setting it down. "At least Owri is on it now. She'll find out what's really going on."

There was a general rumble of agreement, my own voice among them.

It was... by the holy Aspects, it felt *good* to be believed. To have my superior officers actually listen to me, to believe me. To promise to look into something.

I was still a little rattled, but things could have been worse.

They got worse when the conversation began to drift apart, everyone else chatting, while Ruru leaned in on my right.

"So, what are you going to do now?" She asked, swirling her own bright blue drink in its glass.

I blinked, a little confused. "Uh. Drink? What do you mean?"

Ruru huffed, smiling even as she shook her head. "I mean now that the Commander is handling things."

"Oh." I shrugged. "Probably keep looking into the Noroth, maybe see if there's anything on the Keres. They didn't look all that interesting the last time I checked, but maybe I missed something."

Her smile faded quickly into a frown. "What?"

I frowned right back at her, "What?"

"The Commander is handling it." She said slowly, "She said for you to focus on your duties and Strike-Wave, so I'm pretty she meant the whole thing."

"That's not what I got out of that conversation." My head shook, "I'm not saying I'm going to investigate a bloody Arsenal Commander, but I'm not going to let him intimidate me into stopping."

Tarah lowered, and the conversations among the others quieted quickly as they realized an argument was starting.

"Ashe, the Arsenal Commander herself is handling this."

"No, she's handling the officer who tried to intimidate me." I corrected her. "I still want to continue my investigation."

Ruru gave me an exasperated look before turning to the others; a silent appeal for a pack-wide vote on the subject.

"Don't look at me." Fyth replied at once, leaning her head onto my shoulder. "I didn't hear what the Commander said, but I trust Ashe's opinion."

Next in line was Dahj, who held both hands up. "I don't know enough about what she's investigating."

"Yes you do." Ruru retorted. "Come on, Dahj."

Our leader's usual partner sighed, shaking her head. "I agree with Ashe in principle. Something's definitely going on in this colony, I trust her research so far. That being said, I think she should ease up a bit."

I frowned at her. "Meaning?"

"Maybe... less digging into the Notables, while still going out to Northshore?" She suggested. "You can still do some questioning there, can't you?"

I supposed that I could, but it would be a whole lot less efficient than just using an Information Center to do the research.

Tolu quickly piped up at that. "I agree with Dahj. She should continue, but furl a couple of sails."

Across from her was Hely, who took a fortifying sip of her beer before speaking. "I'll third Dahj's suggestion."

"I'm with Fyth and Ashe." Jal spoke next. "I'm curious myself as to what's happening, and I don't think she should back down now."

Next to him, the only other boy among us glanced around the table before groaning. Moriv was the deciding vote and he both knew it, and didn't seem to care for it.

He took a long pull of his own Home-world Hurricane, setting it down with a clatter. "Dammit. Dahj's opinion."

"...fine." Ruru shook her head, looking back to me. "Is that it, then?"

133

Are you going to be a Trahcon, and accept your pack's voice?

That's what she really meant by the question. It was one I'd heard before, from other packs, and one I'd answered in different ways. With my childhood pack, I always went with the group as I should have.

My first new pack I'd been yanked out of too quickly to know, but I doubted I'd have ever gone along with their opinions.

My second had taken me a little while to trust after what I'd just been through, but I'd gotten to that point again.

Packs three through five... not so much.

I let out a slow sigh, nodding once. "You're my pack. That's it."

The way Ruru sighed, visibly relaxing, hurt more than it should have. I wouldn't have thought that she'd think I wouldn't agree, but... I guessed she'd still harbored doubts about me.

More of my drink passed through my lips as I started seriously chasing a buzz that would help me feel better about today's events.

When my glass was empty, my head was light but things still just... ugh.

The waitress bringing me another, plus an extra ration of bright blue liquid in a tube helped. I downed the latter, and finally started to relax when Fyth began hand feeding me bits of bread in between sips of our drinks.

That turned into sips of our drinks between alcoholic kisses, which did a much better job of pushing everything else out of my mind.

At least for one night.

Come morning... come morning it all came back to me.

XV

I was so hungover that I honestly don't know how I got through the next day. It was a real struggle to work through the supply reports we were auditing, and I was pretty sure Tolu ended up doing most of my tasks for the day.

Not that any of my packmates said anything. They just gently guided me along, kept their voices down, and made sure I drank plenty of water.

Thankfully we had the day off from practice, which let me find some time to go off on my own to make a pair of long overdue calls.

The base's communications center was quiet when I walked in. That was partly by design; most of the systems were mounted in little privacy alcoves. It was also because there weren't all that many people who wanted to pay for live transmissions off world, leaving plenty of spaces open.

I still went to the far back of the room, inserting my rank badge into the system before sitting down.

The computer flashed, then updated the screen with a welcome display along with my contact list. Scrolling with my finger, I hesitated over the two names nearest to the top before picking the one I was less excited to talk to.

An automated voice promptly spoke. "Searching for connection, please wait."

With nothing else to do, I did.

It took better than two minutes before the feminine tones sounded again. "Connection found. Agent Rerth'riah, location: classified. Call accepted. Beginning transmission."

And with that, the loading screen was replaced by the attractive features of the woman who'd hauled me out of my childhood pack six years ago.

"Ashe." She leaned back, revealing that she was in a bed. Her bare

chest was even more impressively muscled than Hely's, and was covered in even more wild tattoos than Dahj's. *"I figured you'd have called me months ago."*

She'd used my personal name, good. That meant I could be informal despite her rank. "Evening, Rerth. I didn't see the point this time around."

"Things are finally going well with a new pack then? The Vet seemed like a good fit for you."

The casual admission that she'd picked them out in specific told me everything I'd already guessed. That just because I'd told her off in the past for trying to control my career didn't mean she'd actually stopped controlling my career.

I doubted I'd ever get an assignment she hadn't personally signed off on.

Knowing why she was doing it, the guilt she felt for my spectacularly bad first and third assignments, didn't make it any less annoying.

"They are." I allowed, "I'm welcome among them, and they treat me like a proper packmate. Mostly."

Her left tarah flexed slowly. *"Mostly? Your index or your species?"*

I sighed. "Index, I think. They're supportive, but there's little waves once in a while. They think I'll go against a pack decision, that I'll go too far in my investigations. That kind of thing."

"Can you blame them?"

"Well... no." I admitted, "But it still hurts. Those were entirely different circumstances before. Even you admitted that you'd have done the same if you'd been in my position."

"Yes, because those tides-cursed fools were a collection of prejudiced, corrupt idiots." The Imperial Agent sighed. *"I'm guessing that the Vet don't fully grasp that."*

"I told them about it."

She huffed. *"Telling them about it doesn't make it any easier to*

136

understand. Which leads to them having little doubts, which hurts you because they actually treat you as a packmate, so you're not expecting it."

It was simultaneously relieving yet worrying how quickly she could pick things apart. "...yeah."

"The only thing you can do is keep sailing onward with the current. If they're treating you well, then their doubts will drift away over time. But you already know that."

"...yeah." I said again, more quietly. "I guess I just needed to vent to someone outside of my pack."

"And you thought of me first? I'm honestly a little touched."

I shifted in my seat, "I, uh. May have more questions for you."

She hummed, not looking surprised in the least.

"Did you arrange for our combat transfer to be rejected?" I asked. "You already yanked me from one pack just because they were headed to a combat zone, so I know you'd do it again."

Rerth blinked once, then shook her head. *"I did that for good reasons. You weren't ready for where they were going, but I have not done so again."*

"Swear it?" I asked. "Ruru made it sound like it was definitely because of me that it was rejected, even if she tried to deny it after."

"I swear it." She held two fingers to her chest. *"On Ashahn and Mahkahs both."*

"...dammit. Could you....?"

Her head was already shaking. *"I'm sorry, Ashe. I've got other tasks right now. Most of those officers rotate on a six month cycle though. Have Ruru'vet try again then. If she's denied a second time I should be free to investigate. Just don't get any more demerits before then."*

"I'll try. There's problems in that river too."

"Tell me."

I told her about the odd things I'd noticed around Oshflara, the clear division of species, the oddities about the Notables, the riots, and then how I'd been confronted.

By the time I'd finished she was sitting upright, scowling furiously at nothing in particular.

"Arsenal Commanders don't try to discipline people outside of their formation unless there's a far more serious infraction than what he accused you of. That was a definite shake-down."

"I thought so too."

"Nothing on him, or this local group of Notables?"

"No. And my packmates told me to stop investigating them."

She pursed her lips before nodding once. *"Wise of them. Leave it to your officers. I'm going to contact whoever the local Agent is, and see what they know. Don't do anything foolish."*

I felt my fingers twitch. "I'm not stupid, or a child, Rerth. I know how to investigate things safely."

"No, you know how to get yourself in spectacular trouble." She corrected. *"I'm going to accelerate my current project, and then figure out what's going on there. You focus on being a good packmate and a normal huntress."*

"I-"

"That's an order, Rifle-Experienced."

"...yes, Agent Riah."

"I'll do my best to get out there soon. I'll include you in my investigations if that'll stop you from scowling like that."

I did my best to fix my expression back to something more neutral. "It'll be good to see you again."

"...it will be good to see you again too, little shark. In better circumstances." Rerth sighed. *"I'll never stop apologizing for what I did, and*

I will do my best to keep you safe. Even if it makes you hurl lightning at me once in a while."

I... looked away from the camera for a moment. "...knowing why you do it doesn't make me like it."

"I know. I'll contact you when I'm on my way, or if the local Intelligence Agent finds anything before then."

We exchanged quiet goodbyes, and then the FTL transmission cut off.

Leaving me free to glower at the blank screen. Ashahn's blood, I shouldn't have said anything about what had happened. Should have just asked about the transfer request, made small talk, and then moved on.

Now I had actual orders, even more restrictive ones than the light slow-down my packmates had suggested.

Stabbing my finger down on the controls, I brought up my contact list a second time. A moment later the system was pining away with another call request.

"Connection found. Dual-Commander Huvu'ithi, location: Y4-72-Sho. Call accepted. Beginning transmission."

The leader of the second pack I'd been assigned to couldn't have been more different from Rerth'riah if she'd tried.

Huvu's features bore the heavy scars of the artillery blast that had killed everyone else in her first pack, making her look both wild and dangerous at the best of times. Burns coated the left side of her face, while heavy shrapnel marks still showed on both tarah.

Her sorcery had been crippled by that, something that had occasionally left her weeping into my neck even as I cried about my own failures.

I missed her. Missed Rus, and Olil. And Shiik, and Ghai. I missed being around Guides who... acted like proper Guides. Who'd helped me move on from what had happened to me.

Who'd helped move away from being a child, to being a huntress.

"Ashe!" Her home-world drawl was incredibly thick, as always. *"It's about time you called, I was a few days away from losing my patience."*

I felt myself smiling at the first person I'd ever been with. The packmate I still would have been beside if not for Rerth's interference in my life.

"Hey Huvu. Sorry, I didn't want to bother you while you were on assignment."

She snorted, turning her arm to let me see that she was in full armor. Behind her, a glow in the distance looked like... well, an entire forest on fire.

"More Chezzek pirates, they're already gone and the conscripts have the fire contained. We're in reserve in case another group tries to come in, so I've got time. What's going on?"

"Rerth again."

Her smile morphed into a scowl at once. She had done her best to keep me, only to realize that an Imperial Agent had far more pull than a newly graduated Dual-Commander who had Lost Hunter Syndrome.

"What's that Abantian bitch up to now?"

I told her everything. Vented it all. From how happy I was to be accepted by my new pack, to my disappointment at the doubts they still seemed to have. About the man who'd denied our transfer, about the supremacists who'd beaten me in the Information Center, and the officer who'd tried to intimidate me.

And how Rerth had just ordered me to stop doing what I enjoyed most.

Huvu scowled, groaned, and muttered insults at the appropriate times. In the background I could hear the other members of the old pack doing much the same, occasionally coming in and out of frame as she paced around.

"So that's everything." I said in the end. "What do I do?"

"Well, you start by asking a smart, experienced, and sensible Guide for advice." Her lips curled, twisting the scars on her face. *"So you've finished the first bit of work."*

140

I couldn't help but smile. Even everything she'd gone through hadn't stopped Huvu from being the most boisterously self-confident person I'd ever met. "Well that's a relief to get that first task done."

"*As it should be!*" Laughter in the background saw her grin widen before she went on, "*As for what you should do? Do what your packmates think you should do, do what's best for you, and do what's best for the Empire. If some spy with a guilt complex doesn't like it, tell her to go drown herself.*"

"I'm pretty sure that would kill my career, Huvu."

She snorted. *"Then tell her that I said it."*

We both knew that I wouldn't, but I nodded all the same. "So do what my pack said that I should. Keep up with going out to Northshore, see if I can at least figure out what's going on out there."

"*Exactly. Doesn't sound all that dangerous to me. Maybe some corrupt idiot is running another smuggling ring, Aspects know those bastards in the Reaches are getting Imperial equipment somehow.*"

"...I will."

Huvu chuckled, "*We both knew you were going to anyway. You just needed someone older than you to tell you to do it.*"

My cheeks warmed up. "Probably. I'll try and be better about calling, do you mind if I introduce you to my new pack next time?"

"*Why wouldn't I? Any of them attractive?*"

"A few." I admitted. "I'm dating Fyth'vet right now. She's cute, obsessed with cars, very supportive."

"*That's great! She any good in bed?*"

"Better than you." I teased.

That drew a stunned gasp and more laughter from out of frame. "*Liar!*"

"Maybe." I gave her a grin of my own. "Thank you, though. For picking me up and... telling me what I should do."

"Anytime, little shark. Should be off this rotation in six weeks, call again after and I can get everyone else onto the line."

I made a mental note, "Got it. Will you have good war stories for me?"

Her scars warped as her grin grew vicious. *"Oh you have no idea. It's been fun out here. I got to meet a Void Lord on our last operation."*

My mouth dropped open. "You didn't! Who!?"

"Troba'bahl'gekkot. She got sick of sitting around in her flagship, came down personally to command a raid." Her tarah quivered wildly in excitement. *"I'll tell you the whole story next time. Have to go now."*

"Take care of yourself!"

"And you, little shark!"

The other five members of her pack called out their own farewells before the call ended, leaving me sitting with nothing but the silent echo of their voices.

Ashahn's blood I missed them.

I liked my new pack a lot, liked dating Fyth, enjoyed the company of the others.

But... I missed the first pack who'd welcomed me without reservation.

"Feel sorry for yourself later, Ashe." I murmured, pushing myself to my feet. "You've got work to do."

First thing was first; I had to track down Fyth and tell her what Rerth and Huvu had just told me, and then...

...and then I had to come up with a better plan to learn what was really going on in Northshore.

XVI

On my next day off, I went out just as I had been.

My packmates hadn't gotten any less divided when I'd told them what Rerth had said, or when I'd gone on to relay Huvu's conflicting advice.

Ruru had tried, again, to get me to stop, but I'd refused to change my position. That vote had ended deadlocked; with Fyth, Jal, and Dahj of all people siding with me. Everyone else had gotten nervous at the idea of an Intelligence Agent trying to give direct orders.

Still, without a clear majority in the pack, they'd conceded to stick with Dahj's original compromise.

So once I gain I found myself at the Riverside Cantina, sitting down next to Akari and her husband at a high table for once.

"You're wearing a hat." Ren chuckled after one of the waitresses had taken our drink orders. "Decided against growing your hair out?"

Sighing, I reached up and lifted the regulation cap I'd put on. Underneath my scalp was becoming prickly with a thin layer of fur. When he chuckled again I quickly pulled it back down.

"My packmates talked me into at least trying. They want to see what it looks and feels like when its long." I grumbled. "So now I get to spend the next few months hating what I look like."

Akari shook her head. "You are always dramatic. You will look far more normal with it."

"If you say so."

Her eyes narrowed. "You are not normally so agitated. Did your game last week not go well?"

"No, that went fine." I'd already decided to tell them about what had happened, but I still hesitated for a moment. "It... an officer from another Arsenal tried to give me demerits, and tried to order me to stop visiting

Northshore."

Both of them sat up at once, Ren's voice losing all of his joviality. "Could you tell us what happened?"

I could, and did. I left out everything about my investigation, and about my calls. The rest though... the rest they got, including the Notable Pack of the man who'd cornered me.

"A Keres." Akari murmured, glancing significantly at her husband.

He nodded in a way that struck me as grim, muttering something in a language I didn't know. His wife replied in kind, the two of them going back and forth while our drinks arrived.

I waited until she set the three beers down before asking, "Is there something I should know?"

Ren let out a long exhale before replying. "Yes. The Keres are dangerous. They have no love for our species, you should be careful around those bearing that name."

"It sounds like there is a story to that."

"Yes." His expression stayed flat. "It is not a pleasant one. I am not sure you should be told."

My fingers tightened around my bottle. "Considering that an Imperial officer just tried to shake me down, and left me a nervous wreck for a couple of days, I think I should be."

"That is true, and I understand your need for answers." He replied. "But you are an outside conscript. One protected by your own officers. The less you are involved, the easier it will be for them to shield you."

I glared at him. I'd had quite enough of being 'protected' from Rerth, I didn't need someone I occasionally drank with trying to drag me into a safe harbor.

To my surprise Akari spoke before I could. "Tell her."

He turned his attention to his bonded, "You are certain?"

"Yes."

I took a sip from my beer, waiting patiently when he turned back to face me. He lifted his own bottle to his lips, set it down, and nodded once.

"How much have you learned about the riots that occurred here?"

Leaning back in my seat, I waved one hand slightly. "I know that calling them riots is like trying to call an ocean a lake. It was pretty much a full on insurrection. I'm guessing that it was horribly embarrassing for both the colonial government and the Storm General, which is why no one in my Arsenal was told about it in our briefings."

"Not inaccurate." Akari agreed, "Now simply imagine what a Notable Pack who are primarily hunting enthusiasts would do in such an insurrection."

I grimaced. "They joined the defense then?"

Ren snorted. "That is a most polite euphemism for sniping any Human they saw."

My stomach twisted. "You mean... non-combatants?"

"Yes." A wave towards the exits leading to the riverfront. "They set up across the river, on the tallest buildings. Shot anyone they saw who moved regardless of who it was, or what they were doing."

Akari glanced down at her bottle. "People on the streets. Anyone who stood on their patio's. Who looked out of their windows."

By the most holy Aspects... no wonder the Humans here wanted to stay on their own.

More twisting in my belly left me pushing my bottle away. "And the General let that happen?"

"No." He took another drink of his beer. "I am not the most enamored with the woman, but she has lines she does not cross. She removed their members from the Planetary Circle. They did not take that well."

Akari glanced at her husband. "Now you speak in euphemisms. They delight in harassing any Human foolish or unaware enough to draw near them."

145

"Oh." I bit my lip, trying to work that bit of knowledge into everything else that I knew. If the Keres hated Humans that much, resented the Storm General, and the Noroth were the biggest supporters of our species on world...

The Keres were fond of hunting, of an isolated colony, and were apparently Trahcon supremacists.

The Noroth were automation producers, wanted connections off-world, and were apparently pro-alien.

Yeah. I thought I could see where these currents were going.

"They're rivals with the Noroth, aren't they?"

Both of them narrowed their eyes slightly, but it was Akari who answered. "Yes. How did you come to that conclusion?"

I spread my hands on the table. "I was on a convoy run to a Noroth factory. Talked to a Human employee there, he told me a bit about how much they support advancing us. Seems like something the Keres would oppose on principle."

She tipped her head. "You are not wrong. They are political rivals. The Keres wish for Oshflara to remain isolated, Trahcon dominated. An agrarian and unsettled world to indulge in their hobbies."

I thought I saw where this was going. "They were the first colonists, weren't they?"

"Yes." She confirmed. "This was a world they controlled entirely before the Imperial bureaucracy chose it as an emigration target. Something few of them appreciated."

"And the Noroth showed up later?"

"No, they were also here already." Her husband corrected me. "But they thought Oshflara's location ideal for more than merely being a quiet retreat. They wish for it to become an economic hub within the Titan's Zone. A major center of production, and once the emigration projects began, an example of multicultural society."

Oh. Ashahn's Blood, this was... not great. A spoiling match between two groups of Notables wasn't anything I really wanted to be involved with.

"And the Noroth are on the ascendant right now." I muttered. "They've got a majority in the Planetary Council."

"With a veto from the Storm General, who sides with them ever since the Keres disgusted her." Ren agreed. "It is all too believable than one of their number would find an isolated Human to... take their frustrations out on."

Akari's hand slid across the table, gently touching mine. "Be careful around them, Ashe. I do not doubt he was hoping to draw a more extreme reaction from you. To create an excuse."

I swallowed, thanking all of the Aspects that I'd kept my temper. "You're saying I need to be on watch at all times."

There was no hesitation. "Yes."

By all of the Aspects... I was very, very glad my packmates hadn't overruled me today. This was information I'd really needed to know.

Not that I couldn't have guessed it, I supposed, but it was a very serious confirmation.

"I'll keep that in mind." I told them just as seriously. "What else can you tell me about them?"

Ren shrugged. "Little beyond the warnings we have already given. If you are harassed again, and your officer cannot or will not help, then I would advise sending a request to a member of the Noroth."

"Any particular field I should look for?" I asked. "Are there Noroth officers on world?"

"Assuredly a few, and plenty of Human ones." He replied. "My cousin is a Dual-Commander in the 4th Oshflara Squall. They are out on patrol, but I'll give you his information regardless. If there's an emergency, tell him you're a friend, and that the Keres have focused on you."

"Thank you. Is he a member of the Noroth?"

"He is, as many of his unit are."

A unit on patrol meant Ah or Ae Cycle. One of the many alien units I'd realized were operating outside of the normal rotation patterns... something arranged by the Storm General to agitate the Keres?

No, dammit Ashe. That was a wild guess at best.

I shook myself. "Thank you again, I'll save his number for emergencies."

"I would do no less for anyone else harassed by them." Anyone Human he meant, which tempered my appreciation slightly. "Please be careful, Ashe. They do not dare come across the river, but if I were you, I would have your squad ready to pick you up in the evenings."

I'd only done that on the first night, but it sounded like a wise course to follow in the future.

Ren went on when I nodded. "Could you give us the full name of the officer who threatened you? Perhaps he is one we already know of."

I hesitated. "I... told my packmates that I wouldn't look into him. That I'd leave it for the Arsenal Commander to handle."

"And as I would simply be telling you what I already know," He said, "You would not be breaking your word."

"Semantics." I retorted. "I'm not going to sail around their decision like that."

Ren frowned, but Akari touched his arm gently. "It is how Grayborn are. You will not convince her otherwise, and to do so is a dire insult. Consider if I asked you to betray your brother's trust."

The man grunted once, "I see. My apologies, I merely wish to assist you."

"You're forgiven." Taking my beer in hand once again, I finally took another drink. "I do intend to ask them to rescind that restriction. Would you be able to help in that case?"

"Yes."

His speed of reply made me... wary. "Um. You do mean just doing public research, asking around, right?"

It was his turn to glance at his wife, who folded her hands on the table before her. "That would be our first means of investigation, yes. There are... other routes available, if needed."

"...please tell me it's nothing illegal."

"No. I trust you believe I would not admit to such activities to an Imperial soldier."

"...true, I'm sorry." I sighed and swigged more beer. After the little doubts my packmates seemed to have, I'd gone and done the exact same thing.

Akari was hardly a packmate, but we were friendly enough. She hadn't done anything to deserve that doubt and suspicion.

"Just... been that kind of a week, I guess."

She bowed slightly in her seat. "You are forgiven as well. Say instead that our people keep our own archives, and that the names of those who often act against our livelihoods are often recorded."

A request to see those 'archives' was on my lips before I chased them down with beer.

We were friendly, but not *that* friendly.

"Thank you." I said once I'd set my bottle back down. "Seriously, thank you for this. I'd have stumbled right into some kind of political battle without your help."

"You are most welcome." Akari gave me one of her there-and-gone smiles. "Tell us if your squadmates give you permission to investigate this officer once more, and we will assist."

"I will, I promise. Is there anything else, or can we talk about something cheerier?"

Her expression quickly returned to its usual blank mask. "Sadly, there is. Korokek will be back next week. He has not forgotten you."

"He's not going to try and sleep with me, is he?"

To my dismay, she tipped her head to the left. "If you show any sign of interest, he may."

My mouth worked. "Naule aren't even... you know, compatible with Humans. Or Trahcon."

"Traditionally, no." She agreed. "There are alternatives for the more adventurous, and he is... both open minded and lecherous."

...Ashahn's blood. "Should I avoid the bar next week?"

"No, he will simply arrive unannounced then." Akari nodded to our left, where Ramos was working the bar proper. "We will be there at this same time, with a seat reserved for you. Our presence, and that of Louis, will keep him at bay."

"Thanks. Feels like I'm owing you more every time we meet."

Ren smiled at me. "Aid for a Human looking to connect with her people is more than worth it, and you are good company. Simply regale Korokek with stories of other worlds, and he will be content."

I nodded, "Got it. Anything else?"

"No." He paused, "If you wish to relax, might I educate you as to why Football is superior to Strike-Wave?"

"You can certainly try, but be prepared for me to educate you as to why no sport is better than Strike-Wave in return."

Akari smiled into her beer as her husband and I began an hour long debate that cost three more beers, two loaves of bread, one plate of chips, and which ended up resolving exactly nothing.

It was... more than relaxing after everything that I'd just been told. After everything I now had to think about, had to find a way to research that didn't violate the word I'd given to my packmates.

An hour of nonsense banter about sports was... wonderful.

XVII

"This is getting really serious." Fyth put her hands on her hips, staring across the river. The setting sun highlighted the Riverside Cantina, revealing plenty of people already taking spots on the patio over the water. "I'm worried."

Pursing my lips, I let out a heavy breath before adjusting my cap. "It's not that bad."

There was a snort from my other side, Jal mimicking Fyth's pose. "You sure? Because I'm positive those two women were following us from the base."

"It's a straight road. Everyone walking west from the base looked like they were following us."

"Uh-huh. Tell me I'm wrong then."

Well, when he directly called me out like that... I couldn't. I was pretty sure they'd been following us too. "Don't be smug about it, Jal."

"Lost cause." Fyth muttered. "He's always smug."

Jal shrugged modestly. "Find me a man who isn't and I'll tell you he's got issues. Point is that if we're wandering into a political fight between two Notable Packs, we should start asking for everyone else to come with."

"I won't say no if you want to call Ruru." I shook my head. "That's going to be your call. I'm already late for whatever this is. The sooner I figure out what's going on with this supplier, the sooner I can try and figure more of this puzzle out."

Fyth glanced up at me. "I thought you pretty much had it."

Another shake. "I've got the broad course each side is following, but there's more here. There's still the strange unit assignments and the smugglers to figure out. Plus exactly what laws both groups might be ignoring."

"I'm as in favor of finding out the truth as you are, Ashe." Jal said.

"But I'm starting to think we're a bit past a harmless hobby."

"So what? I should just give up?"

He grimaced. "No, just... dammit. I don't know."

"Fyth?"

My usual partner sighed. "I don't know either. I'm not going to tell you to stop, but... he's kind of got a point. So does Ruru. This really feels like a river that conscripts shouldn't be swimming in."

"Maybe it is." I bit my lip, chewing on it for a long moment before I said. "But if I give up now, we'll never get told anything. I'll never know what was actually going on."

There was a quiet groan from her. "And you have to know, don't you?"

"...yeah. I think I do."

"Dammit Ashe. That's kind of hot, and all kinds of annoying."

I huffed out a startled little sound. "My curiosity is attractive?"

"A little. More your determination." Rising up to her toes, she gave me a quick peck on the lips ."Go on. We'll call the others, and be at that bar just down the street. If anything happens..."

"I'll call." I promised.

They both retreated back, Jal's wrist-comp already online, leaving me to make my way across the bridge.

As I'd been able to tell even from the far side, the Riverside Cantina was busier than normal. Several small groups were waiting outside, while even more were packed into the entryway to do the same.

Thankfully I wasn't the only conscript in uniform, so I didn't draw much attention as I carefully moved my way through the crowd. Which was an extreme relief; I felt my nerves starting to falter with how many people were pressed into the space.

Especially since I couldn't understand anything any of them were saying.

I got a bit of relief when the man acting as the host recognized me from my prior visits. He waved me on before I could say anything.

"At the bar!" He called over the numerous conversations around us. "Waiting for you!"

"Thank you!"

He smiled and gave me a thumbs up, then went back to listening to an older man growling something at him.

Letting that conversation go on behind me, I walked past filled tables to find the bar just as overflowing with other members of my species. The sole exception was noticeable for his volume if not his size.

He was at a corner seat, with Akari and Ren to his left. Letting them more or less face each other despite being seated at a very crowded bar. Past them I could see Ramos bustling around, serving drinks, with another man who looked rather like him assisting.

And as I noticed them, they noticed me.

Korokek rose, both of his left arms waving at me when I approached. "And she finally arrives!"

I held my own left arm up in apology, waiting until I was closer before speaking. "Sorry! Got held up by a few things at base."

The Naule laughed, waving for me to sit. "Don't worry about it. You're a soldier, you have duties. We have all gone through such things!"

Smiling politely, I took the seat that Akari and Ren had left empty between them. With my two usual drinking partners acting as shields, I felt myself relaxing a little despite the sheer numbers of other Humans around.

Ramos was already moving a coaster in front of me, smiling as he usually did. "Ale or something stronger tonight?"

"Just an ale, please."

Nodding, he quickly retrieved a dark bottle. A twist of his wrists popped the top off, letting me take a grateful sip when he handed it over.

Then he was off to serve other customers, leaving me to see exactly what this was about.

"It's a pleasure to see you again, Ashe'lori." Korokek gave me a sharp-toothed grin, one hand brushing some dark fur back from his eyes. "I delight in meeting new people."

"It's... good to meet you too." I managed after a moment. He was dressed just as well as he had been last time, something that made him stand out just as much as his species. "What are you drinking?"

That was a safe enough question to lead with, and from the way his grin widened he didn't seem to mind.

"A dark beer that I'm particularly fond of." His own bottle rose, "From an Ark Fleet colony in the Near Reaches. Very difficult to get out here."

Was he trying to impress me by showing off a very expensive drink? I'd have thought his wardrobe enough of a statement.

"How did you even find beer from that far out?" I asked. "I thought the Empire only traded with Alum and the Cathian Crescent."

"There's unofficial channels as well," He chuckled, "But those are both expensive and unreliable. No, you are quite correct. There is a corporation on Alum who facilitates limited trade in Human and Xenthan items."

"Ah. Probably still pricey though."

"Very, but, it is good, and so I drink it all the same."

To my right, Ren snorted quietly into his glass. "Are we going to spend all night listening to you brag about your wealth, old friend?"

Korokek laughed more loudly, "You know that I never tire of it, old companion. Nor do I tire of trying to convince you both to accept my offer. There is wealth enough for you in my employ."

Akari shook her head immediately. "We are not joining your Clan, Korokek. That has not changed."

"And it brings me great despair. Your talents are being wasted." He sighed, disgusted before turning his sunken eyes to me. "Have you heard of the foolish things they waste their days with?"

I sipped some ale, choosing my words carefully. "They've told me a few stories."

He promptly launched into one I hadn't heard, apparently one that involved a Naulian Clan who'd decided to find... unconventional uses for their automatons.

I was ready to call him a liar before I saw Ren burying his face in his hands, and Akari shaking her head.

"Wait, they didn't..."

"Oh they did!" Korokek loved to laugh from how often he did it. "The amount of hair that got yanked out was beyond belief! And then these two poor little Humans walk in on half a clan to find them too embarrassed to talk!"

I couldn't help but smother a laugh of my own. It was a ridiculous story, and a fairly funny one. I still didn't quite believe it, but still. Funny.

"I told you never to tell that again." Ren groaned when he'd finished. "I couldn't even look at any of your people for a month."

"Come now, it was hardly that bad." Korokek grinned, "What of you, Ashe? Any amusing stories from your time as a conscript?"

Lowering my ale, I debated for a moment before shrugging. "I've got a few about my second assignment."

"Come! Regale us!"

Knowing that Huvu and the others completely lacked in shame, I launched into a story involving the time I'd been escorting a newly assigned Arsenal Commander around our base. And how we'd walked into the entire pack having a little too much fun in the garage.

That drew some chuckles, but the laughter started when I got to the rather inventive ways the senior officers had devised to punish everyone.

"Ha!" Hands slapped the bar when I finished, Korokek entirely pleased from the looks of it. "A good tale! There are times when I truly appreciate this Empire."

I remembered some of the first words I'd heard in this building, and I didn't miss several dark looks his loud words earned.

Not that he seemed to care, shaking himself in amusement. "Come Tell us another! Or perhaps Akari can break her taciturn silence!"

Akari gave him a rather prim look, pointedly saying nothing. Her flat expression drew another smile out of me, and I found myself telling another story of a time that Rus and Olil had gotten lost exploring a city.

"We had to hose them down after." I giggled at the memory of the two men's suffering expressions. "While the entire base watched."

Korokek snickered before launching into a story of his own; a tale of another squad of Naule who'd run afoul a paint trap.

Ren had apparently heard this one before as well; he started correcting the other man when he tried to exaggerate some of the details. Their back and forth was nearly as amusing as the story itself, and I found myself relaxing as the banter went on.

I was still a little confused as to why he'd wanted to meet me, and how everyone seemed to know him, but this wasn't proving to be as bad as I feared.

We swapped a few more stories before Ramos came over to take our second drink orders.

"Busy night." I told him when it was my turn, "Is there an event today?"

He smiled as he took my empty bottle, already replacing it with a fresh one. "It's New Years Eve."

No it wasn't. It wouldn't be New Years for... oh. "Earth calendar?"

"Yeah!"

"Any different from what I'm used to?"

"Nope!" His grin widened. "Eat, drink, have fun! Seems to be pretty universal."

Korokek's endless smile seemed to falter a little. "Would that all things were."

I frowned a little at the change. "What do you mean?"

"Oh, the usual." He seemed to sigh. "For every good officer, such as those in your tales, there are as many who look at nothing but our species when it comes to assessing our worth."

My own mood fell quickly. "It... can happen, yes."

He shook his head, dark fur rippling. "Foolish. This Empire could be so much, it is a true shame it so discriminates against our peoples."

"It's..." I worked my jaw for a moment, then distracted myself with more beer. I remembered the glares he'd gotten earlier, and I didn't want those glares turned on me next.

Still, it wasn't easy to say anything overtly negative either.

The Empire wasn't always perfect, but nothing I'd heard about the alternatives made me think they were anything but worse.

"...it's certainly not perfect, no."

He nodded agreeably. "That it is not. For every good story there is a more troubling one. When I was your age... I cannot recall the amount of times I was feared to desire slaves, or it was believed I would murder others in sacrifice to bloody gods."

Memories of history lessons on the old Naulian religions made me shift uncomfortably. "Can't say I've ever been accused of either of those."

To my surprise he merely chuckled. "Be glad for it, Ashe'lori. Though I feel safe in guessing that your own accusations run towards subversion, perhaps with snide comments about piracy."

"...occasionally." I admitted, not really sure where this was going, but not at all liking the darker shift the night had suddenly taken.

I think Ren noticed because he shifted slightly in his seat. A moment later Korokek stirred as if he'd been nudged; maybe kicked around the side of the bar.

"But you didn't come here to complain." All four hands folded over the man's chest. "Forgive me, I soured the mood."

"It's all right. It happens."

His sharp-toothed grin returned when he tipped his head. "My thanks. Now, to better stories! Tell me about this Strike-Wave tournament going on in Green River Zone."

I blinked a few times, "Uh, sure. Every Arsenal on our side has put together a team, I think the plan right now is for everyone to play everyone else once. Then maybe some kind of seeded tournament after."

"And they did not invite the populace to watch?" He almost sounded like he was pouting. "The first example of a proper sport here in years, and I cannot even watch!"

Akari huffed. "Cannot profit from it, you mean."

"Are they not one in the same?" Korokek asked innocently.

She snorted while Ren chuckled, and I managed a small smile as our casual banter resumed.

We chatted, traded stories, and generally relaxed for nearly an hour. That sole moment in the deeps not repeated.

Still, by the time I made my excuses and left to reunite with my packmates... I didn't know what it had all really been about. Why the wealthy alien had wanted to meet with me. He'd certainly never flirted with me, Akari had indicated he might.

And... none of them had ever told me how they'd met either.

Another mystery on a world that already held far too many.

XVIII

Korokek showed up at my usual night each of the next two weeks. Each time he wore a new suit, drank a different kind of expensive liquor, and regaled me with amusing stories. Some of his time in the Imperial Army, others about more recent events.

He had yet to actually do anything to have warranted Akari's warnings, which paradoxically just made me all the more confused and wary.

I wasn't anyone someone like him should have been bothering with.

I was... well, pretty much no one. I had a decent number of honors, a few too many demerits, but nothing that made me stand out in either direction. The only thing that made me noticeable was the fact that I was the only Human assigned south of the river.

Fyth and I debated it for a few days, with Jal and Dahj chiming in, but we didn't really come up with anything.

So that left me pleading my case to Ruru and Dahj during Strike-Wave practice.

"I'm not asking to look into the Notables." I batted aside another ball, palms stinging from the blow. "Just into Clan Wuqtin."

Ruru grunted, spinning another in her hands. Normally she wouldn't have been present, much less helping, but the rest of the team was working on mock-scrums. Since those had nothing to do with goalies, the Dual-Commander acting as our coach had agreed to let my packmates run me through my own drills.

"...not happy." She said finally.

"I know, but-" I shot to my right, punching aside Dahj's sudden throw before it could get in. "-but he's definitely up to something and I can't figure out what."

"So you've been saying." Winding up, she hurled the next ball at the bottom right corner. It wasn't fast enough to be a difficult save, but my chest hitting the ground felt as unpleasant as always. "Did you try asking him?"

Grimacing, I got back up. One hand rubbed an aching breast while the other threw the ball back to her. "I tried, but he deflected."

Ruru grunted, glancing to her partner. "Dahj?"

The other woman shrugged as she picked another ball of her own out of a box. "Seems like a safe enough ask to me. It definitely relates to what's going on over in Northshore, and it's not like she went out looking for him."

Our Half-Sword Leader heaved out a heavy sigh. "...fine, fine. Whatever. Just be careful."

I fought down the urge to sigh of relief. I hadn't been entirely sure she'd give in without an argument.

"Thank you." I said, and I meant it. "How did the briefing go today?"

"Arsenal 715 is in real trouble." She started to wind up, then suddenly stopped so Dahj could abruptly kick one to my left. I'd started to buy the fake, and only just barely got my fingertips out to deflect the actual shot. "Nice save! Anyway, they managed to misplace three entire crates."

"Wow. That's definitely demerit worthy." When neither moved to shoot again, I started moving my arms to stretch them out a bit. "What did they lose?"

Ruru rolled a shoulder, "Two crates of auto parts, and one of automation parts. Apparently they got a little too focused on last week's game and completely botched their daily assignments."

Ouch. That was definitely going to leave a giant black mark on whatever pack was discovered to be responsible.

"Drop it off at the wrong location?" I guessed.

"That's what it looks like." She snorted, one tarah lifting in dark amusement. "They're still trying to track down who picked them up. So we all got our tarah's yanked about our record keeping. Plus another lecture about getting too distracted with games over duty."

I glanced around the pitch, at the sweating members of the team struggling in a heavy push at the far end. "Strange. I wonder why."

Dahj snickered, kicking a lazy shot high to make me jump to push it up and over the top of the goal. Relaxing as well, Ruru grinned and kicked another ball my way, then a third.

"Low left for the rest, please. I think that's my weakest zone."

They both obliged, varying up the speed and strength of their efforts. Ruru added in a few sorcerous twists to her throws, giving them wicked curves that made them a lot harder to predict.

I got most of them, but after the twentieth my left arm started to seriously ache from the number of times I'd landed on it.

"Ow. Ow. All right." I groaned, pushing myself up to my knees for the last time. "I think that's enough. Dammit Ruru, if you could work those spells faster you'd be a solid sail-runner."

Her tarah quivered in pleasure at the compliment. "Maybe when I'm at the Academy I'll have the time to practice that. What's next for you tonight?"

"Stretching. And making sure we get everything put back so we don't get demerits for misplacing anything."

That earned me a snort from Dahj, "I think a couple of Strike-Wave balls are less of a priority than entire crates of machinery, Ashe."

"You still laughed."

"Yeah, it was a little funny." She grinned, idly kicking one of them up into her hand. "Anything else going on, Ruru?"

Ruru stretched out her arms with a quiet groan, "Yeah, plenty. Let's get this done, then we can talk about it in the baths. Or do you two not think you need one tonight?"

"Ashe definitely needs to wash her fur with how long it's getting." Dahj teased.

I scowled at her, self-consciously bringing a hand up to touch the bristles. Over the past month it had grown about a finger's width, covering my

161

normally brown scalp with increasingly thick black. Fyth said it didn't look nearly as bad as I made it out to be, but she also admitted to really wanting it be longer before she decided if she liked it or not.

"Stop teasing her." Ruru ordered lightly. "She's uncomfortable enough with Tolu's newly discovered fetish."

"Ugh. Don't remind me." I muttered, stepping back into the goal to start kicking balls their way. "She keeps trying to pet my head now."

"I did tell her to stop."

I nodded gratefully, kicking another one. "And thanks, but... I'm really regretting letting Fyth talk me into it."

She huffed, holding a hand out. The scent of ozone tickled my nose as gentle spells began to nudge balls towards Dahj, who was amusing herself kicking them up into her grasp so she could drop them into the box.

"You indulge her too much." Ruru chided.

"Or you don't indulge her enough." I countered.

That drew a wince. "Maybe... in our defense, we're in our eighties now. It's... about that time we start to drift apart."

About the time even Trahcon were getting tired of one another's company she meant.

Nudging the last of the balls her way, I watched her flick it over to Dahj with her mind. "Yeah. I guess you are. Sorry, that might have been too harsh of me."

"No, you're right." A hand waved off my apology. "She's more enthusiastic than everyone but you about her hobbies, that's not a bad thing. Maybe I'll make Tolu ride with her on the convoy run tomorrow."

I couldn't help but smile. "You know she'll be even more... enthusiastic than normal if it's Tolu."

"Hey, you and Fyth both want her to stop trying to pet you." Ruru grinned, "And you're right that the rest of us should appreciate Fyth more."

"I didn't mean appreciating her ability to terrify everyone." I said, but I laughed all the same. "I think she'll appreciate it though. I'll be back, telling the coach we finished."

She gave me a lazy salute, then told Dahj to stop laying around so that they could put the supplies away.

Jogging over to the far end let me find that the rest of the team was pulling into harbor for the night as well. Stepping around people stretching, groaning, or drinking water, I assured the officer acting as our coach that I'd gotten plenty of shots in.

She nodded, then had me describe how it had gone. She cheered up at once I told her I'd worked on my weak left side, clapping me on the shoulder before giving me permission to leave.

A half hour later found me dropping my aching body into hot water, Dahj and Ruru quickly sliding in after me. All three of us groaned in near unison, which drew giggles when we'd realized we'd done it.

We helped each other wash off as quickly as we could, eager to get that over with so that we could simply enjoy the bath.

It was only when we were all cleaned, seated, and relaxing in the steam that we really started talking again.

"So." Dahj said once she was settled in next to Ruru across from me, "What else happened at the briefings? Anything on the officer who went after Ashe?"

Ruru shook her head, "No, and I did ask for us. Arsenal Commander said the bastard did formally send her demerit requests that she rejected out of hand, and that the Squall Commander signed off on her denial."

"Thank the Aspects..." That was beyond relieving. "...best Commander I've ever had, just for that."

"Owri is damned good." Ruru agreed. "She's wasted in a garrison unit like this. Anyway, she said she doesn't have anything on why just yet. Said to not worry, he's probably just a petty bastard with a grudge against Humans."

I sighed. "That doesn't help me not worry."

She nodded tiredly. "Yeah, I know. Sorry. If he shows up again we're to call her immediately, regardless of the circumstances. So you've got a shield."

Good. That was good.

"You haven't seen him again, have you? Or heard anything about him?"

"Just what I already told you about the Keres."

Ruru flexed her right tarah. "All right. Keep an eye on the horizon all the same."

"Already doing that." I replied.

"Good. Apart from that," Water splashed a little as she adjusted herself, scooting a bit closer to Dahj. "not all that much going on. Still haven't had anything sink down to our level about the smuggling."

Dahj perked up. "That's a good thing though. Better odds they'll still be active when it comes time for us to rotate to Ah-Cycle."

"If we're lucky." Ruru agreed. "What about you, Ashe? Your last trip give you any hints?"

I sighed. "Not really. Not many people really want to talk to me, even now. So I pretty much just chat with Akari, Ren, and Ramos. And I guess Korokek now. If I asked them about smuggling..."

"They'd think you were just trying to use them for information?"

"Yeah." Which I guessed I kind of was... I mean, I'd only gone out there in the first place to try and figure out some of the oddities of his colony. But I did enjoy their company, it was fun drinking with them.

And I sympathized with a lot of what they'd gone through. Appreciated the respect that Akari had given me in return.

"Nothing at all?" Ruru asked. "Nothing really strange over there?"

I rolled a shoulder. "Unless you count expensive Human drinks from the Reaches coming in, not really. I think Korokek just orders those from

Alum to show off his wealth."

That drew snorts from both of the others, a sound I echoed. After a moment, Ruru tilted her head. "You think he's involved in the smuggling?"

"I don't know what to think." I admitted. "He's definitely rich, and definitely involved in some kind of trading and supply business. He really shouldn't be the type to frequent a place like Riverside Cantina."

"So he's strange." Dahj noted.

"Very." I agreed. "But he's the polite kind of strange. Beyond that? No idea. He's really good at being funny, being engaging, showing off his money, and saying a whole lot of nothing about himself."

Dahj hummed, shifting a tiny bit so that Ruru could rest her head on her shoulder. "What do you even talk about with him?"

"Old stories mostly. Recaps of the Strike-Wave games." I gave them another shrug. "Apparently he was trying to get a league set up right before the riots, but the whole separation of the districts cut him out afterward."

Ruru closed her eyes, huffing out a breath. "Not like the Naule don't have games of their own he could sponsor. Or that weird kick-ball thing other Humans play."

"Football." I corrected her. "Everyone at the bar is obsessed with it."

"Fun to watch?"

I thought about it. "It's refreshingly simple, I guess. It's not bad, but it's not Strike-Wave."

"Nothing is." Water dripped as she brought a hand up, covering a yawn. "Keep us updated on your research, and make sure you don't go alone to the Information Center."

"I'll ask Fyth and Jal when we get back. No practice tomorrow, so I may drag them over then."

She nodded, closing her eyes. "Sounds good. Dahj? Wake me up in ten minutes so we can go to bed."

I smiled as Dahj lowered her own head, resting it on top of Ruru's. "As you order, Half-Sword."

XIX

Clan Wuqtin were an oddity in the Imperial economy; they ran an export-import business.

That didn't mean they imported things from other Imperial worlds. Such things were supposed to be done through the regional bureaucracies. Same for sending goods off of Oshflara.

No. They sent and bought things from outside of the entire Empire, which was... well, I wasn't really interested in economics, but even I knew that we didn't really trade with outsiders. No one had seriously traded with the other Compact nations in centuries, and the scattered worlds of the Reaches were very far away.

Which left the question...

"So how do you really make your money?" I asked Korokek directly the next time I saw him. He'd finally missed a week, leaving me free to spend an evening bickering with Ren and Ramos about the effects of weather on sports.

They thought sports should be played under domes, and had gotten insulted when I'd rightfully accused them of insanity.

Now, the week after that, I'd decided to open with a direct question. It certainly seemed to take him off guard, his glass pausing before his lips. Tonight it was just the two of us, plus Ramos, the bar fairly quiet apart from the usual elders at the far end.

"Well," He chuckled, "That is certainly a first. I don't believe I've heard someone open a conversation that way between friends."

I gave him a smile and a little shrug. "You keep trying to get people to work for you, but never actually say what you do. I looked up your clan. Your DataNet site says you do a lot of importing of goods from the Reaches."

"That we do." Korokek agreed.

"And you make money off of that?" I pressed. "I mean, this is the

Empire. Why go outside of it for goods?"

Sipping his amber drink, he set his glass down before spreading all four arms. "We don't always. In truth most of our business comes from supplying my fellow Naule with goods from our homeworld. Sadly 'specializes in shipping from Shaidan' doesn't quite have the same note to it."

I considered that before admitting, "All right, I wouldn't call it that either."

He chuckled. "Glad that you agree."

"But Shaidan's an Imperial holding, so why go through you and not just send a request up the technocracy?"

"Priorities, dear Ashe'lori." Those same arms folded back in once again. "Getting Naulian specific goods into a backwater like Oshflara is hardly an Imperial priority. As I was able to secure a few small cargo ships for myself, I was equally able to secure a few trade contracts."

"Ah." That made far more sense. "So the Regional Circle uses you instead of having to allocate their own shipping."

"Precisely!" He beamed at me. "Quite beneficial for all involved. There are other such interests, on other worlds, but I have largely cornered that business in our little sector."

Interesting. Sort of. Maybe.

"So food and drinks mostly?"

"Along with clothing, furniture, and conversion kits to make vehicles more agreeable to us." Four hands rose in example. "My people may have been members of the Empire longer than your own, but a great many industries are still concentrated in the worlds of the old kingdoms."

Which we were pretty far away from at the moment. "So you charge a whole lot to get things shipped here, and profit."

"We mostly buy in bulk, but you have the general idea." Korokek settled back in his seat, sharp teeth on display. "Goods from the Near and Far Reaches fetch very high prices as well, especially as the number of Humans here has grown."

I hummed, considering that.

It was mostly plausible. Most Humans I'd met would probably pay quite a bit for goods made by the Ark Fleet, or by independent colonies in the Reaches. Even if the quality was worse, they'd still prize it.

If the local Naule felt the same, he could have made a pretty good amount of money importing things for them. Except...

"This isn't a very rich colony." I frowned. "Who could really afford that kind of thing?"

He chuckled. "Come now, Ashe'lori. You are a clever woman. Who here *could* afford that kind of thing?"

The wave struck the beach in my mind. "Oh. The Noroth."

"Indeed. They are by far and away my primary buyers, with those few officers of our respective species being second. They are less wealthy, but willing."

That made... wait. No. No it didn't make sense. Unless the Noroth were bringing a lot more Humans and Naule than any other group of Notables I'd heard about, they'd be dominated by Trahcon.

Why would they buy up specialized goods for aliens? To resell them? That didn't track either; their specialization was automation production. What would they be doing buying and reselling anything else?

I was about to ask when Korokek casually added, "The Keres pay a great deal as well."

My mental ship slammed into a sandbar. "What? The alien-hating Keres buy from you?"

"A great deal."

I blinked, utterly baffled. "Why?"

His amusement only seemed to grow, "Why, to stop the Noroth from buying it of course. To answer your original question, little bidding wars between them is how I made a great deal of wealth for my clan."

"What do they do with them though?"

"Ship them right back off world at a markup to improve their own wealth." He flicked a dismissive hand. "They hold no great Imperial contracts for production or trade, given their focus. They are always in need of hard currency, especially as the Noroth continue to expand their own operations."

I could only shake my head at the oddities of interstellar commerce. And as, yet again, everything here seemed to come down to the petty rivalry between the two Notables.

"Is anything on this planet not a competition between those two?"

Korokek barked out a laugh at my groaning complaint. "I have asked myself that very same question, in much the same tone at times!"

Sipping more of my beer, I set my bottle down before asking. "Did you come up with an answer?"

"There are still many things that do not revolve around them. Not that they would ever admit as much." Two hands folded over his belly, while his upper pair fiddled with his drink. "It did not always used to be that way. Things were once calmer here."

I met his eyes for a moment, "Before the Human emigres began to arrive?"

He shrugged, an odd motion on his little body. "Yes. I don't blame your species, it was hardly your choice. In truth your arrival only accelerated what was already going on between the various local groups."

"But we still got blamed for it."

"Such is the way of things." Korokek sighed. "Before Humans arrived, my people were the emigre newcomers. The ones blamed by the Keres for despoiling their pristine little world. Still, they were less aggressive about it, so things did not seem quite so tense."

"Were they actually less tense?"

His chuckle was quiet, regretful. "Likely not. I was younger, more focused on growing my clan's enterprises. In truth Oshflara has likely been in conflict ever since it was founded."

I nodded. "You just miss when there were fewer factions involved."

"Well put." His bottle rose in a little salute. "Speaking of other factions, how goes your own endeavor?"

My investigations? No, my 'reconnecting' with my species.

"I don't know to be honest." I said. "I like Akari well enough, and Ren. Ramos is funny and helpful. But I'm still... uncomfortable when it gets crowded in here. When I can't understand almost anything that's being said."

The businessman nodded agreeably. "I can't claim to understand all that you feel, but I do a little. One of my first actions upon buying a ship was to take it to my own peoples homeworld. I thought it only proper."

I perked up. This was a story he hadn't told before. "How was it?"

"Not at all what I thought it would be." He admitted. "Before, I thought myself as much a Naule as anyone. Yet when I arrived... my accent was suddenly too thick. That I preferred Caranat turned business opportunities into shut doors. Everyone seemed to pine for things I did not understand or desire."

Licking my lips slowly, I picked my beer up and took a long pull. "I... yeah. I think I know what you mean too."

His bottle rose again, "To understanding."

I mimicked his motion, "To understanding."

We both drank again, and then settled our bottles down. He spoke once we had, "What of you? Any desire to visit your homeworld?"

"Ashahn's blood no." I shook my head at once. "I mean, I don't know much about Shaidan, but it's supposed to be pretty peaceful. Prosperous."

"It is." Korokek agreed. "Lost in the past, but accepting of the Imperial present for the most part."

"Yeah. Earth... Earth isn't." At least as far as I knew. Everything I'd heard about it made it sound like a... well, like a giant mess. Isolated pockets of decent living under Imperial garrisons, a whole lot of ruined land, and constant low-level rebellion everywhere else.

"I'd probably be shot the moment I left a garrison just for only speaking Caranat."

"From what I have heard, that would be all too likely." He said. "A true shame. No people should be so treated upon their very homeworld."

I shrugged. "Not something that will be fixed in my lifetime, I think. I'd rather see Zulflara to be honest."

Korokek blinked, then chuckled. "The legendary world itself? Do you wish to see the ruins left by the Airalon invasion, or simply enjoy being drenched by the monthly hurricanes?"

"The first. And... maybe the old temples."

"Not the Strike-Wave leagues?" He teased.

I snorted. "I mean, the ancient stadiums would be fun to see, but if I wanted to watch the best, I'd have to go to Gathahn. You know that."

He grinned, "Of course, but you seemed to like history so I was curious if you preferred old buildings to better teams."

"I like both." I paused, then admitted with a small smile. "But I'd rather watch the best play in person."

"As would we all. Speaking of, how goes your little league?"

We chatted for a while longer, mostly about the upcoming game my team had against Arsenal 841. It was going to be our first real challenge, and we spent a little way debating the best way to attack their rolling style of defense.

I still wasn't at all sure what to make of him, but it was pleasant to talk with someone new who actually knew the game.

Eventually it came time for me to depart for the evening, and we said our polite farewells.

When I got near the door, I had to step around a few late arrivals, which briefly had me looking back the way I'd come. That let me see him and Ramos in quiet conversation, both of their heads close.

And... I silently realized that Ramos had only come over once during our nearly two hour conversation. He'd given us new bottles, smiled, and then gone back to... doing what?

There were hardly any other people at the bar, so why hadn't he been talking with us as he usually did when it was slow?

Biting my lip, I focused on that question as I stepped out to make my way back.

Fyth, Jal, and Tolu were waiting on the far side of the bridge. They'd apparently picked up some food to go from the bundles in their hands, all four of us falling into step once I arrived.

"What did you find out?" Jal pressed before I could even ask what they'd gotten to eat.

"I need to think on it."

He groaned, "Ashe..."

I sighed. "Some of what he said made sense, some of it didn't. I think he's older than he looks, and he's pretty well traveled. Apart from that... I may need to ask for an exception on the research ban."

Fyth groaned. "Ruru's not going to like that."

"Understatement." Tolu piped up, shaking her head. "We agreed, Ashe."

"I'm not going to dig for details. I just need a member check on the Noroth. Count of Trahcon, Humans, Naule."

The shorter woman twitched one tarah, frowning. "Back to your species oddity theory?"

"I think it might be relevant." If Korokek really was selling a lot of alien goods to the Noroth, that would only really be viable if they were a large number of wealthy aliens among them.

If there wasn't, then the Noroth had to just be selling them on, which would be beyond their focus. Apparently the Keres were already exceeding theirs... but I didn't know if he'd been telling the truth on that.

He may have just been biased and trying to make them look bad.

Well, worse. The Keres already looked pretty bad to me.

"You voted against me expanding my research the last time. What do you think?"

Tolu groaned. "You have to ask when I'm surrounded by people who agree with you?"

"You wanted to come with." Fyth noted.

She pouted, twitched both tarah, then sighed. "That seems harmless enough, but have one of us do the check instead. That way none of the officers can say you're swimming where you shouldn't be."

I considered that for a moment, shrugged, and nodded. "That works for me. I can use that to check basic economic data. Should tell me if Korokek was telling the truth or not."

Fyth nodded once. "And if he's not? Mean he's up to something?"

"I'm pretty sure he's up to something." I frowned. "The questions are what that is, and why he keeps talking to me."

XX

The next day Dahj wandered off to the Information Center after our duty hours ended, and came back with a hand written list of data.

Sitting down at a mess hall with Fyth and Jal, both of whom now seemed at least as invested as I was in this, the three of us started to pour over what she'd found.

"He was telling the truth." I muttered, tapping my finger along each line she'd written. "If her math is right, the Noroth are forty percent Naule, and more than twenty percent Human. Only the highest levels here on Oshflara are Trahcon."

Jal was already frowning, "The Naule I could see, I mean, they've been here a while. But Humans haven't been here for more than a decade, right?"

I nodded. "So far as we know. Ramos said his grandmother has been here longer, but I think the serious emigration only got started recently."

"So how did that many of them manage to specialize enough in automation design to get invited into the Noroth?"

That was a very good question. "Corruption?"

Fyth leaned forwards, frowning at the notepad. "Maybe. To what end though? Notables rise and fall based on their reputation, so why gamble on taking in people who aren't qualified?"

"More support among Humans, I would guess." I frowned as well, then nodded slowly as I thought about it some more. "Especially since the city has separate councils for each district. Even if the Keres got enough of their people up the technocracy in Green River Zone..."

She nodded slowly. "Then the Noroth could still be sure they could have control of the other two."

"Giving them a strong level of local control." I mused. "Even if the Keres manage to get their majority back in the planetary council in a few decades, the Noroth will still have options."

Another set of nods, then a deeper frown from Fyth. "But if the Noroth are corrupt like that, why haven't the Keres done something about it? And why send someone to intimidate you?"

Those were... good questions.

"Korokek said he sells to the Keres as well... which is outside of their focus, unless they're strictly buying hunting weapons or supplies. Maybe they can't expose the Noroth without drawing attention to themselves."

Jal hummed. "Yeah, I think that makes sense. And maybe intimidating you was just... what do they call it. An attack of opportunity?"

I tilted my head, "Just some idiot harassing the first Human he came across?"

"Maybe."

Grimacing, I grabbed the pen Fyth had given me along with her notes and started writing my own. I needed to get my thoughts organized or else I'd just keep jumping from one factor to another as I found new information.

"First, smugglers on Oshflara." I glanced between my packmates. "We've heard more rumors, but nothing else. So they're still a mystery. Right?"

They both nodded, Fyth speaking, "Right."

"Second, the unbalanced assignments that started this whole thing." The pen tapped the paper. "In theory that's because of the Storm Generals' orders splitting the assignments, but it's still lopsided. There are more Trahcon units on Ah-cycle than there should be."

"Right." Fyth repeated. "No theories on that?"

"Nothing that doesn't accuse the Storm General of things I'd really rather not."

Her tarah lowered at once. "Let's... not go there."

"Agreed. Third, the Noroth and Keres are involved in pretty much every level of rivalry that two groups of Notables can have. Both are probably skirting more than a few laws to try and make Oshflara how they want it."

Jal held a finger up, "Which I think we've solved at this point."

I pursed my lips. I didn't really agree, I thought that there still might have been more there. But if Jal thought we'd found as much as we needed to in that river...

Our last vote on my research had been four to four. If he sided with Ruru then that would be it.

"For now." I said after a moment. "Fourth, Oshflara is filled with tensions between the species far past what we could have expected. That kind of ties into points two and three, and... isn't something we can really investigate further either."

Both of them indicated their agreement, Fyth looking cheered. "So it's really just the smugglers."

"Five," I corrected her, "Korokek seems to be involved in a lot more than he's told me. He might have been telling the truth about his income, but he still just... *feels* like he's got some kind of game going."

Fyth's tarah drooped. "Oh, right. Him. Still no idea what he wants with you."

"It's annoying." My lips twisted. "There's times when I think he just wants more people to talk to about Strike-Wave, then there's times when I think he's trying to see if I'm as bitter and angry as a lot of other Humans."

"Maybe he is?" Jal suggested. "Maybe he's doing smuggling on top of his legitimate business."

I groaned. "Don't put that idea in my head. You don't go in with a theory without facts to back it up."

He quickly brought a hand back up, ticking off points. "He's too rich to be hanging around in that bar. He's the wrong species to be there. He's strangely interested in the only Human assigned to our base. Seems to me like he's trying to see if you'd be a useful contact."

My own rose in a counter. "He's their main supplier of off-world liquor, he's old friends with my drinking partners, and I'm their new reclamation project."

"So it's a coincidence?" Jal asked skeptically. "I could see that if he'd showed up more often before, but where was he the first few months?"

That... was a point. Had Akari and Ren been trying to sound me out first? No, that didn't track. They seemed to like Korokek well enough on his own, but they were equally wary of him in ways I knew I didn't appreciate.

Ramos though... no. Well, maybe. I could just be overreacting to what I'd seen last night.

Dammit. This is why I didn't like theories before I was sure I had all of the facts.

I glanced at Fyth to see her biting her lip in thought. After a few moments she sighed. "I don't know. He seems weird, definitely has something going on like you say. But I don't know if it's related to anything else."

"So I focus on him?"

"I think so."

We both turned to Jal, who shrugged. "Apart from things that you can't investigate, I think he's the only option."

At least I still had something to investigate. The others wouldn't be able to say I wasn't still focusing on Northshore. Well, so long as whatever Korokek was up to didn't end up involving me in more.

I wasn't sure if I hoped he would or not.

"Hey," Fyth asked, "Did you want to go out tonight? It's still early."

"Sure. That sounds fun." I glanced at Jal. "Are we inviting him?"

She hummed, turning to eye him as well. "He has been rather helpful lately. I suppose a night out is the least we could do."

Jal took on a wounded look. "I'm helpful all the time."

Fyth and I snickered, my usual partner clapping him on the shoulder as she stood up. "You can come with, Jal. Can we dress up? It's been a while since I got to see you in your nice clothes."

I felt myself frowning. "With my fur like this?"

Her tarah lowered as she put on the saddest expression she could. "Please?"

"I'd really rather..."

Jal lowered his chin to the table, mimicking Fyth's expression perfectly. "Please?"

An hour later found me in the lovely outfit that Fyth had bought me, my arms threaded through my packmates' as we walked together towards the eastern exit.

We'd invited the others, but Moriv had apparently convinced them to join a card game with pack Ishpon. Thankfully Hely hadn't left the room yet, and she'd come through to save me with a silk scarf the same dark green as my clothes. Tying it around my head hid the unsightly fur, and left me feeling far better.

"So where are you taking us?" I asked Jal as we walked.

"Riverfront Thunder." He replied cheerfully. "Tolu and I found it last week. Not quite as nice as Storm's Love, but a lot more upscale than most of the closer places."

Fyth perked up at that. "You mean better food?"

"I mean better food." He agreed. "And all of the seating is outdoors on decks over the river."

That sounded delightful. "Good, I'm starving."

"Me too." Fyth agreed. "Come on Jal. Stop making us walk so slowly."

Our male companion scoffed. "It's not my fault you're both so damned tall."

I smiled, "Could you imagine us being as short as you?"

He shuddered, "No thanks. I don't understand why alien men like their women shorter than them. It's just weird."

We both snickered, then fell professionally quiet when we got to the security gate. The guards at this particular one recognized Jal but not the two of us, which obviously meant they had to make sure our rank chits checked out.

If two armored women had to spend an extra minute or two chatting up Jal, watching Fyth flex, and complimenting my tattoos, well... that kind of thing happened.

The unfamiliar eastern streets didn't look all that different from the other areas I'd already been through. Well decorated, rather pretty, but also a little more busy. Probably because there seemed to be more apartments on this side.

I started drawing the usual looks after the first block or so, though thankfully the fact that I had packmates on either arm stopped anyone from approaching.

Even more thankfully I thought most people looked more interested and curious than hostile. It could have been far worse.

"Here we are." Jal grinned when we reached our destination. "Nice, isn't it?"

"Looks it." Fyth agreed, a sentiment that I echoed a moment later.

There wasn't actually much of a building. Just an entrance gate with a greeter, then a sheltered but largely open kitchen to one side. The smell of cooking meat filled the air, bits of smoke rising from fires and pans.

Just beyond was a multi-layered patio over the river, filled with candle-lit tables.

"Wow." I smiled as we joined the line. "This was a great find just for the view. Good work, Jal."

He beamed, "I'm the best, I know. Feel free to keep saying it though."

I was still laughing when we stepped up, the host smiling politely.

"Late arrivals?" She asked. "The rest of your party is already here and in talks with the Keres. I'll have someone brought over to guide you up right away."

Fyth blinked and spoke for us, "I'm sorry? Party?"

"The negotiations?" The host prodded, blinking as well. "Is that why you're here, Notable?"

It took us a moment to realize she'd directed the question at me. "Um, I'm not a Notable."

A blank and confused look settled over her features, tarah twitching up and down. "Oh. *Oh.* I'm sorry, I'm not used to seeing your people south of the river unless they're with the... my pardon. Are you from the base?"

Negotiations? Between who? The Noroth and the Keres? Had to be, from what she was saying. But why hold it here of all places?

"Yes?" Fyth tried, "We're Rifles from the 711th. Our packmate said you had excellent food."

That made her polite smile return, "That we do! Table just for the three of you, or will the rest of the pack be coming later?"

Fyth shook her head, tugging a little at my arm when I started to try and look around. "Just us tonight. Table rather than the bar, please."

"Of course! This way, please!"

She set off at once, leaving us to follow. I kept my head moving, eyes searching.

I found them after twenty seconds or so; a large party on one of the elevated platforms off to the left. A host of Humans dressed in what I thought counted as our species classical finery, several Naule dressed much like Korokek did. They were seated at a long table opposite of Trahcon dressed up just as well.

Well, some of them were dressed up. At least half of the Trahcon were in uniform. They must have come from the base as well. Was the man who'd tried to intimidate me up there? If he was then-

"Ashe." Fyth muttered as our host guided us away from that platform, "Stop staring."

"Sorry." I forced myself to stop looking over my shoulder. "What's that about?"

She glanced up at me. "Ashe. No hobbies tonight, please. We can stare into that reflection tomorrow."

"I..." Stopping myself, I sucked in a breath, then blew it out. "I'll try."

Waiting until we reached our table, she tugged at my arm to stop me from sitting. When I turned she rose on her toes and pushed her warm lips against mine for a moment. "Be good or I'll drive like a maniac on tomorrow's convoy run."

"You'll do that anyway."

She grinned. "No, I'll drive like what *I* think of as driving like a maniac."

I shuddered at the very idea. "All right, all right. I'll be good."

"Good." Another quick kiss had her relax, breaking away. "See Jal? It is possible to get her to stop investigating something for one night."

There was a snicker from our packmate as we all sat down, "Does that mean I get to start kissing her when she won't relax too?"

"We'll have to find you something to stand on first." She teased.

Laughing, we settled in for a good dinner with better company. I did my best to stay focused on the meal. To flirt with them both a bit when they did, to tease them, to praise the meal and the view.

But no matter what I said, what I did... I couldn't shake the feeling between my shoulders.

Someone watched us through our dinner, through dessert. Through the quiet kisses the three of us shared when we rose to leave. It didn't fade when we left, joining the general crowd of soldiers heading back to base after their night out.

Someone followed us at least as far as the base.

That night I laid awake between Jal and Fyth, wishing the sex had done more to make me stop thinking.

To stop worrying that I was dragging my pack into something I didn't yet understand.

XXI

At first, I didn't think anything really happened over the next few days.

We participated in several large convoy runs. Both bringing materials to more isolated outposts, as well as escorting supplies coming back in. Then we spent a day helping do inventory of a shuttle hangar.

I spent the evenings practicing with the team, then recovering from those practices. My packmates indulged in their own hobbies during their own limited free hours.

To make a long tale far shorter... we had no reason to expect the Arsenal Commander to arrive in the garage in the evening of the fourth day after our dinner, just as we were cleaning things out before going off duty.

"Pack form up!" Ruru's shout had me scramble back out of the truck I'd just gotten into, Fyth doing the same on the far side with cleaning towels dropping from our hands. "Salute!"

"Commander!" All eight of us chorused at once, fists before our throats.

Our commanding officer returned the salute, glancing around at us all before speaking. "Calm the waves."

Once we all shifted into a relaxed stance, she spoke again. "Half-Sword Vet. Confirm your report from three days ago."

Ruru blinked once, looking confused, but did as she was told. "Commander. Three days ago we conducted a standard supply order. Utilizing four trucks, we moved eight crates of marked supplies from this base to Outpost 17-May. Following that, we took four crates to village depot 23-Jah and picked up eight replacements, which we returned to base."

Commander Owri nodded. "And you confirmed the contents of the crates?"

"We had no orders to do, sir." Ruru replied. "We scanned the crate

ID's per standard procedure, local officers signed off as usual."

"You say this when your daily orders clearly indicated you were to open and inspect each crate?"

Oh no. No. We couldn't have missed something like that.

It took Ruru a moment, but she recovered. "I do not remember those additional orders, sir."

The Commander stared her down, then turned to her left. "Rifle-Experienced. Pull up Day Twelve's order."

Hely's left arm rose, tapping on her wrist-comp. A few quick motions and another tap brought the daily orders up.

I could have guessed what she would find even before her tarah lowered in shame. "...instruction fifteen; Half-Sword Vet-Lori to confirm contents of all shipments against checklists provided by local officers."

My throat was dry, and so was Ruru's from her quiet response. "...no such checklists were provided, sir."

"Did you request them?"

"...no sir."

The Commander's tarah rose, her expression briefly showing her anger before she got it under control. "There is your first demerit as an entire Half-Sword."

Ruru looked agonized as we all got a black mark, but she bowed her head. "Sir. I understand, sir."

"You, personally, will receive a second for a command failure." The Commander wasn't finished. "Thanks to you, your team managed to move empty boxes from one base to another for absolutely no reason, leaving agricultural automations to sit pointlessly in warehouses."

"...sir."

She went on as if Ruru hadn't spoken, which she more or less hadn't. "Hely'vet. Read that same day's instruction thirty."

"Yes sir." Hely sounded as miserable as I felt. "Half-Sword Vet-Lori to transport materials from Outpost 17-May to Depot 23-Jah. Contents to include... to include *eight* crates of automation supplies."

How did we miss that? It wasn't possible that we'd missed all of that!

"Second Half-Sword demerit, and the third for yourself, Ruru'vet." Our Commander's voice was merciless. "You managed to not only miss half of your quota, but in doing so you completely jumbled the supply orders for the rest of the day's shipments."

Ruru didn't say anything that time. Neither did anyone else.

"You are all confined to base for the next month." Owri stated, voice flat. "Half-Sword Ruru'vet. As this is your first official command mistake, you will not lose your rank. You will, however, be assigned to retake your HSL training. Anything less than an exceptional response will result in another demerit and a demotion."

"Sir."

The Arsenal Commander snapped her gaze from her to me, "Rifle-Experienced Ashe'lori.."

"Sir." I said the only word I could, making sure my stance was as perfect as could be.

"I have reviewed the security footage from your involvement with Arsenal Commander Cura'tin'keser." Her tarah twitched sharply. "I cannot give you a merit for merely not losing your temper before a blatantly racist superior officer, though I dearly wish that I could. Instead I have ensured you will remain on the Arsenal's Strike-Wave team despite today's demerits."

"...sir." I bowed my head, "Thank you sir."

She nodded once more, then swept her eyes around the garage. Made sure the each and every one of us present knew that she was still furious even if I'd earned a tiny mercy.

"You were among the best Half-Swords in this entire formation." She growled. "I did not expect this from you. I will not tolerate anything like this again. Understood?"

"Sir!" Eight voices rose in unison.

"Resume your duties." Turning sharply on a heel, she stormed out of the garage without another word. The almost oppressive weight of her anger went with her, leaving us all to slump and groan.

Ruru fell to a knee the second the door closed. Dahj was beside her in a moment, wrapping her arms around her. The rest of us quickly moved in as well, everyone touching someone else.

"How did I miss that." Hands rose to cover her face. "How did I miss two entire instructions like that?"

"You can't have." Dahj said at once. "Ruru, you haven't missed an order in the thirty years you've been our Half-Sword."

"Evidence says otherwise."

I shook my head sharply, falling to a knee in front of her. "No, Ruru. Those orders can't have been like that. We've made that trip two dozen times, and we've never had to open the crates. Why would we? We're just the truck drivers."

"Did you not hear Hely?"

"There is no way." I cut a hand between us. "Ruru, you read each one of those stupid instructions every morning. You don't skip even a single one. Swear to me, by any Aspect that you want, that you *honestly* think you missed those."

Ruru hesitated. "I... no. I remember reading them to Tolu before we left. It was just our usual orders. I mean, maybe I missed the eight instead of the four, but... I don't remember instruction fifteen at all."

There was a huff from Tolu. "So what are you suggesting, Ashe? That we got the wrong orders, and someone updated them after?"

"That or someone changed them after to make us look bad."

Seven sets of eyes turned to stare at me.

I quickly held my hands up, "I'm just saying it's possible, isn't it?

None of us think that you actually missed those orders, Ruru. Right?"

The agreement was quick and unanimous.

"So if that wasn't what happened, the only alternative is that someone changed the orders *after* you read them. Either because they sent ones without new updates on accident-"

Morith quickly spoke, "Meaning someone else deserves to be drowned for not sending an alert that the orders were updated."

"-meaning that," I agreed, "or that someone changed them after we got them on purpose."

"Why?" Tolu piped up. "Why would someone do that?"

There was a huff from Jal. "Could be someone over in the 715th covering themselves after they got humiliated for losing a shipment a few weeks back. Or..."

I nodded, agreeing with his current of thought. "Or this is how the smugglers get what they want to get."

Hely shook her head irritably. "Would you two please stop being so clever and just speak plainly?"

"Sorry." I settled in and explained, "Smuggling is dangerous, risky, and can be very expensive. You want to cut down on all of that as much as you can. The easiest way to do that is to have someone on the inside to set things up."

Ruru narrowed her eyes, "Figured this out on your last assignment?"

"Yeah, and I think it makes sense here. Blaming conscripts for equipment going missing sounds like a really convenient way to make things disappear."

That time Hely got it, groaning. "Automation parts. That was what we were supposed to be shipping. That's what the 715th lost too."

"The only thing Oshflara really produces." I sighed.

A quiet chorus of growls and curses followed, Fyth leading the discussion. "We should tell the Commander."

"Are you joking?" Dahj countered. "She'll think we're just trying to blame someone else. And she'd be right."

"We can't just *not* say anything." Jal countered.

Tolu quickly brought a hand up, "You're assuming they aren't already looking into it. They wouldn't just ignore missing equipment."

"But what happens if they find out we guessed what was going on, and didn't tell them?" Fyth retorted.

"Quiet!" Ruru's snap had everyone shut up. "Let me think for a moment!"

Silence lingered as we waited patiently, our nominal leader closing her eyes and steadying her breathing.

I didn't blame her. Three demerits, for command mistakes? This late in her career as a conscript?

She'd probably just seen her chances to be promoted to full Sword-Leader sink just in sight of land, and saw any chances of applying to the most prestigious academies go down with them. Now she'd be stuck going to a smaller school, and her career would be far slower to advance.

Ruru had just been cut in both hearts, and we gave her all the time she needed.

After a few minutes she exhaled. "Ashe?"

"Yes?"

Her blue eyes met mine. "You're done investigating."

I flinched. "Ruru!"

"No!" She hissed. "I think you might be right. One of those stupid local notables or the other is up to something. Trying to sink barbs into one another."

It didn't take me long to realize where she was going with this. "You think that someone thinks I'm involved?"

"You said it yourself." Ruru growled. "Someone followed you from the restaurant. Someone saw you there at the same time some kind of negotiations were happening. Someone apparently thought you were there to spy on them."

Ashahns' blood. I'd considered that, but I didn't think it would lead to something like this. I tried again, "But-"

"I don't care that it was a coincidence!" Her voice rose, "I don't *care* what is going on in this stupid colonial backwater, but I'm starting to think they targeted us for what you've been up to!"

Tolu shifted, looking at her feet. "She might be right, Ashe. The officer may have been the polite way to make you back off. And when you didn't..."

"But I still don't *know* anything!" I protested. "I barely know anything!"

"You apparently know enough to get us all demerits!" Ruru snapped. "We're voting on it, and we're voting now! Hely!"

Our tallest member flinched at the shout, not quite looking at anyone. "I... Ashe? We need your opinion."

Swallowing, I struggled to find the words. This wasn't anything I'd considered, anything I'd thought or prepared for.

"I... if we were targets, then we need to prove it. We need to get those demerits removed." I flailed in the water, trying to process all of this. "If something is going on here that's so serious they'd go this far, then we've got to figure it out. They might not stop at just punishing us like this."

Hely bit her lip, right tarah lowering a little. "And... do you think you *could* figure it out? You said it yourself, you don't know anything yet."

"I... I'd need time. More information."

"To dig into the Notables. The officers." Closing her eyes, she shook her head. "That's... that's too far. I'm sorry, Ashe. Stop."

I winced, then winced again when Ruru barked a new name. "Tolu?"

"...stop." Came the quiet mutter.

"Morith!"

He sighed, shaking his head. "Stop, at least for now. Let things calm down."

"Dahj!"

Two hands rose, rubbing tiredly at her face. They stayed there, muffling her word. "...stop."

And that was that. It didn't matter what Jal and Fyth said, much less what I said. Not that it stopped Ruru from turning to them, forcing them to make their opinion clear.

Fyth swallowed audibly, then put a hand on my shoulder. "Ashe is right. They might not stop just because we do. We should dive into the river, not flee to the heights."

Ruru grunted, then everyone turned to our last member. "Jal?"

His own groan was long, pained. "I... fuck. I shouldn't have brought us to that stupid bar."

No one else spoke.

"...hiatus." He tried at last. "We vote again when the month is over. Not like we can do anything until then anyway."

"No." Ruru's voice was flat. "Vote yes or no, Jal."

"...dammit." His shoulders and tarah both drooped. "...stop."

It hurt. Everything hurt.

Everyone turned to stare at me, waiting for my response.

What else could I say?

"I... I accept my pack's voice."

XXII

I tried to live my life as if I wasn't Human. As if I was a Trahcon like every friend, packmate, and lover I'd had.

But once every couple of years... once every couple of years I found myself acting like a Human.

We couldn't leave the base, but there was still a bar within its walls. The entire pack had gone straight there once we'd finished our cleaning duties, everyone fully intending on getting utterly drunk to try and forget what had just happened.

Everyone but me.

I'd quietly told Fyth I needed to be alone, and then slipped away.

Walking two laps around the interior walls to burn off frustrated energy didn't do as much as I'd have liked. I briefly checked out two of the weight rooms only to find them both fairly busy, legs carrying me on after brief looks.

An hour later I was alone in one of the outdoor arenas, the walls surrounding the small pitch cutting me off from the thousands of people all around.

It would do.

A short trip to a storage shed let me grab a practice target and three Strike-Wave balls. Setting the former up against a wall let me start kicking the latter as hard as I could at it.

"Fuck!" I swore with each successive boot. "Fuck! Fuck!"

What was I supposed to do now? My pack had been challenged, and had decided to back down.

But *I* didn't want to back down. Sure, there were times you had to. Times when you had to duck your head, had to take getting a spell to the back. Tune out the stupid things people said about you.

Sometimes... sometimes you had to stand your ground. You had to accept the pain, and then respond in kind.

Just because we'd decided to back down didn't mean that whoever had screwed us over would *know* that we'd backed down. Wouldn't decide to find a new way to make sure that we weren't a problem.

Now every day would become a mess of paranoia and worry until we finished this stupid cycle.

"Listen to you." I muttered, retrieving the three balls so that I could kick them again. "Making sure we aren't a problem? How could we possibly be a problem when you're so stupid that you can't figure out what the problem is?"

That was the question. I had my notes. Had theories. None of them made any sense.

None of the currents seemed to lead to the sea.

"What does it matter?" Grimacing, I slammed my foot into the first ball, hammering it into the target. "They said to stop. That means thinking about it isn't going to do anything."

It would just frustrate me all the more.

Three kicks later had me stalking off to retrieve everything once again, trying to use the time I had to waste doing so to help calm me down a little.

I guess it worked a little. I spent most of an hour just repeating the same actions; kicking three times, setting the target back up, retrieving all three balls, and then doing it all over again. More words tumbled out as I tried to just... get rid of all of the thoughts in my head.

Get rid of every theory I might have had, as if merely saying it would help me stop thinking about it in the future.

Was Korokek a smuggler? Maybe, it didn't matter now.

The Noroth were corrupt? Definitely, it didn't matter now.

The Keres were breaking laws? Probably, it didn't matter now.

Someone in the army was selling to smugglers? A theory, it didn't matter now.

Someone had been following us? I thought so, at least twice, but it didn't matter now.

All that mattered was that my pack had spoken, and now the only thing to do was wait for Rerth to show up. Wait for her to rebuke me further for not doing as she'd told me. Maybe she'd give me another demerit, leaving me with even worse odds of getting into an Intelligence Academy.

Maybe I did need to start searching for a middling colony with a Strike-Wave league. It wasn't really what I wanted to do for the rest of my life, but I needed some kind of plan for my post-conscription career...

I was working myself into a thoroughly morose mood when someone opened the gate and walked in to my little hideaway.

A familiar someone.

Arsenal Commander Cura'tin'keres closed the gate behind him, one tarah lifted as he smirked at me. "Rifle Lori."

"Arsenal Commander." I saluted, something he returned only after a long moment. "I apologize if you reserved this space, sir."

"I did not." Turning, he took a few steps to one side, and then leaned against the outer wall. "Carry on."

"I was just finish-"

His voice sharpened. "Carry on, Rifle. I am curious as to how your kind reduces stress."

A little bolt of anger rolled through my belly, but I held my tongue in favor of nudging the three balls into line with my feet.

I drove the first right into the center of the target. Then the second. Then the third.

"That's it?" He drawled when I walked forward to reset and retrieve yet again. "You've been kicking those things into a stationary target? Not all that useful of a talent for a goalie."

"I know, sir." I replied without looking his way. "The repetition is meditative."

A snort. "Meditative. I'm sure."

I didn't reply. I just got set again, this time picking up a ball to try throwing them instead.

The first one left my fingers, sailing straight... and then abruptly curved to smack into the fencing. A light scene of ozone made me turn, unable to stop myself from glaring at the man who'd just affected my throw.

"Humans shouldn't be playing Strike-Wave." One tarah slowly flexed outwards before tucking back in against his head. "You couldn't even hear me gathering power, much less wielding it."

"That does not stop me from playing goalie, sir." I said in reply. "And I can smell the effect just fine."

Blue eyes rolled, "So useful, that. Being able to smell a spell long after it has already been cast."

Once again I said nothing. When he didn't go on, I reached down and picked up a second ball. Letting out a slow breath, I wound up, and threw again.

That time he twisted it off course the moment it left my fingers, making it bounce hard off the ground before fetching up in a far corner.

"Sir." My temper rolled further. "If you are merely here to disrupt my exercises, I request you allow me to depart."

Tin'keres' smile was anything but pleasant. "You might be the most polite of your kind I've ever met. I suppose you deserve some credit for that, or whoever raised you properly does, at least."

"Sir." Stretching down, I picked up the last ball but tucked it under an arm rather than throw it. If all he was going to do was make comments, I was going to do my best to leave.

He kept speaking as I started walking to retrieve the two balls he'd sent flying off target.

"How does it feel, knowing that you crushed seven more careers through your own negligence?"

My mouth went dry, and I was glad to be looking away from him. "I... would not know, sir."

"Oh I think you do. I've read your Index, Rifle. You're a lightning storm that burns everything she touches." I stopped walking, lowering my head, which seemed to encourage him. "Your first squad of fellow Humans? All sent to a penal colony for supposedly attacking you."

"...there was nothing *supposed* about it, sir."

He ignored me and went on. "Your third pack? Several demerits for supposed supremacist behavior. Fourth? Mixed Naule and Humans who all earned a dozen demerits each. Fifth? They were well primed for professional careers as soldiers before you dragged them into one of your little investigations."

I flinched without turning. "...they were trying to cover up corruption, sir."

"And now your sixth pack. The Vet." The Commander kept speaking, footsteps sounding as he began to walk around the small field. "Yet another promising set of careers doomed to be held back, all because you were assigned to them. I'm sure each and every one of them is cursing Khash for the ill-luck he blessed them with."

My fingers curled into fists for the barest moment before I forced them to relax. He was trying to do this. Trying to make me break down.

Either to gloat and relish if I collapsed, or to have the perfect excuse if my temper broke.

It was working... it was working very well.

"No." I whispered. "Can't let it happen. Can't."

"What was that, Rifle? Speak louder than a mutter when a superior is speaking to you."

I swallowed. "Nothing, sir. My apologies, sir."

"Come now." Tin'keres strolled into my view, smirking up at me. "Out with it."

Another dry swallow. "It was nothing, sir. Clearing my throat."

That earned me a quiet snort. "I'm sure. I would have thought someone with an Imperial Agent hovering over them, even a useless alien, would be better at lying."

"...we don't speak much, sir."

"Clearly." That dark smile returned. "One of my packmates is good friends with the local Agent. Perhaps I can arrange for them to give you better tips."

Ashahn's blood. Of course they would know the local Agent... so much for Rerth's report.

By the Aspects, was that what this was really about? Was I being targeted simply because I'd told Rerth, and she'd tried to start an investigation based on my call?

Maybe that started it, and us accidentally walking into the wrong restaurant on the wrong day had simply been the final grain of sand.

"Now tell me, have you learned your lesson about involving yourself in things beyond your place, Rifle?"

It wasn't quite an admission of guilt, but it was close.

Some stupid part of me dove into that at once. "Sir. I'm not sure what you mean, sir."

When he opened his mouth, I spoke again. "And it is *Rifle-Experienced*, sir."

"...for now." His voice lowered to a growl at once, that condescending smirk gone. "Now, there are two rivers before you, *Rifle*. You can take the calm waters, keep your furry head down, be a good little conscript, and you will leave this world with that rank intact."

"I feel I must remind you, sir, that I am not in your unit."

"Such things can be changed." Even the limited back-talk was apparently too much for his self-control. "Be less useless than the rest of your kind, keep your dull little eyes on your feet, and there will be no future problems. If you try to get back into the rapids, I will personally make sure you, and your entire pack, drowns. Understand me?"

I worked my jaw. "I understand, sir. Should I report this conversation to Commander Vahl'owri?"

He snorted. "I was merely assisting you in your practice to make up for my prior rudeness."

No cameras in here. Or recording devices. And considering that I'd just been given two demerits, even if Commander Owri believed me, he could drag in someone else who wouldn't. An Arsenal Commander against a recently disciplined Human conscript?

I'd be lucky to not get another demerit for accusing him.

"...I understand, sir. Am I dismissed?"

He regarded me flatly, then nodded once. "Clean up your mess first."

"Sir."

I wasn't surprised that he didn't leave as I collected the balls and target. It was more surprising he held back from being truly petty and scattering them around with his sorcery, or hitting me directly with a spell.

Instead he just stared at me, tarah flexing in and out in a display of his own frayed temper.

Maybe he realized that he'd practically admitted that he'd been behind what had happened today.

Maybe he thought I wouldn't be able to do anything about that.

I... was going to prove him wrong.

XXIII

Grandiose promises to myself aside, there were plenty of practical problems with my plan to resume investigating.

The most obvious was that my pack had just told me not to.

Decisively.

The equally obvious solution was to simply not tell them. Even thinking about that made me want to throw up.

Not telling my last pack what I was doing hadn't been that difficult of a choice. They'd disliked me from our first meeting, and had despised me by the time I'd realized what was going on. Further, since they'd pretty much ignored my existence, getting away with it had been easy.

I didn't want to hide things from my pack now. I didn't want to have to be a paranoid mess going against their voice.

I wasn't sure what choice I had. The Keres didn't seem like they were simply going to let us be. Telling the others about what had happened would just make them even more determined to not draw any more attention.

But that sort of led into my second problem; I was confined to base for the next month. That was going to make doing any kind of digging into Tin'keres, and the Keres in general, rather difficult. Especially if I wanted to buy myself time by making it look like I was being a good little huntress and just doing what I was told.

Difficult... but not impossible.

I just had to break a few laws of my own.

My opportunity came two weeks later, after Strike-Wave practice.

Everyone in the Arsenal had heard about what had happened, so none of them was surprised when I started volunteering to help clean up after practice. I got a few sympathetic looks about our pack's plight and troubles, and then grateful words when the rest of the team went off to bathe.

While I did start putting all of the gear away, I slipped into the bathing facility after a few minutes.

"There we go." I muttered on seeing my objective. This was my second attempt at this, and yesterday no one had left their wrist-comp in the entryway rather than taking it into the baths.

Not wasting time, I knelt down beside the jumble of clothing and tugged the device out. A tap of my finger on the mesh brought it online, and more importantly revealed that its owner hadn't locked the thing.

Thank the Aspects for two mercies at once, I supposed.

Rummaging in my own pockets, I pulled a small data-drive out and linked the two.

Knowing I didn't have much time, I started with my searches and downloads without letting myself actually look at what I was grabbing.

"Base unit roster... got it. Keres list... got it." Clearing that search, I tapped out the next. "Noroth list... got it. Officer indexes..."

I almost gasped in relief when the last one finished, quickly disconnecting the drive before clearing the recent history of what I'd done.

Then it was a simple matter of putting the comp back where I'd found it, slipping back outside, and rushing around to get everything put away.

Climbing into the baths just as everyone else was leaving left me... feeling relieved at the lack of confrontation, yet terribly alone at the same time.

I spent a little while feeling sorry for myself once again, then went through the motions of getting clean, getting dressed, and walking back to the barracks.

I got there just as Hely was closing the door to our room, her tarah lowered a bit.

They perked up a little on seeing me, at least. "Oh, there you are. Helping clean again?"

"Yeah. Are they all...?"

She sighed. "Yeah. Maybe I'm just hitting the Guide stage early, but I'm not in the mood. You?"

I glanced at the door, considering. Mindless sex sounded sort of good. It would at least bury a few of my feelings for a while, make me feel like one of the pack. Let me stay connected to them.

Make me feel like I wasn't going against their word... no. I'd feel a thousand times more awful tomorrow.

"Not really." I sighed. "I think I'll just go to the lounge, or the library. You?"

"Bar." She twitched a shoulder. "Looking for a new hobby?"

"Maybe." I evaded, already turning around. "Want me to come help you get back to our room later?"

"Sure, might as well get totally drunk." Hely shook her head, using her long legs to catch up and fall into stride with me. "This bloody month. Here I thought things were going well."

"...me too."

My tallest packmate grimaced. "Yeah. This has to feel like the same old waves to you, doesn't it?"

"...yeah." I said. "I'm sorry if I haven't been a very good packmate the last few weeks. Just... feels like the same old waves again, like you said."

Her head shook. "Ashahn's blood. I'm sorry for that."

"For voting against me?"

"...well, no." She admitted quietly. "I don't think diving into that storm is the right thing to do right now. I'm not against you starting up again, just... later. Like Jal said."

That was a little better than a flat no, even if it left me feeling even worse for what I was doing behind their backs.

I think I was about a breath away from telling her something. I wasn't sure what, but *something*, when she went on before I could.

"Maybe finding a new hobby will be better for you though." Hely suggested. "Investigations... sound like dangerous things to me. Seems like they've brought your packs trouble before."

"...maybe." The word was a murmur, my single heart very not in it. "I'll see what I can find. See you in a few hours?"

"Sounds good." She gave me a hesitant smile before we split apart; her leaving through the nearby doorway while I kept going down the long hallway.

Brought my packs trouble.

It hurt more coming from Hely than it had from Tin'keres.

Maybe they were right... maybe I was a lightning storm. Just a stupid little Human that brought nothing good, just sound, blustery wind, and collateral damage.

"Maybe." I took a deep breath, counted to five, and then let it out. "Maybe. But if that's what the Aspects have guided me to do, then I'm going to drown doing what I'm best at."

The walk to the base's small library wasn't a long one. Although calling it a library was kind of overstating things.

It was more of a large room, with plenty of windows and couches, and several shelves where people could leave books they'd finished, then pick up new ones.

A couple of men and women from other units were lounging, reading. Enjoying their time after their duty hours.

I made my way to the back corner where a reclining chair sat empty and alone. Settling in, I spun it around so that I could see anyone approaching, fired up my wrist-comp, and got to work.

A short link to the drive I'd used later, and I had what I needed.

"Question one." I murmured, "Why are the Keres the ones harassing me?"

I'd have expected it to be the Noroth. They were the ones I'd been more certain were corrupt. More likely to be involved in the supposed smuggling.

"So apart from being Human, why come after me?"

Hesitating for a moment, I decided to start with the Arsenal Commander's Index rather than anything on the Keres as a group.

Cura'tin'keres had been born on a minor colony in the Abantia Sector. He'd earned no honors or demerits in his childhood pack, which wasn't surprising. Few did.

His life as a conscript had been more exciting. He'd spent nearly forty years in the Stormshroud, and unlike Ramos he'd actually seen combat. Several times in fact, earning merits in several engagements against both Thondian and Human pirates.

"That got him above the acceptance limit, accepted at the Officer's Academy on Altair." I pursed my lips, shaking my head as I kept scrolling down. "Off to the Contested Region to fight the Chezzek... what's he doing out here?"

I found it after a bit more reading, and I honestly should have guessed.

He'd had a bright and promising career until he'd been assigned under one of the few Naule to reach Storm General... in a Naule majority unit.

Within a year he'd gotten four demerits for disobedience, failure to respect superiors, and the abuse of troops under his command.

"Must have been assigned here as a punishment." My free hand rose to rub tiredly at my face. "Forced acclimation."

It clearly hadn't worked.

After those last demerits the only note in his index was that he'd been invited to the Notable Pack of Keres five years ago. No honors or demerits since.

Why a group like the Keres would invite a recently humiliated officer into their ranks was a question as well. Especially since he'd... Ashahn's blood. He'd been on world for less than three months before being invited in.

"So they really are just a bunch of supremacists. That's not enough time for him to be seriously considered otherwise."

Letting out a frustrated breath, I flicked over to the roster file I'd found on the Keres.

There were quite a few for a 'hunting lodge' organization confined to a single mixed-species colony. And... a whole lot of them had military ranks before their names.

Ten... twelve... seventeen Dual-Commanders, Five Arsenal Seconds, Eight Arsenal Commanders, two Squall Commanders, and equivalent numbers of Naval counterparts assigned to the system defense fleet.

That was... that was a lot of the senior leaders on world.

Biting my lip, I flicked over to the Noroth to check their own list. Their list of names was substantially longer, and just as substantially alien. Just as as Dahj's research had indicated they seemed to be dominated by both Naule and Humans as far as Oshflara went.

A few were officers, but only a few. Maybe half as many DC's as the Keres, and only three Arsenal Commanders. No one above that rank at all.

So even if the Noroth dominated the local technocracy, the Keres clearly had the edge in the military. And since this was a mere colony, the Storm General's word was law.

"And she's not a friend of the Keres, but if she's ever reassigned... they've got good odds of having one of theirs promoted up."

Maybe that was what the negotiations were about? Trying to avert a political struggle? No, that was a guess at best.

I had to focus on the immediate question; why the Keres had targeted me, targeted my pack, and how could I stop that from happening again?

Leaning back in my chair, I double-checked that no one had noticed me muttering to myself. When I was pretty sure that no one had, I went right on doing it.

"Keres. Supremacists. Hunters. Lot of military members." That last struck me, and put a second stone on top of the first. "None of those are wealthy positions. Korokek says he sells to them."

If Korokek was telling the truth, and the Keres were buying up Human and Naulian goods to deny them to their rivals... where were they getting the money?

Officers were paid very well, but not so well that they could waste cash on petty things like that. And since they were hobby focused, rather than economically focused, it wasn't like the Keres were pulling in wealth through their little hunting parties.

"Fact." I whispered. "Two otherwise reputable packs have been accused of sloppy reading of their orders, leading to missing goods. Theory... the Noroth aren't the ones trying to expand their wealth illegally."

The Keres were.

XXIV

I had my working theory. Probably sooner than I should have, but I was in a rush.

Either way, now I had to see if all of the facts suited it.

The first extra research I could do even while confined to base, and without drawing too much suspicion; I jumped on to Clan Wuqtin's marketing board, and then starting price comparing. His public wares, those few rivals his clan had, along with the local manufacturers.

Once I had that down, I did some quiet asking about the salaries of the officers.

That earned me a few tarah-twitches, and gentle comments that I probably would struggle in officers' training. Still, they'd believed me about considering my options, and I'd gotten both our Dual-Commander and even the Arsenal Second to talk to me at length about it.

I'd considered calling Huvu... but I couldn't bring myself to do it. She'd support me still pushing on, I was pretty sure, but she'd definitely be against me not telling my pack about it. So I didn't, and was glad when her own call was a short one to tell me our long conversation would be delayed because of her duties.

Ashahn's blood I was a terrible person.

My awful mental state only got worse over the next couple of weeks.

I honestly expected Ruru to confront me about what I was going around asking. Just to ask what I was up to, at least. Maybe to compliment me for considering going with her into a proper military career. Maybe just to discuss things.

Instead she... didn't seem to notice. She rarely spoke to me anymore, beyond during duty hours.

Honestly that hurt nearly as much as everything else. How fast I'd gone from being one of the pack to... being back into my usual state of quasi-isolation. Even Jal was pulling away, though in his case I thought it was guilt for not siding with me like Fyth had.

By the time our period of confinement to base had ended, Fyth was the only one who actually sought out my company anymore.

Not that I was being ignored entirely. Everyone was still happy to talk with me, to help with duties, or to chat about their hopes of what we'd do when we were free to leave the base again.

They just... needed me to be the one to start every conversation. If I sat quietly and said nothing, no one but Fyth seemed to remember I was there.

"They just need some time." She told me over a meal at the mess hall. "It's... it just sucks right now. We've spent a decade being one of the best Half-Swords in our unit, and now we're... well, you know."

"I know." I sighed, staring down into my tea. "I just... I don't know. I try so hard, but it always seems like things go wrong. Thought things were different this time."

Fyth's tarah lowered in pain. "They *are*. This is just... a rough squall, that's all. You'll see."

"Hope so." It felt like it was going to get even rougher soon. Especially since I was...

Shaking my head, I pushed aside my cup. "So. First night free. We still going out?"

She perked up at once, grinning. "Of course. I'm scheduled to get a test drive in. You sure you don't mind watching?"

I smiled. "Watching you cover the stands in water by way of reckless driving?"

"Yeah!"

Even my gloom couldn't quite withstand her enthusiasm, and I started laughing. "Sounds like fun. Finished?"

Nodding eagerly, she bounced up to her feet. I followed her far more sedately, and then we got going.

The sentries let us out without any issues now that our punishment was over. Then it was a quiet but companionable walk to a public stop, where we caught a shuttle to the other side of the city.

Since the ability to drive a hovercraft transcended species, the race-track was one of the few things that similarly transcended the river. Half of the course was on the south side, half was on the north, and both had plenty of bleachers for an audience.

Today they were pretty much empty. It made sense. This was time set aside for amateurs and rookies to practice in rentals and personal vehicles, and not many people would want to watch that.

I stood around providing a bouncing Fyth with moral support as she confirmed her reservation, then smiled as she gushed over her assigned car.

Then I was in the stands, alone, half-watching as she tore out of the garage, sent up a plume of dust banking onto the track, and then roared down range like the maniac she was.

"Cute." I smiled as she shot out of sight around the corner, making for the river. "...glad I'm not in there with you, though."

I watched her do a few breakneck laps before I brought my wrist-comp online. Now that I was finally off base again there were people I needed to see as soon as possible.

The first of those people accepted the call after a few moments. *"Ashe'lori."*

"Akari." I smiled at the small image hovering above my arm. "Hey. Did you get the message I sent you a few weeks ago?"

"I did." Her always dry voice turned more so. *"I would have contacted you far earlier to see what had happened to you otherwise."*

"Right." Shaking my head, I tried to get a little more comfortable on the metal bench and wished I was surprised when I couldn't. "I'm guessing you were able to tell everyone what happened then?"

She nodded once. *"Yes. Korokek was most distraught, he has not ceased complaining about missing your company."*

I gave my wrist an arch look. "Please tell me you're joking."

"Of course I am." One of her rare smiles came and went. *"Everyone has been a conscript, and all of us have received demerits in our own time. We understand."*

"Thank you." I blew out a quiet breath, glancing up to see Fyth's car forming up with a few others to start a race. "Let me know if you can't hear me, I'm at the races with a packmate."

"The hovercraft obsessed one, I assume." Akari shrugged. *"It is background noise, nothing more. Much like Korokek's voice. While I exaggerated, he has complained about losing the only other person who likes Strike-Wave. He wishes to know when you will be returning to our company."*

That was a complicated question.

"I... don't know." I said, biting my lip for a moment before lowering my voice. "My pack and I think that the Keres set us up because of my visits to Northshore."

It was easy to tell that her attention sharpened immediately. *"Set you up? For a demerit?"*

"For several." Hesitating for only a moment, I pushed on with the partial truths that I'd drawn in the sand. "Someone changed our duty orders after the fact to make it look like we were both negligent and lost several crates worth of automation parts. Afterword, I was trying to calm down and ran into the same Arsenal Commander who tried to give me demerits a couple of months ago."

"And he admitted to being responsible?" She guessed.

"He certainly implied it. He came close to... well, threatening a lot worse than just demerits if I didn't shut up and be a good little conscript in the future."

Her mouth twisted in distaste. *"And you intend to do as ordered?"*

"No." I said at once, before I felt myself grimacing as well. "My pack disagrees. They agree that we were set up, but they want to avoid attracting any more attention."

Akari hissed. *"I believe I understand. That is a difficult position."*

It was. "I'd like to talk with everyone again in person, if I can. At least one more time."

"You would go against your pack in this?"

My free hand rose to rub at my face. "I don't want to, but... I'm getting the feeling that this officer isn't going to just let us be even if we shut up and swim in circles."

"Extremely likely." She replied. *"The Keres are as petty as they come. If they have already struck you twice, that implies that you have been marked as a target. Obedience will not equal safety."*

I couldn't disagree. "You've seen this before?"

"Yes."

When she didn't elaborate, I tried to push. "Did you report it? Is there anything you think that I can do?"

Akari went silent, simply staring at me through the connection. If not for the feed status telling me we were still on the call I might have thought that it had locked up on us.

"I think we both know how well reporting such an incident would have gone." She said finally. *"As for what you can do, that question is difficult."*

My jaw clenched. "Akari. There's something going on here. Something I've apparently ended up involved in."

"Yes."

That she admitted it freely made me blink... and then scowl when she didn't say anything else.

"What do you know about what's actually going on in this colony?"

"More than I would like to." For a second I thought she would stop again, but that time she actually kept going. *"Your pack is right in this. It is*

not something you should be involved in. Sadly it would see that you are regardless. When is your next day of rest?"

"Three days."

She nodded. *"Are you explicitly forbidden from coming to Northshore?"*

"Not explicitly, but I doubt it would be a good idea." Both my pack and the Keres would be on top of me if I tried to go back. Maybe... "I could try to arrange another shopping trip. Frame it as getting back into everyone's good will, but I'm not sure."

"A gamble." She agreed. *"I am unfamiliar with the Green River Zone. Is there a place that would be safe for multiple Humans to gather?"*

"Here, probably" I glanced around the race track. "It connects to both sides of the river. I can see a balcony over the river for observing the racers when they're over the water. Would that work?"

"Very open... too open." She shook her head. *"Attempt to use the shopping excuse. If that does not work, I will arrange to meet you at the track in two weeks, on that day off. Agreed?"*

"Yes. If I can arrange it, when should I meet you at the bridge?"

"At the eighth hour. We will be there to discuss matters. Do you have an excuse for your pack?"

"That I'm visiting you one last time to catch you up on what happened, and to thank you for everything. To buy some things for the officers to tone down their anger, and make sure the other units still appreciate us."

All of which was technically true, even if it still made me extremely uncomfortable with what I was doing. What I would have to say to my pack.

What their reactions would be when they found out what I was up to.

"Do not thank me. This will likely not end well."

The heavy roars of engines made me look up as the amateur racers shot past this half of the stands. Fyth's was far in the lead... it was easy to imagine the wild grin on her face as she accelerated along the straight-away before making the next turn.

"...it won't." I replied quietly. "But I have to know what's going on. I can't not know."

Akari closed her eyes for a moment, shaking her head in a tiny motion. *"Such determination is dangerous, Ashe. I will tell you what I can, but do not be reckless with that knowledge."*

She closed the call before I could reply.

Great. I finally had gotten what I'd wanted from my little trips, my bar visits. I had the trust of someone who would tell me what was really happening on this colony.

And from how she was acting... I was pretty sure I wasn't going to like the answer.

XXV

My pack wasn't happy about my planned meeting. Not even a little bit. In principle they all liked the idea of me trying to restore our reputation. In practice... the idea of me going alone into Northshore made them all exceedingly wary of the idea.

In the end it was the Arsenal Commander approving my request, and giving me another shopping list for the officers, that had made them all back down.

Still, they weren't happy about it, and Ruru seemed especially suspicious that I might not be letting things go like I'd promised.

I'd done my best to deflect, but each time Fyth had stepped in to defend me had made me feel even worse about what I was doing. I couldn't even eat the morning of; I'd have just thrown up anything I managed to force down.

The one thing that had seemed to calm everyone down was when I'd sworn this would be the last time I even went near the other districts.

If everything went well today, if Akari told me everything I needed to know, that would be an easy promise to keep.

If not... I didn't want to think about if not.

Arriving at the bridge in the early morning, I wasn't surprised to find myself the only person crossing. In a final bit of punishment Commander Owri had changed around our days off; now our schedules had us free in the middle of the work week rather than on one of the usual rest days.

Meaning what tiny traffic ever actually crossed the bridge was absent, and I was very alone when I stopped in the middle of it.

I felt even more alone when I stopped in the middle with no one else present. Just fifty yards of empty street in both directions, and a silent river below.

"Well... this is unsettling."

That unpleasant feeling didn't get any better as the minutes ticked by. As Akari and Ren failed to come strolling down the far side to join me.

Akari was a lot of things, but late to anything she agreed to wasn't one of them.

Crossing my arms, I leaned against the railing and did my best to be patient. The quiet rumble of vehicles in the distance was the only real distraction that I had. I tried to busy myself by keeping track of how many drove past on either side, but... well, my heart really wasn't in it.

Three quarters of an hour later someone finally appeared around the corner, walking in my direction.

It just wasn't either of the Humans I was expecting to see.

"Ashe." Ramos smiled as he approached, hands resting in the pockets of a casual jacket. "You're out here early."

"Ramos." I tried not to put any stress on his formal name. He'd never quite taken the hint that I didn't like him using my personal one, but I didn't want an argument about it right now. "I could say the same about you."

He casually walked the rest of the way over, stopping a polite distance away. "Enjoying my morning before we open for the day. You waiting for someone?"

I rolled a shoulder in a shrug. "Akari and Ren. They're helping me with another shopping trip."

"More drinks for your officers?"

"Plus a few other things." Putting my hands on the railing, I tried to relax a little. "How are things at the Riverside Cantina?"

To my discomfort he moved to the railing as well, mimicking my pose a few feet to my right. "About the same as ever. Things are a little less interesting without you around though."

"I'm hardly that interesting."

"You'd be surprised." He smiled again. "Not many grayborn even make an attempt to get to know regular Humans. Lot of people were curious about you. Well, that and they enjoyed your interest in sports."

I hummed rather than offer a proper reply. Where, exactly, was he going with this? And where was Akari?

"Are we going to start seeing you around again?"

"...it's not likely."

"Because of your squad, or because of the demerits?" When I frowned at him, he gave me a shrug of his own. "Akari told Korokek, and he told me about it. Something about your unit messing up a supply order and getting punished for it."

Dammit. I hadn't really wanted that story to spread. "Something like that."

"Did you?"

I blinked. "Did I what?"

"Did your squad actually make a mistake." He clarified.

The question made me hesitate. I'd already told Akari, so telling someone else probably wouldn't hurt. That being said, I trusted her more than him or Korokek.

"We're not sure." I said finally. "Our Half-Sword isn't the type of leader to make that kind of mistake, especially since she's striking for officer."

He huffed out a breath. "Meaning someone who's both powerful and petty would have to be behind something like that. Meaning you think the Keres might be the ones."

I licked my lips. "Maybe. How'd you guess that?"

"There isn't a Human on Oshflara who doesn't know someone those bastards have screwed over." Ramos shook his head. "Or who hasn't heard the stories of what they got up to during the riots."

That made sense, I supposed. It was probably an instinctive reaction for him; a fellow Human gets screwed over? The Keres would be the first suspects.

"What are you doing about it?"

"Right now?" I waved my right hand around us, "Doing a shopping run to help get us back into the good graces of our Commanders. After that, we decided to keep our heads down for a little while."

The plan made him frown. "They aren't just going to stop if they've marked you. They don't let Humans go who've drawn their attention."

So I'd been told. I was about to reply when my wrist-comp chimed with a new message.

Giving him a polite smile, I brought my arm up and checked it while he just as politely waved for me to see what it was. For starters, it was from Akari, which was good... though the high priority marker she'd attached made me worried even before I read it.

Events in motion. Korokek on way to pick you up. Accept his offer to learn our version of events. Reject or return to base at once to remain uninvolved. ~ Sato Akari

Korokek was coming to pick me up? What?

"What's up?" Ramos asked when I just kept staring at my forearm, trying to figure out what was happening. "You look surprised."

"A little." I replied. "Akari can't make it, so she apparently asked Korokek to escort me instead."

"Huh. Strange."

He tried to sound casual, but there was something in how he said it. In the way he tried to smile as he said it...

What *was* he doing here? I couldn't remember him ever mentioning going for walks in the early morning. Especially since he usually worked late. Why wasn't he still asleep? Or with his family?

"Strange." I repeated. "Oh well. He's tolerable enough company, I suppose."

Ramos hummed. "He's pretty good company, but I don't think he'll be too much help to you shopping. Unless you want to go over to the West Bend instead."

"Maybe he'll have Ren with him." I suggested.

"Maybe." He shrugged again. "Why don't you and I go handle things? You can meet up with them at the bar tonight. Make a party out of it if we're not going to be seeing you for a while."

Yeah. There was definitely something going on right now.

"I think I'll wait on Korokek." Before he could reply, I went on, "Not that I don't mind your company, but Akari told me that you have a bond."

"Wife." He corrected at once, a bit of annoyance creeping into his tone.

"Wife." I amended. "I know our people tend to be more... strict about that kind of thing. I don't want to cause you or her any trouble."

Ramos shook his head, "It wouldn't be. She's entirely supportive of people learning more about their origins. I could ask her to come with if that would make you feel better. Let you meet more people."

I gave him a somewhat blank look. "Ramos, this is probably my last day visiting the Northshore while I'm assigned here."

That annoyance crept back in. "We can still talk by message, Ashe. And you could use more Human friends in your life, couldn't you?"

This conversation was getting increasingly uncomfortable. Not just because he kept using my personal name without permission, but how insistent he was being.

I tried another probe. "Why not just wait for Korokek, and all three of us could meet with your bond?"

A twitch in his cheek. "My *wife* and Korokek don't really get along. Come on, what's the harm in meeting her?"

The fact that I was becoming certain he didn't want me to meet with Korokek. And I wanted to know why.

"Why don't they get along?"

Annoyance became frustration. "They just don't. It's a personality thing. If we don't get going the shops are going to get busy, and I know how you hate that."

He was right about that, but I wasn't about to go anywhere with him.

I was saved from having to come up with a new question for him by the quiet rumble of a low-flying hovercraft. From the luxurious make of the thing I didn't doubt it was Korokek's even though it came up from the south side of the bridge.

It slowed to a stop between us, a back door swinging open to let the wealthy Naulian out.

"Ashe'lori!" He beamed, showing off his sharp teeth. "Louis! How fortunate to see you both this morning!"

"Korokek." Ramos didn't even try to hide his displeasure. "Ashe and I were just about to handle her shopping trip."

The other man's smile seemed to grow. "How gracious of you to offer! Fortunately I have a great many staff who can handle such drudgery. I had hoped to speak with Ashe'lori one last time before she is forever confined to the south."

"And I," Ramos retorted, "Was going to introduce her to my wife for the first time."

"Perhaps she will have time to do both." Korokek suggested, turning to me. "Will you?"

"No. I'm lucky to have even this morning free."

Ramos grunted. "Then you'll have to choose, I guess."

I would, and it was looking to be an easy choice. "I'm sorry, Ramos, but I do need to speak with Korokek as well. I'll message you later, all right?"

He stared at me, voice turning harder than I'd ever heard it. "You sure you'd rather go with him?"

...that sounded like an ultimatum, but not one that I truly understood.

"...yes."

The first Human I'd thought of as a friend scowled at me, scowled at Korokek, and then pushed off from the railing. He walked north without another word, hands back in his pockets.

I waited until he was too far away to hear us before I turned to Korokek. "What in the Aspects' holy names is this about?"

"The politics of Oshflara." His smile had vanished. "You have well and truly found yourself in the middle of unfortunate events."

"How?" I demanded. "I've just been trying to figure out what's going on, and now Ramos is giving me ultimatums about going with you or going with him. I thought you two were friends!"

His chuckle was grim as he stepped back, waving to the open door of his car. "Our relationship is complicated, and has soured most recently. Come, quickly. I will take you to my Clan's Home. Akari and Ren are there, they shall help me explain."

Dammit. This didn't sound like a good idea either. But I needed answers, and this was apparently the only way to get them.

Clenching my jaw, I took a final breath... and got into his car.

XXVI

Korokek's driver brought us through the Northshore at a good speed, sweeping us over in the West Bend within ten minutes or so.

Trying to ask questions during the ride only saw him asking me to wait until we arrived. With nothing else to do, I stared out of the window and tried to take in my surroundings

I'd never been inside of a Naule city before. It was... well, about the same as the other two in terms of what it seemed to hold. Lots of restaurants, shops, and other small businesses. The only real difference was a clear preference for tall but narrow homes that left it feeling more crowded and built-up than it probably was.

My host's home was much the same. Six floors at least, made from stone, and half covered by fruit vines. Passing my shopping list to the driver, who Korokek assured me would be able to retrieve it all, we got out and walked up to the building.

Two more Naule with the same dark hair and a similar look to Korokek opened the front doors for us. Both were in suits much like the ones he normally wore, but I could see where their hidden body armor ruined the lines.

And both clearly had pistols holstered to their waists.

Clan Wuqtin was apparently preparing for something violent... and that left me even more concerned than I already was.

He rumbled something in their Trade Tongue, got an answer back. Nodding once, he turned to me, "They are on the patio above us. Come. We shall share good food, good wine, and you shall learn."

"Thank you." I tipped my head and followed him through a luxurious entry hall. Paintings of people I presumed to be important Naule, and a few Trahcon, covered most of the walls. More plants were set up here and there, giving the entire space a fairly pleasant appearance.

I was too busy enjoying the ambiance to realize that the stairwell had been built for Naule rather than Humans.

While Korokek easily ambled up the narrow steps, I nearly fell on my face on my second step, and stubbed my toe twice.

My face was hot by the time I stumbled my way the rest of the way up. Korokek merely chuckled when I caught up with him, waving for me to follow down a hall.

A doorway opened out onto a patio, where I found Akari and Ren sitting at a small table filled with snacks and wine glasses.

"You arrived. Good." Akari seemed to relax on seeing us arrive. "Any issues?"

I was opening my mouth to reply when Korokek beat me to it. "Ramos attempted to co-opt her."

Her eyes narrowed at once. "Did he?"

"He did." I confirmed. "I'm not entirely sure what it was about, but he was very determined that I should go with him instead of coming here."

Ren let out a quiet grunt. "You declared that you were a loyalist in his eyes."

Well, I was a loyalist if he was referring to the Empire as a whole. "Meaning he isn't?"

"Few Humans here are." He replied. "My wife and I are not, but we recognize that there is nothing to be done about it. Our only goal is to move to a quieter colony where we might raise a family in peace."

I swallowed, thinking that I saw where this was going. "Meaning you don't think that Oshflara is going to stay peaceful?"

Akari shook her head. "No."

"Oh." Finally sitting down beside her, I glanced between them and Korokek before taking the nearest wine glass for myself. "So Ramos is a rebel, then?"

Korokek hummed. "It is difficult to say. I believe his entire clan, pardon, his entire family is involved. To what extent? I do not know for certain. At a minimum they use their place of business to identify recruits."

That made me groan. "Meaning the bar I randomly picked all those months ago just happened to be the center of a rebel cell?"

That earned me a snort and a wry look from Ren. "Lori, *any* bar you could have picked in the Northshore could count as a center of rebellion. Did you think the dislike for the Empire simply went away after the riots ended?"

"Well, no." I admitted before sipping some of the wine. "I just... I don't know. Thought everyone realized that trying again wouldn't end well."

"It won't." Akari agreed, voice grim. "Not that many care."

I drank more wine. "That's... did you tell any of the officers about this? Anyone in the government?"

Korokek chuckled. "Many are very aware of the situation, but are doing their best to delay and defuse it. Others, however, are causing problems. Which is where you have become involved."

Since there was only one group actively trying to ruin my, and my pack's, career, it was an easy guess. "The Keres? Why?"

"Is it not obvious?" Korokek's upper hands flicked out in a dismissive motion. "Another rebellion on the Storm General's watch? She was lucky that she was able to bury the first, divert the attention. She will not be so fortunate a second time."

And with that the water went still, and I felt myself seeing the entire horizon clearly.

The Keres wanted Oshflara under their control again. Wanted their quiet hideaway returned, the aliens gone or firmly suppressed. The Storm General and Noroth stood in opposition to that.

But as a fairly minor group of Notables, their options were limited.

"They're behind the smuggling." I heard myself telling them my theory, now certain that I'd been right. "Stealing profits from the Noroth and pinning black-marks on local units not aligned to them. Are they using that money to sponsor Human rebels?"

The fur above Akari's eyes rose slightly. "It cannot be proven, but Korokek believes it likely."

A glance at him saw a nod. "I believe their plan is rather simple. Engineer a second Human insurrection, ensure as many of their officers are in place as possible to take credit for putting it down."

I groaned, nodding as well. "Forcing the Storm General to be relieved or transferred, and ensuring one of their people is promoted. And the Noroth will be humiliated since so many of their people are either Human or trying to encourage assimilation."

Ren snorted. "Assuming that many of them are not tragically killed during the fighting."

My stomach twisted a little, and I took another gulp of wine. "They'd go that far?"

"Considering what they have done so far?" Ren shrugged in the Human way. "Likely."

It was... extremely unpleasant to consider that Imperial citizens could do something like that to one another. Then again, I doubted that many in the Keres saw we mere aliens as being fellow citizens in the first place. Which was what all of this seemed to actually be about.

"Is that why there are so many alien-majority units being kept out of the capital?" I asked, hoping to finally solve the mystery that had started this whole mess.

Akari tilted her head, "What?"

Korokek let out a quiet laugh. "Oh? Noticed that did you?"

"Yes." I rolled a shoulder. "When we first got assigned here I did a bit of research on the other units after our early supply runs seemed weird. Noticed that there were too many Trahcon on Del-Cycle, and a lot of Naule and Human ones on Ah and Ae."

"Indeed there are." He agreed, still looking amused. "Officially it is simply the luck of the assignments."

"And unofficially?"

He waved his upper hands in the little motion again. "The Storm General is being careful to keep several Naule-majority units, along with those Trahcon formations she is certain of, ready and outside of the city. To move in again if needed."

"Ah." I nodded, getting it. "And she's keeping the Keres units stuck inside of the city on support duty, keeping them mostly disarmed in case they get too eager to keep the peace?"

"Indeed." Korokek repeated. "She would rather not have them disgrace themselves or the Empire as they did the last time around."

Yeah. I was definitely seeing the entire horizon now. It was all starting to make sense.

I'd been half right about this being a mess between the Noroth and the Keres. I'd just missed that the Storm General was far more involved than I'd previously considered, and that the Human District was far more ready to erupt a second time.

I needed to tell Rerth about all of this, as soon as possible.

Korokek went on. "As for your own people? They're being kept away from the city because she does not trust them to not cause problems. Or to sympathize too much with the locals."

Next to me, Akari scowled. "Why did you not tell us this, Korokek?"

The Naule shrugged. "Because you refused to be my agents until this morning. Now that you've accepted employment I would of course told you in good time."

I felt myself blinking. "Agents?"

Ren sighed and sipped his own wine. "He has been trying to convince us to report on events within the Noroth and within the Northshore for some time. We have done our best to remain uninvolved."

"Did... I change that?" I asked hesitantly. I hadn't meant to cause problems for them.

"Through no fault of your own." Ren assured me. "Several of our neighbors... informed us last night that we were to aid in co-opting you into a viable agent. They further warned us that we were too friendly with the aliens within the city, and that our home was very lovely."

Ashahn's blood. "Why didn't you report... by the Aspects, are the security forces in Northshore corrupt too?"

"Define 'corrupt'." He replied. "They keep the peace, but their loyalties assuredly lay with the insurrectionists."

Of course they did. "What about you? I mean, why are you doing all of this? I... don't think you're a loyalist."

Korokek smiled genially, hefting his own glass up. "It would depend on how you define loyalty, Ashe'lori. I am loyal to stability, to peace. It is what is best for my clan. So long as the Empire provides that, I shall remain faithful to it."

Well, that was good.

"And yourself?" He asked. "Are you loyal to the same Empire that has caused you and your species so much pain?"

Oh dear. That was the direct, and dangerous, question that I'd managed to avoid for so long.

But now that it had been asked, I didn't see how I could avoid answering.

"...yes." I said quietly.

Akari regarded me steadily. "You do not sound certain."

I sighed. "No, I am. I just... I understand why a lot of people have problems with it. I... empathize with other Humans, and I don't like how some Trahcon treat us."

"The Keres." She supplied.

They'd hardly been the only ones I'd run into. "People like them, yeah. But I still... I still believe in the Empire. Have faith in it."

She stared at me for a few moments before tipping her head. "I thought so. Were you hoping to find fellow loyalists in our district?"

"I don't know what I expected to find." I couldn't tell her why I'd really gone. I couldn't. "I guess that I hoped that I would at least find other Humans I could talk to without being hated on sight."

Akari exhaled through her nose, a single hand moving to gently pat my arm once before withdrawing. "I believe I understand."

"Thanks." I replied quietly.

Ren sighed from across the table. "Do not thank us yet. We've told you a lot about what's going on, the question is what do you intend to do with that knowledge?"

I bit my lip. That was the question. "Do you have hard evidence?"

"Yes." Korokek answered. "But none that I can give to a mere Rifle-Experienced. No offense intended, young one."

"None taken." I *was* just a conscript after all. "Does Imperial Intelligence know?"

His fur shifted as he shrugged. "It is hard to say. The local agency is rife with Keres, so I do not doubt they are the ones behind much of the smuggling. As for the organization as a whole? Impossible to say. Why?"

I hesitated, then said, "The woman who pulled me out of the facility I was raised in was in I.I."

All of them seemed to sharpen their attention towards me, though it was Korokek who kept speaking. "And you are in contact with her?"

"Sort of." I hesitated, then went with another partial truth. "She's the one who got me put on my first assignment. The one where I was almost..."

Akari's lips twisted. "Raped."

"...yes." I swallowed, pushing those memories back into the deeps, then pushed on. "I've never really forgiven her for that, but she says she owes me for that mistake. I could call that in."

Korokek made a thoughtful sound. "That has some potential, but it could be dangerous for you."

That earned him a flat look from Akari. "Merely being in this building has put her in danger."

"She still will have a chance to keep her head down." He countered. "Those in the Northshore could do nothing if she remained on base beyond this point, and so far as I know the Keres do not know or care that my clan is involved."

"Dangerous." Akari insisted.

"Her choice." Korokek replied, and once again all three of them turned to me.

I swallowed once, let out a slow breath, and nodded.

"Get me back to base. I'll call her."

XXVII

Deciding to tell all of this to Rerth, to get a proper Agent to investigate Oshflara, was easy.

Deciding how exactly I was going to do that was a little harder.

The easiest way would just be to have Korokek drive me right back to base, drop me off, and I could head right in to the communications center. I'd make the call, and then try to quietly stay with my pack until Rerth could arrive to handle things.

My problem with that plan was the second part.

Showing up in Korokek's car would be anything but subtle, and since I knew there were Keres officers assigned there they'd be able to pull the communications logs.

What would happen to my pack? To me? Would they try to cover things up further?

I didn't like that risk. If I was going to ever make it into Imperial Intelligence myself, I had to be subtle once in a while. That meant doing things carefully.

On that day, it meant living up to what I'd said I was doing.

"Drop me off here." I said once we'd crossed the bridge back into Green River Zone. "Can your driver bring everything here as well?"

"He can." Korokek confirmed from behind the wheel. Rich or not, apparently he had only the one driver, and so he had volunteered to drive me back when I'd told them my idea.

For their part, Akari and Ren had stayed behind at his place, and hadn't approved of this plan at all. They both thought I should have taken the direct route. "So. You will return with your various groceries, and inform your Arsenal Commander of events?"

"Yes." I confirmed. "And I'll ask her to accompany me to the

Communications Center to talk to my contact. She's a good officer, I can't see her saying no, and she'll be able to cover for my pack after."

He hummed as we slowed to a stop beside the very bridge he'd picked me up from. "I will trust that you know what you are doing."

"What about you? Will you be all right?"

"Me?" An honest laugh came between his words. "Lovely little Lori, I have been quite enjoying this game for the past year or more. I dearly wish that things were different, but I find myself loving it all the same."

I blinked once. "Oh. But you'll be all right?"

"Of course, of course. The Keres may have duped your people, but mine are wiser." When I gave him a flat look he merely laughed again. "I doubt I will be leaving the West Bend anytime soon, but yes. I will be quite safe, and I will ensure our dear friends are as well."

"Thank you."

"You are quite welcome." He nodded to a nearby restaurant. "I believe that is a reputable business. I would remain inside until my man returns with your cargo."

I nodded, pulling the door open. "I'll send you a message once I've made the call."

"Thank you." He echoed, "I wish you good fortune, Ashe'lori."

"Calm seas, Korokek."

One of his many arms waved in farewell when I got out and shut the door. Then he pulled smoothly away, heading west, leaving me alone.

I watched him go, then blew out a single breath before walking to the door.

A battle-scarred woman greeted me when I walked in, guiding me over to a booth without any troubles.

Ordering tea and paying with some of the hard currency I had on me, I brought my wrist-comp up to call my pack.

"*Ashe.*" Fyth looked relieved when her face came up, the background telling me she was in one of the training yards. "*Finally done with your trip and farewells?*"

"With the farewells, yes." I told her, "Not the shopping yet."

Her tarah drooped. "*Really?*"

"Korokek insisted on taking me wine sampling along with the others." Yet another half-truth made my stomach twist. "He sent one of his people to do the shopping for me. I'm at the diner by the bridge waiting for him."

"*Oh, that's good then. Were they understanding?*"

I shrugged. "They weren't happy, but they understood."

Which was true in all regards, at least.

"I've got a call to make with an old packmate when I get back." I pushed on before I could feel any worse for what I wasn't saying. "After I'm done with that, did you want to do something?"

She seemed to perk up a little. "*Like what? Finding you a new hobby?*"

"How about helping with my Strike-Wave game?"

Her tarah rose further. "*Helping you flex your muscles for a few hours? How could I say no?*"

I huffed out a breath, then turned to smile when a waiter brought over my snack. "Thank you. Anything else going on with the others?"

"*Just some light sparring.*" Fyth turned in place, letting me see Ruru and Heley trading some light blows in the background, while Jal and Moriv were wrestling just beyond them. "*Tolu's sleeping in, so I'm the odd one out right now.*"

I sipped my warm tea, smiling. "Lucky me."

"*Lucky you.*" She teased back. "*So some Strike-Wave practice, then maybe a nice dinner?*"

Leaning back in my booth, I nodded once. "That sounds good to me. Are we inviting everyone else, or just us?"

Fyth hummed. *"How about we invite everyone to both? If we force Tolu to get her little ass out of bed, we could play a four on four game in one of the smaller fields. Or maybe an alternating offense-defense game?"*

"Either sounds like it would be good practice for me." I tapped a finger against my cup, hoping that Commander Owri would agree to let me try and pretend things were normal.

And that Rerth wouldn't spit lightning across space to kill me when she found out I hadn't stopped.

"Games and dinner then." She beamed, *"Will we be having fun into the night as well?"*

"Depends on my mood." I retorted. "Unlike you I'm not always ready to jump into bed. Speaking of, Tolu's been sleeping in a lot lately. You think she's...?"

Her head tilted in thought. *"Oh. Yeah, she might be. Would explain why she hasn't really been involved with the others at night as much."*

"Her first?"

"Third or fourth maybe?" Fyth shrugged. *"We haven't really been keeping track."*

I snorted. "You could spend ten seconds to check her Index."

"I could, but then I'd have to stop looking at your exotically lovely face."

Another snort. "That's a bit much, Fyth. You're going to have to work harder at getting my shirt off so you can stare at my arms while we practice."

She gave me a pouting look. *"I thought that was a good line!"*

"It was terrible." I grinned before glancing outside. "I think he's finally here. You've got until I'm done to come up with a better one."

"Well fine then." There was a huff, but she was grinning too. *"See you soon, Ashe."*

"See you soon."

Closing the call, I picked up my tea, braced myself, and then guzzled as much of it as I could. No sense wasting the sugar and caffeine on what was probably going to be a long day.

Leaving the nice little diner behind, I headed back outside to find Korokek's driver politely waiting next to the hovercraft. The back doors were already open, letting me see several bags stuffed full of various goods.

"Everything on your list, Rifle-Experienced." His accent was a lot thicker than his employers, but I could just about understand him. "Will you need help carrying it further?"

"I don't think so." Carefully reaching in, I slid my left arm through the straps of two bags, and took the last one with my right. They were heavy, but manageable. "All of the liquor is in this one, right?"

He nodded. "Indeed. The other two hold all of the dry goods and snacks that were requested."

"Thank you, and tell Korokek thank you again."

"Of course. Safe travels, Rifle-Experienced."

I returned the pleasantry, made sure the bags were settled, and then started on my way back to base.

After the first block or so I started regretting not asking him to drive me at least a little closer. It wasn't that the bags were too heavy, they weren't, but the straps seemed designed to cut into my hands as much as possible.

Adjusting them every couple of yards got pretty old, pretty fast. I blame that distraction on what came next, on making me not realize what was coming.

Later I would realize just how professional the attack was.

My only warning a bit of movement to my right. I glanced over in time to see a woman in a conscript's uniform lurking between a pair of bars still closed this early in the day. A hand was already raised, and I had no chance at all to react before the Strike hit me.

It was a hard spell, a strong one. The point of its impact was right above my stomach, and she'd clearly aimed up from the way it hurled me off of my feet and into the alleyway I'd just been walking in front of.

My breath tore out of my lungs, stopping me from yelling when another spell hit my back.

I expected it to throw me up again, but instead it just slowed my descent as I came down onto the concrete. The impact still hurt but I managed to stop my head from slamming into the ground.

At the same time, something else ripped at my hands, and even as confused as I was some part of me realized they were stopping the bottles from shattering when they hit the concrete.

I tried to get up.

I tried to yell.

Two other Trahcon in military uniforms grabbed my arms before I could do more than start to sit up, shoving me down.

"Stop-!"

A boot slammed into my cheek before I could finish my shout. That time I *did* hit my head onto the ground, hard enough to leave me gasping in pain.

"Pathetic short-fur." A man growled from somewhere nearby. "Did you really think us that stupid?"

Before I could try to do anything else there was a sharp pain in my right shoulder, the cold feeling of an injection... and then darkness.

XXVIII

I woke up slowly, painfully. My head and shoulders ached atrociously, and my mouth was completely dry. Trying to move added pain to my wrists and ankles; something sharp digging into both.

Cracking my eyes open let me see a dimly lit room with... nothing at all to see besides myself, the chair I was cuffed to, and the door. They'd at least left me in my uniform, which I appreciated, but they'd taken my wrist-comp, which I didn't. And a second check told me they'd taken my rank badge as well.

Trapped in a room with no way to call for help, and no way for anyone to track me.

Ashahn's blood... this was all kinds of bad.

Twisting my head around and tugging at my left arm let me see the dark red band wrapped around my wrist, a metallic chain connecting it to the chair. A look down showed the same set up for each ankle.

Experimental flexes didn't do anything besides hurt and jangle the chains a bit.

Aspects. Whoever had me... had me.

"Whoever." I whispered, "Heh. You know who has you."

Swallowing to try and get some saliva into my mouth, I licked my lips and tried to find a way to get comfortable. That pretty much proved impossible, so I tried to find a way to sit that was... well, tolerable was the only word that seemed close.

I kept talking to myself as I did, "Your pack will be missing you. So will the Commander. Focus. Stay calm. Stay relaxed. Watch for a chance."

It turns out it's a lot easier to say and think that than it is to actually do it.

I don't know how long I sat there, but from the feeling in my bladder and the general aching of having to sit there it was at least a few hours before the door finally opened.

The tallest woman I'd ever seen in person walked in. She had to be well above six feet, easily beating Hely. She also had her beat in raw bulk; her uniform visibly strained to contain her muscles. Despite that her features were a bit plain... but her left hand looked like someone had shoved it directly into a fire.

Oh. And that uniform she was wearing bore the markings of a Squall Commander.

I swallowed, straightening up as best I could on reflex despite the fact that she'd clearly had something to do with my abduction.

"Do you know who I am?"

Pretending like I did or didn't wouldn't get me anywhere, so the truth it was. "One of the Keres SQ's, but I don't know which one."

Walking to a spot just in front of me, she crossed her arms to better stare down. "Interesting. I guess that little fool was right. You were investigating our activities."

She wasn't wrong, but I wasn't sure what to say. I fell back on more instincts; when you don't know what to tell a superior officer, say nothing at all.

"What were you doing in the West Bend this morning, conscript?"

I had a brief, irrational urge to correct my rank... but I managed to hold that response down. "Visiting drinking companions for the last time, sir."

"The last time?"

"My pack told me to stop investigating the local situation." I replied honestly. "So I went to tell them I would be staying on base for the remainder of my assignment here."

One of her tarah twitched. "I would consider believing that if not for the identities of your so-called drinking companions."

"Sir?"

"Do not play stupid, conscript." Her voice lowered to an angry growl. From someone her size it would have been intimidating at the best of times, but when I was tied to a chair it was... extremely so.

"Do you honestly expect me to believe that your 'drinking companions' just happened to be members of a powerful Naulian Clan? One set in complete opposition to my Notable Name?"

I didn't expect her to, even if it was honestly the truth. "Yes, sir."

A breath huffed out of her nose. "You're polite for a furry beast, I will give you that much. You know your place."

In a normal situation I might have offered some back-talk to that. In this one I kept my mouth shut once more.

Several long moments of silence passed before she spoke again. "You regularly visited Northshore. Were you looking for fellow rebels there?"

"I am a loyalist, sir."

That made her sneer, "None of your kind are ever loyal. What were you doing there?"

"Following my pack's voice about finding tolerable Humans." I replied. "And purchasing Human goods for anyone who wanted them."

One tarah twitched irritably. "What were you doing there?"

"I told you sir."

"You lied." She stated, burned hand sliding free to point directly at my face. "You will tell me the truth, or you will regret it."

I swallowed nervously. "I am telling the truth, Squall Commander. If I met with rebels it wasn't by my intent."

Her pert nose flexed with a breath, then she brought her hand forward. I tried to flinch but couldn't move away, leaving her free to touch cup my cheek with the four fingers of that hand.

"I am an certified Disciple of Velshen, member of the Order of

Night." My guts turned to ice water. "Tell me the truth, or you will not enjoy this."

My resolve broke. "I didn't intend on any of this. I just wanted to know why so many aliens were assigned here! I didn't intend to-"

"Lies."

Her tarah twitched outwards once... and blue flame wreathed the fingers touching my face.

Everything went white with agony.

I screamed.

I think I tried to jerk back. Tried to tip the chair over. Her other hand grabbed my uniform shirt, keeping me in place.

I honestly can't tell you how long it lasted before she let go. Minutes or seconds, it didn't matter. All I knew was that it hurt. It hurt more than anything I'd ever felt before.

When she finally stepped back, it took me a while to realize that sobbing sounds were coming from me.

And that the smell filling my nose was my own burned flesh.

It hurt. Most holy Ashahn, it *hurt*.

"Tell me why you were in the Northshore."

The scary thing wasn't how much it hurt to cry, or the fact that I'd lost control of my bladder somewhere in the screaming. Or even the fact that I didn't know if anyone was coming to find me.

The scary thing... was how bored she sounded.

This woman... this officer... was going to torture me until I told her what she wanted to hear.

And wouldn't care how much I screamed.

"Didn't..." It hurt to talk. It hurt so bad. "...intend. Trying... to learn..."

"Learn what?" My vision was blurry, but I saw her holding her burned hand up as if she was idly checking to see if she'd gotten my blood on her. "Speak clearly, beast."

"...learn what was... happening." I managed to gasp. "Wanted to... know enough to stay away. Keep pack safe."

She huffed. "You failed spectacularly if that is the truth... but I doubt your kind understands how to be loyal to a pack. Tell me why you were in the Northshore."

All I managed in reply was another sob.

"Very well then."

"Please... don't..."

My fur was just long enough for her to grab onto it with one hand, returning the other to where it had just rested on my cheek. "Try not to wet yourself like a child this time."

"Please-"

A deeper voice cut in. "Enough."

The Squall Commander froze for a brief moment, then exhaled and slowly let go. I made another pathetic sound, letting my hand hang low as if to protect it.

"Mother of god... really?" He was... Human. I managed to notice that, somehow, even through my crying. "You couldn't have waited five more minutes for me to arrive?"

"She lied. Repeatedly." Came the bored reply. "She is either aligned with the Noroth or is a targeted recruit for them. Regardless, she knows too much about our operations here, and her Index has her being observed by Intelligence. She may be working for an Agent."

An irritated sound, but I couldn't bring myself to look up to see what he looked like. I was too busy choking on my own spit, gasping for breath as the tears made my cheek throb in even greater agony.

"You should have simply left her to her own devices. She was a bumbling amateur, nothing more."

"Unlike your kind, mine does not take foolish risks, beast."

"Fucking grays... well, nothing to be done for it now but make the best of it. What are you going to do when the Agent arrives?"

"That will be handled, so long as you dispose of this one properly."

Ashahn's.... no...

"The timing is terrible, and we don't have the facilities to preserve a body." Footsteps shifted around. "We'll have to move her back to one of our facilities. She'll be found, tragically killed by your kind. That should galvanize support."

"Enough for what we need?"

"Can't say."

By the Aspects... they were going to kill me and make it look like Trahcon had done it. All to rile up the other Humans. All just to spark a pointless revolt.

And... they were talking about it right in front of me.

Like I wasn't a person to either of them.

"...very well." The Commander said. "Bring your beasts in and handle moving her. I'll ensure she isn't missed for some time."

Her footsteps faded away, replaced by several more sets. I finally managed to get my head up, trying to see through the tears and pain just who was grabbing me.

More Humans. All men. All wearing masks that stopped me from seeing their faces.

One of them muttered something in another language, waving at my lower half. Another struck him on the arm and pointed at my face instead. That made man number one grunt something that sounded like an apology, but I couldn't follow any of it.

I tried to speak, to beg them not to do this.

Another needle struck my arm before I could.

That time... that time I almost welcomed the darkness.

It meant that I stopped hurting for a little while.

XXIX

When I woke up again I was laying on a cold floor. The right side of my face was throbbing slowly. It was distracting, but not enough to stop me from thinking clearly as I slowly focused my mind.

Opening my eyes a crack let me see the familiar tiles of a barracks' bathroom. A careful glance around confirmed that I was alone, again, giving me a chance to take stock of things.

Sitting up with a groan, I felt my back press against the base of the sinks.

"Smaller room." I muttered with a little bit of a slur. The right side of my mouth not quite moving as it should have. That wasn't good. "Smaller than ours. Maybe not a full base. Outpost?"

A Human-dominated outpost outside of the city maybe. Not smart of them. There'd be at least a few Trahcon officers around... unless they were all off site, my captors would have to keep me out of sight.

I was probably only here temporarily. Maybe just to clean me up.

Taking a deep breath, I checked my arms and legs. They'd changed my cuffs to a more standard pair of bright red bindings, locking my wrists together in front of me... but they'd removed the ones from my legs.

"So I can move."

Another breath, then a third, and finally a fourth gave me enough to slowly force myself to my feet. My legs were stronger than I'd have thought, but my balance wasn't quite as steady. I had to lean on to the sinks to stay upright.

I stared down at the faucet before jerking my head up to take in the damage.

It... was both better and worse than I'd thought. I had three branded imprints on my cheek from where she'd lain her long fingers, and a smaller mark from her thumb near my nose. The skin there wasn't... it wasn't pretty to look at.

Still, someone had covered it in some kind of ointment, which was... good.

Probably had some kind of anesthetic in it from the fact that I wasn't flat on the floor sobbing, even if it still ached.

"Buy why?" I shook my head a tiny amount. "Why bother?"

Confused, I checked myself and confirmed they'd also changed my uniform. I appreciated that... but if the whole point was to kill me, why clean me up?

Not that they'd cleaned me up *that* much, they clearly hadn't properly treated the burns beyond whatever they'd slapped on... but they'd still done something.

"Focus." I reminded myself. "Focus. You're loose."

I was. I was confined to a bathroom, but I was at least loose. Even better, they'd made the mistake of binding my hands in front of me rather than behind. Which gave me options.

Not many options... but at least I wasn't utterly helpless this time.

Slowly pushing myself away from the sink, I took a few experimental steps. When I didn't tip over, I upgraded to more confident ones as I checked my surroundings.

Four tubs, all empty. The bay of sinks, no soap dispensers, and the faucets were recessed into the stone. Sixteen lockers, all sealed shut.

One camera that was clearly newly installed, placed in the ceiling well above my ability to reach.

Nothing I could use as a weapon, or even as leverage.

"But you can move."

Steadying my breathing once again, I forced myself to try and come up with a plan. Nothing in my training really covered the 'being abducted by your own military' scenario, so I was going to have to improvise.

I didn't have any packmates, any sorcery of my own, or any weapons. So I wasn't going to win any kind of protracted fight. No armor meant that even if I did steal a gun, I'd likely die well before I managed anything.

So I wasn't fighting my way out of this.

Sneaking? There was only one door in and out of this particular room. The only air vents were all in the ceiling, and even if I could reach them they were far too small to even attempt to get into. That narrowed my options down to leaving by the same door my captors would be using.

Plus, getting out of this room wouldn't help if I had no idea where on Oshflara I was.

That meant I had only one real option; I had to call for help, and then survive until it got here.

"This is a bad plan, Ashe... Ashahn's blood, this is a bad plan." I tried to bite my lip, wince at the pull on my cheek, and then settled for muttering. "No. Like they say in training. If you do nothing, you'll die. So do something."

Swallowing against my nerves, I rolled my neck once, and then started stretching out my legs as best I could. As I stretched, I thought furiously, glancing up often at the camera that was definitely tracking my movements.

That camera would stop any chance I had of just playing dead and jumping the first person to come in. Would stop me from hiding behind the door. But maybe...

When I got through as much of my usual pregame routine as I could, and no one had arrived, I got started on my actual plan of action.

It was a bad, desperate plan... but it was the only thing I could think of besides trying to jump the first person through the door. Since that sounded like an even worse idea, the desperate route it was.

A quick test of the nearest bath confirmed that they hadn't shut off the water in here. Good. Twisting the knob all the way around set the water to its hottest, and I left on as I went to the next tub in line.

Once all four tubs were filling with steaming water, I went to the sinks and repeated the process. While the air started to fog up nicely, it definitely wasn't going to get to the point where it actually made it hard to see.

That was fine. I wasn't expecting that much luck.

When no one came in to stop me just yet, I swallowed, and then started with part two of the plan.

I took a deep breath, and then carefully stepped into the first tub I'd started filling. The water was painfully hot, making me grimace... which just hurt my face even more. Feeling the water soaking my uniform wasn't any more pleasant.

Taking a final moment to steady myself, I deliberately raised my head so I could stare into the camera. Then I brought both hands up, gave it the rudest gesture I could think of...

And then I started furiously working my arms back and forth, digging the hard edges of the cuffs into my skin.

It didn't take much to manage to cut myself. Bits of red and pink started to stain the water as I bled. The sight of it had me start working harder, clenching my teeth against the extra pain I was causing myself.

I could only pray to the Aspects that this would work, and that I wouldn't actually tear open an artery.

The water turned redder. Pain got worse.

I was just starting to doubt my mad plan when the door abruptly slammed open, two pale-skinned Humans rushing in with panicked features.

Both were in uniform, both had pistols on their belts.

"Stop!" The first shouted as he ran towards me, "Stop!"

I worked my shoulders, as if I was still trying to end my own life before they could. I don't know if it helped make them panic more, but either way it went perfectly from that point.

Instead of coming at me together to try and haul me out, they got in each other's way. The first man dropped into a slide, and tried to grab my arms to pull me out of the water.

The moment he touched me, I sprayed water in his face as I brought my own up and around his neck. He gaped at me for a second before I hauled him into me with all the strength that I had.

He tried to stop me, but laying out on a wet floor didn't let him brace himself properly.

We both fell back into the broad bath, the scalding water adding a whole new pain to my face in the process.

He started to thrash at once, trying to get free. I'd already started to pull my arms up when he shoved them away, easily overpowering me.

I didn't mind. I hadn't been gambling on an underwater wrestling match.

He rose at once to get his head out of the water, probably to clear his lungs.

It made it very easy for me to yank the pistol off of his belt with both hands.

My thumb hit the safety the moment I managed to get it turned around, and I yanked the trigger far harder than I should have once it was settled.

The man jerked violently once, then twice when I shot again. Blood immediately began to billow out of the holes in his body, and coated me when a hand shot down to grab my fur and yank me up.

I don't think the other man realized what had happened to his partner or he would have been ready for me to shove the pistol into his face when I came to the surface.

He had enough time to gape before I shot him too.

That time... that time I had much a better view of what happened when you shot someone. Shot them in the throat, specifically.

Shot them in the throat when I wasn't more than a few inches away.

My vomit added to the mix in the tub when I turned and simply heaved up everything I still had in me.

I don't really know how I managed to focus enough to keep going with the plan. To crawl out of the tub, yank the man's wrist-comp off, and then get upright.

To not look back as I tottered over to the door, vaguely knowing that the gunshots would draw attention.

"Focus." I heard myself muttering when I got to the door. When the floor dried, and I could start moving faster. "Standard outpost layout. Move right."

I started running as best I could when I came out of the doorway. The familiar rows of doorways marking a barracks welcoming me as I ran.

No one poked their heads out.

No armed sentries came running.

At least, not at first. I made it to the first corner intersection before an alarm started screaming over the loudspeakers. Flinching at the sudden sound, I forced my legs to keep going to the very next doorway.

For once Khahsh's luck was with me; the Dual Commander's office for this wing was right where it was supposed to be.

Even better, the door was wide open and no one was inside.

I'd probably just killed him.

The thought made me lose my stride, and I didn't quite manage to stop before running into the desk in the center of the room. Throttling a yelp of pain, I backtracked to the door and rammed the butt of the pistol against the controls.

It slammed shut with a reassuring clang, and a more careful poke of the controls set the first lock. Resetting the safety on the gun, I tossed it onto the desk before using my freed up fingers to grab the emergency latch and haul it over.

Even heavier thuds sounded as solid bars were set to barricade the room entirely.

"Step one... worked. I will pray to you every night, Khahsh." I gasped. "I'm sorry for ever doubting you!"

If only the Aspect of Luck would stay with me a little longer, I might actually live through this.

Staggering my way back to the desk, I moved around it to collapse into the chair there. His console was still online, which saved me from having to try and use his wrist-comp for the next step.

At that moment it was showing a live video feed of a foggy bathroom with two corpses... and more people piling inside, waving and presumably shouting at each other.

I didn't have much time then.

Working the controls with my hands bound was hard, but I managed to open up his mail application.

I typed as quickly as I could given the situation.

THIS IS RIFLE-E ASHE'LORI. AM CAPTIVE. PLANNED TO BE KILLED. KERES ALLIED TO-

Sharp knocking on the door made me jump, adding a typo I couldn't risk correcting.

-TOZ HUMN RBLS! SND HLP!

Jerking my hands around, I added the officer's signature which thankfully included the outpost-designation.

Then I started adding every single mailing list I could find to the send-to field. Every military list, every civilian list. I wasn't sure how many people I was sending this to, beyond 'a lot'.

My movements got jerkier as the knocking progressed to pounding, then shouting. A warning alarm flashed from the door when someone tried to override the lock, only for the emergency setting to prevent that from happening.

"Until they get an officer with a higher override." Swallowing, I sent up a final prayer that I'd added enough people, that they hadn't cut my access... and hit send.

A helpful message immediately popped up, a progress bar scrolling as it politely informed me that it was working on dispatching it to all seventeen-thousand recipients.

"Alert sent." I whispered, looking up as another sharp clang came from just outside. "Last step of the plan. Survive until help comes."

XXX

I prepared as best I could. I used my hips and legs to shove the desk back as far from the door as possible, got the chair out of the way, and then I knelt down in cover.

Alone, my uniform coated in... well, a disgusting mix of water, blood, and vomit. My face was beginning to hurt more with each minute that passed. I'd probably washed off the ointment with my soaking.

"Still alive, Ashe." Settling one knee on the ground, I braced my stolen weapon on the desk with my hands. "Still alive.'

People kept moving around outside for a little while. There were a couple more frustrated attempts to get through the lock I'd set, but no one seemed to have the proper code to open it. Either the senior officers weren't in the conspiracy, or they just weren't present.

I'd take it either way.

The desk's computer abruptly shut itself off about a minute or two after the message sent, so they definitely knew where I was. Sooner or later they'd realize I'd already sent a distress call, and I had no idea what would happen after that.

Considering how quickly they got on that, it was kind of surprising how long it took them to realize that I had the officer's wrist-comp. Nearly twenty nervous minutes passed before it began to emit musical ringing in my pocket.

Tugging it out, I spread the mesh out on the ground before tapping the blue section to accept a voice only channel.

A man immediately began snapping something in the same language the others had been yelling in.

Swallowing, I said nothing.

He seemed to take the hint after a couple of seconds. When he spoke again it was in Caranat even more thickly accented than what Korokek's driver had spoken with.

"Do you have any idea of what you've done?"

That time I did reply, speaking as best I could as the pain got worse. "Lived a few more minutes."

"You'd have had a few more days." He growled. *"I went through the trouble of cleaning you up, making you comfortable. And you repay me by killing two of my most loyal men."*

"Why?" I asked in return. "Why do that? I heard your friend. You're going to kill me and frame the Noroth anyway."

"Because you are Human, and even race traitors like you deserve some dignity." There was an irritated huff. *"Which is why I'm giving you one chance to open the door and yield. Do that and I'll make sure you die without any pain."*

I swallowed. "And if I refuse?"

"I let my men have a few rounds with you before we clean you up and put you out of our misery."

The full-body shudder ran through me before I could stop it. It was the expected threat, but that didn't make it any more pleasant to hear. Or think about.

In the interest of buying myself time, I asked another question. "Why are you even doing this?"

"To free our people, obviously."

"How?" I didn't have to fake the bafflement in my voice. "You think starting a rebellion on a tiny colony in the middle of nowhere is going to do anything?"

A heavy snort. *"I wouldn't expect a loyal pet to understand. We will be the first spark that ignites the inferno of revolution."*

By the Aspects, they had to be insane if they actually thought that.

"Those Keres think they're using us. We'll show them exactly how

strong we are. How we're wise to their little games." Apparently I'd just needed to poke him once to start him ranting. *"We'll take out those disgusting hunters first, decapitate the grays before they even know what's happening. The four-arms will join us if they know what's good for them, and then Oshflara will be ours. Our message will spread, and every Human in this pathetic Empire will know that we can beat them."*

Yeah. He was insane.

"And you will be part of that spark. You should be rejoicing that your death will give your useless life some meaning!" His voice rose. *"You'll actually do something to help your species, instead of just worshiping those gray animals for the rest of your pathetic days!"*

I risked looking away from the door to check the clock on the wrist-comp's display. Twenty-five minutes since I'd sent the message.

Was there a ready-action force on Oshflara? Protocol said there should be, but who knew if they'd gotten my message. If they believed it. If they would actually do anything.

I swallowed and kept talking. Buying time was literally all that I could do, so I'd keep doing it as long as I could.

"If it's so glorious, why don't you let someone burn your face and then die for the cause?"

"Leaders are required to advance Humanity."

"And none of your people volunteered?"

His sneer was audible. *"No true Human need die when there are plenty of traitors who we can use instead."*

The snort came out before I could stop it, and drew an instant flinch as white-hot pain ran through my face.

Right. Laughing at his stereotypical lines was a bad idea.

"I don't think we're traitors." I had to slow down my delivery, trying to move the right side of my lips as little as possible. "We're just realists."

"You are traitors! Humanity should never have bowed! We shall be

free or we shall die!"

"Then you'll die." Shifting my knee onto the edge of the wrist-comp, I dragged it closer so I could lower my voice as well. That seemed to help with the pain. "There's... what? Forty Trahcon for every Human? We're an afterthought in the galaxy."

That sneer came back. *"Spoken like the coward you are, but I think I've let you stall long enough. Make your choice, bitch"*

I closed my eyes for a long breath... and used my knee to end the call.

Then I settled in and braced myself for the door to open.

It didn't take very long for the override chime to sound. Clanks and thuds sounded as the emergency bolts retracted into the walls, freeing the door to be opened.

After that it slid upwards just enough for someone to roll a grenade in before it slammed shut again.

I had just enough time to duck before the stunner went off.

White light and a wall of noise made my head feel like it was about to explode, and I didn't even realize it when I fell over. That came a while later, when I blinked slowly to find myself staring at the ceiling.

Panic made my heart pound in my chest. My hands were open. I couldn't hear anything. I could barely see for the white spots flashing around all over the place.

I'd dropped the gun.

I tried to get up, rolling onto my left side. "...gun. Need... gun."

I had to find it. Had to find it.

It was the under the desk.

I fell over when I tried to crawl to it. It took me another try before I managed to get my fingers wrapped around it, tucking it against my chest.

I had the gun. Good. That was good. Wait...

My mind cleared a little as I realized something else. I... really should have been dead already.

Getting my knees under me, I slowly rose to look over the desk to see the door open, but... no one was there.

What?

I stared at the open space in blank confusion longer than I should have. There really should have been a host of soldiers ready to rush in and grab me. To kill me, disarm me, violate me, torture me... whichever one they felt like.

I'd been helpless after the stunner had gone off.

So... where were they?

I was just about to stand up when an armored form appeared, and I tried to shoot them on panicked reflex.

Fortunately for me I hadn't actually gotten the gun settled in my hands properly. So instead of shooting the battle-ready Naule who'd just walked in, I shoved a finger against the grip and accomplished nothing at all.

All four of their arms spread, holding their shotgun away from their body. Their full coverage helmet stopped me from seeing their face, but from the way their head was moving I thought they were talking.

Right. I couldn't hear anything.

Remembering that seemed to clear some more of the fog floating around in my skull.

"Can't hear." I rasped. "Grenade."

The helmet bobbed in a nod, one of their lower arms pointing at the pistol in my hands.

I really didn't want to let it go, but a second, sharper gesture had me fumble it onto the desk.

After that things got blurry again.

They quickly ambled around the desk, grabbing one arm and pulling me along. I vaguely remembered moving through the outpost. More Naule in full kit were everywhere, with a few Trahcon mixed in among them.

Humans were everywhere. Mostly dead. Some were prisoners.

I came around when a Naulian medic jabbed me with several different drugs in short order, making me flinch and gasp for breath. Had I been holding it or something?

Inhaling rapidly, I blinked a few times and realized that I was in the courtyard of a standard outpost.

Two heavy combat shuttles loomed to either side of me. The scorch marks and deep gouges in the concrete told me that they'd landed hard.

My chin was abruptly grabbed and jerked around, the man treating me giving me an annoyed look.

"Sorry."

He rolled his dark eyes before getting back to work. Two hands rose to shove things into my ears, while his other set pulled canisters and tools from his belt.

"-stay still." The hearing aids switched on almost at once, bombarding me with noise. "Confirm your identity."

"Ashe'lori. Rifle-Experienced."

He grunted. "Keep your voice down, you're shouting."

I'd thought I'd been speaking normally, but I tried to speak quietly. "My message was received?"

A woman's voice came from behind me. "It was."

Even knocked around, I knew who'd just spoken, and I flinched on reflex. The medic promptly smacked me in the belly with one hand. "Stop moving dammit."

I mumbled something apologetic, bracing myself as Imperial Agent

Rerth'riah angrily strode into view.

She was in full kit too, but her armor was sleek, almost skin-tight compared to the bulky plating of the soldiers around us. One of her hands was fully raised as if ready to slap me across the face before she got a good view of my wounds.

That made her freeze for a moment... then actually reach up and grab both of her own tarah, tugging them down in complete and utter frustration.

"Dammit huntress!" She swore. "What in the Aspects' holy names happened here?"

Well... I'd survived. That was good. But... there was no way I was getting out of this one without enough demerits to drag me into the deepest depths for the rest of my life.

XXXI

I spent the next few days alternating between recovery and debriefing.

Between Rerth, my Dual Commander, my Arsenal Second, my Arsenal Commander, the Squall Commander above her, and even a packmate to the Storm General... I lost track of how many times I had to tell the exact same story.

To make things worse, I was officially under confinement. They didn't even let my packmates in to see me. Assuming that they would even want to after they found out I'd gone against their voice.

Ugh.

On the fourth day Rerth strode in to find me leaning against my room's window, staring out at the city.

"Watching the assault shuttles?"

"Yes." Sighing, I turned and saluted. She returned it before waving for me to relax. "How has the fighting been?"

The Imperial Agent rolled a shoulder. "It could have been significantly worse. The Northshore is under total lockdown, with combat teams going house to house looking for armaments."

"Fighting?" I asked again.

"Some." Her expression told me she knew what I meant. "That bar you liked didn't make it. They tried to use it as a firebase to hold a nearby bridge."

I swallowed, bowing my head. Dammit Ramos... I'd liked you once. You were kind, helpful, funny. Why did you have to turn out to be so foolish?

Then again, he'd probably thought the exact same thing about me.

"What about Korokek? Clan Wuqtin?"

"Being given honors for loyally reporting activity to the Storm General. They'll be getting a monetary reward as well, I think that entire clan plans to migrate to a calmer world in this sector."

Good. Akari and Ren would get what they wanted then. They'd be able to find a quiet world to settle down on. To have children in peace without worrying about insurrections and fighting.

"Any others?"

"A few units on the patrol cycles also tried to resist being disarmed." Rerth walked up to stand beside me, the two of us watching as more shuttles came and went across the city. "It didn't go any better for them."

"Human ones only?"

"All but one. A unit fanatically loyal to their Keres officers tried to advance into the Northshore against orders. They fought for an hour before yielding."

I could only shake my head. "All of this for what?"

The spy let out a heavy sigh. "Wounded pride, mostly. Resentment that the Naule were settled here a century ago, and anger that more aliens came in later. They couldn't stand that their quiet hunting retreat was turning into something more than that."

"Are the Keres...?"

"The Storm General has already sent the official request for the name to be revoked." Rerth confirmed. "Each and every one of them will be evaluated. The ones who were less involved will just have to move. The rest... penal colonies or exile."

"Good... good." I nodded. "What the officer who... did this to me?"

I looked to my right in time to see her scowl. "No Squall Commander matched that description on Oshflara."

"What?"

"Neither did any Arsenal Commander, Dual Commander, or any other officer in the database." Her head shook. "I've got one of my packmates running through everyone else right now, but I doubt she'll be there."

I swallowed, fighting against the urge to touch the bandages covering half of my face. "Then who was she?"

"Right now? A shadow. I've got more Keres to interrogate still, along with the rebels smart enough to surrender." A shoulder rolled. "First guess is that she's a mercenary they brought in. Maybe a member of the Order of Silver disguising her origins."

"I thought they only worked in the Reaches."

"A few of those mercenary fools make it to the Empire." Rerth corrected me. "Not many, but a few. Either way, she's at the top of the wanted list at the moment."

"...good." I murmured again. "Um, how's your pack doing?"

"They're fine, though they'd laugh themselves sick at how pathetic that attempt to divert my attention was."

I winced, then did so again when she turned and stalked into my personal space. Even though I'd ended up being a bit taller than her, I still felt like a little child when she scowled at me.

I'd avoided it for a while... but the punishment for what I'd done was apparently pulling into harbor.

"I've avoided this conversation out of courtesy for your wounds." She began, her bright eyes locked onto mine. "But you're lucid, patched up, and ready to hear just how much chaos you managed to cause with your bungling."

"...yes, sir."

Her nose flared as she let out a heavy breath before beginning. "First. You went against my direct orders to remain uninvolved until I could arrive. You're getting another demerit for disobedience for that."

That wasn't good, but I'd expected it. "Yes, sir."

"That's your *second* level one demerit. " Her voice sharpened. "You understand that? You're running out of chances, and I can't protect you forever."

"I know." I swallowed. "I know, sir."

She took another deep breath. "Second. You, a conscripted Rifle-Experienced, attempted to undertake a clandestine mission without the approval or knowledge of your officers, your Half-Sword Leader, or even your pack. For that you're getting another demerit for reckless behavior."

Not as bad as one for disobedience of an officer, but still not good. "Yes, sir."

"For a double-demerit of those levels, you're demoted back down to Rifle."

"...yes, sir."

Rerth went on, "Third, through your lack of communication with local officers, you completely upended an ongoing project by the local Storm General. She was entirely aware of local events and was preparing to take action when you managed to set off a partial uprising on your own. That's another reckless demerit."

At this point my Index would be nothing *but* demerits. "Yes, sir. Am I demoted to Conscript?"

"Shut up, I'm not done."

I flinched. "Yes, sir."

"Fourth," Her jaw worked, "You went against your pack's voice, hid your activities from them, and also failed to inform them of what you were actually doing. Your entire pack, yourself included, are getting a demerit for failure to control your reckless behavior."

My heart ached, but I kept my mouth shut.

"I thought you'd learned from the last time you did that." She growled, "But apparently you just can't resist repeating the same mistakes. The only thing that saved you then was that you were right about the smuggling ring... and the only thing saving you this time was that you managed to be right once again."

I... had been?

One of her hands rose to rub tiredly at her face, her tone softening at once. "Ashahn's blood, Ashe. I don't know what to do with you. You manage to uncover things, do the *right* thing by the Empire wherever you go. But you always manage to do it in a way that frustrates everyone and causes complete and total chaos."

I... wasn't sure what to say, so I kept saying nothing.

Rerth leaned her head back, groaning. "Moving on from your demerits. For alerting Imperial Intelligence that the Storm General tried to downplay and cover up a prior revolt, and that she did not alert the proper channels of the ongoing problems here, you're being given one merit."

"Thank you, sir."

"For deducing that the Notable Pack of Keres was behind the theft of materials and blaming it on newly arrived units, you receive two merits." She sighed and relaxed, meeting my eyes again. "We've already traced the replacement orders. Seventeen Half-Swords, including yours, are having a large number of demerits erased from their Indexes."

I perked up a little more. That would knock off some of what had happened. At the very least it would help my pack, and seriously help Ruru's Academy placement requests.

"Thank you, sir."

"For bravery and quick thinking while under extreme duress, and having the intelligence to alert the entire world to the alliance between the Keres and the Insurrectionists, you receive another two merits and are promoted back to Rifle-Experienced."

So my career wasn't dead then. That was good.

"Don't look so happy." She clearly noticed my thoughts from her reaction. "Your Squall Commander has already requested you be transferred out of her unit. Your Arsenal Commander protested, but your Dual-Commander wants you gone as well."

I wasn't surprised at the first or the third, though I did smile faintly at the idea that Commander Owri had actually wanted to keep me around.

Well, I smiled until she added. "It's going ahead since your Half-Sword didn't offer to speak on your behalf."

And just like that, my heart crashed right back onto the stony shores.

Ruru hadn't defended me... of course she hadn't. I'd betrayed her trust, betrayed my pack.

I'd kept doing exactly what they'd told me to *stop* doing, and even if I'd avoided directly lying to them, I'd still never told them the actual truth. I'd be lucky if any of them, even Fyth, came to tell me goodbye.

My shoulder slumped at once. "I understand, sir. Where am I going next?"

"To be decided." Rerth replied flatly. "Your second unit has a standing request for you to be transferred back, but that will be up to the transfer board as soon as one can be assembled."

"How long will I be alone for?"

"A few more days, at least." Her chin jerked to the situation outside. "Week at most to resolve most of this, and get enough officers free to examine your Index and potential landing spots."

I bit my lip, then asked, "May I put in a request?"

Rerth rolled her eyes, "Of course you can. Back to Dual Commander Huvu'ithi's unit?"

"Yes, sir."

Her head shook tiredly. "Ashe, there's no way they'll send you to a front-line officer's pack while she's in combat. Not with your record."

"...I still request it, sir."

"I'll enter it." She sighed. "It's pointless, but at least it will be on the record that way. I have to warn you, Ashe. For all the honors you manage to grab, you've got so many demerits that you're about to drown. If you screw up again you'll be dismissed from the service. You know what that means for a conscript?"

"...I'll be assigned to a penal colony."

"How much investigating and Strike-Wave do you think you could do on one of those?" Her jaw clenched for a moment. "Aspects damn your need to know things, huntress."

I shifted my balance. "I'm sorry, sir."

"Just..." Eyes closed, her head shaking. "...try to relax and heal. The local network should have the latest Strike-Wave matches from Gathahn loaded for you. I'll be in and out as things progress."

"Thank you, sir." I paused, then asked more quietly. "If... any of my pack... can you ask if any of them would visit?"

For the first time her expression became one of pained sympathy. "I'll ask, but... don't get your hopes up."

I could only nod, and turn back in time to see muted explosions within the Northshore.

As the chaos I'd started went on.

XXXII

I spent the next four days with only Rerth's occasional visits for company. I didn't really count the doctors, who came and went a few times a day to check on the burns.

When they finally took the bandages off for good it didn't look nearly as bad as I'd thought it might. Instead of having a horribly burned face, I just had three jagged lines on my cheek, along with the smaller mark near my nose.

Enough to make me handsome even with my head fur growing out, but thankfully not so bad as to seriously affect my life.

"You got lucky that those fools gave you some early treatments." The doctor told me during our last meeting. "We patched up your muscles and contained the top level damage. Put this ointment on it after you bathe every day for the next two weeks."

I'd thanked him, and then gratefully left the tiny hospital room that I'd been confined in.

The message indicating I'd been officially rotated out of my Half-Sword had come that morning. My pack... my former pack, had already collected my things and shipped them to the transfer station on world.

But since I wasn't due there until the evening... I'd sent a final plea, and then made one last trip to the Storm's Love.

It wasn't that busy at midday, and I managed to get a seat alone.

I was about halfway through my beer when Fyth pulled out the chair across from me, dropping into it without a word.

Risking a glance at her eyes let me see her furious glare, and I quickly dropped mine back down.

"I'm sorry."

Her huff was disgusted. "You're sorry."

I winced, looking to my right. "I'm sorry. I fucked up."

"No. Shit." The chair shifted, then she growled out. "Why did you do it, Ashe? Why go against the pack? Why... dammit, why didn't you at least tell *me* about it?"

Taking a deep breath, I told her. "That Keres officer cornered me again, after you all told me to stop. He said... he said a lot of things. Tried to make me lose control. Basically admitted he'd set us up."

"So you decided to go after them on your own?"

Another wince. "I... kind of. He said that they knew the local Imperial Agent. I figured that they had to be covering up all of this. I had to know more to warn Rerth."

She didn't sound any more impressed. "You had to know. That stupid determination of yours."

No point in denying it. "I... I had to know."

"And what? Keeping me out of it was to stop me from choosing between you and the rest of the pack?"

I swallowed and looked down once again. "Yes."

The frustration in her voice only seemed to grow. "Do you have any idea how badly I want to slap you right now? No Trahcon would have done what you did."

"I... I know. I'm sorry." Hands rose to rub at my face, the scar tissue still strange to feel. "I try so hard to be a Trahcon, as close as I can be, but I always manage to fuck it up."

Fyth's own fingers drummed on the table. "If you're so self aware why do you... ugh. Why am I asking when the answer is that you just can't help it."

"...I'm sorry."

There was a deep, heavy sigh. "I know. I... fuck. I'll try to forgive you, but it's hard right now. Just... stop looking like you expect me to actually hit you. We both know I couldn't."

It was hard, but I managed to raise my head back up to see her looking more exhausted than angry. Well, mostly. Her tarah were still twitching a little, even if she was slumped in her seat.

She'd stolen my beer when I hadn't been looking, and took a deep pull from it. I waited until she finished before asking, "How is everyone else taking it?"

Fyth sighed. "You betrayed our voice, got us all a demerit, and we were all convinced you were dead when you vanished. Spent most of a day panicking, then your message started getting broadcast everywhere. Knowing you were alive was... such a huge relief, but then we realized what you'd been up to."

"...I'm sorry."

Her head shook. "But... you also got those fake orders revealed, got those demerits removed, and turned out to have been completely right. It's incredibly frustrating. Oh, and Ruru's convinced you saved her future career by knocking off that severe demerit, plus the minor ones."

"She is?"

"She is." Fyth gave me a dry look. "I think part of her wants to have the most violent sex she can with you, and then never see you again. The rest of her is too livid to even hear your name mentioned."

I tried to smile but couldn't really find it in me. "Everyone else?"

She waved the bottle around. "I'm the only one who came. Pretty sure that should tell you how they feel."

"Oh." I supposed that it did. "I guess I won't be seeing anyone else before I leave then."

"...probably not." Her tarah lowered for a bare moment before she visibly forced them back to a neutral position. "When do you leave?"

"Tomorrow, I think." It was my turn to shake my head. "Transfer board meets in the morning. They're going to reject my request to go back to Huvu, so... who knows where I'm going next."

"No idea at all?"

"No. I think I used up all of the good luck that Khash felt like giving me already." I bit my lip for a moment. "Between being assigned to all of you, and then surviving all of this. Now, I'm... I'm getting very close to getting dismissed."

She fully winced that time. "Oh. It's that bad?"

"Two severe demerits for disobedience already." I said. "So... if I can't get my curiosity under control on my next assignment, that'll be it."

"Oh." Fyth repeated more quietly. "Damn. Ashe... you *were* right though. Don't your honors help?"

"A little. I think. I would probably be fine with more standard demerits, even more than I already have. But any severe ones..." My voice trailed off.

She glanced down at the bottle in her hands, then sighed and pushed it back to me. I took it, downing what was left.

"Did you get to see any action?" It was a blatant change of subject, but I wanted to try and enjoy my last bit of time with her.

"A disorganized brawl when a few officers tried to order the base to mobilize." Her tarah perked up a little. "The sentries blocked the armory, so it was just fists and sorcery. And there weren't that many of them."

"But you got some hits in?"

A sly smile appeared. "I may have broken the arm of a certain officer who threatened you."

I finally felt my own smile return. "You didn't."

"I did." She openly grinned. "Saw his name on his uniform when he started yelling and couldn't stop myself. Jal got a few hits in too, and then Ruru knocked him out with a Strike. Slammed him right into a doorway."

"Awesome!"

We both giggled, for a moment packmates again as she described everything else that had happened.

In all honesty it wasn't much. As far as she knew, my message had sparked some kind of chaos over in the Northshore. Some Humans had gone to arms to try and rebel again, while others had started demanding to know if their leaders were really working with the Keres or not.

When word had gotten to the base about the chaos, the Keres had tried to suppress both my message and orders from the Storm General in favor of rushing to 'suppress the rebels'. Unfortunately for them, there had been only a dozen or so officers, and most of their troops had already seen either my or the general's messages.

Chaos had erupted as conflicting orders began to spill out, at least until our Arsenal Commander had lost her temper completely.

"It was probably the hottest thing I've ever seen." Fyth said. "She beat down two Keres with her sorcery while shouting orders at the same time. Then she started screaming insults when everyone was too stunned to actually do what she wanted."

I smiled at the image. "Sounds like she got control quickly then."

"You have no idea. That was when we jumped in and caught that jerk. Our whole Arsenal assembled and rallied around her, forced everyone else to yield. By the time the Storm General herself showed up with the ready response group we'd locked the entire base down."

"You saw the General?"

She nodded eagerly. "Yeah. Tough looking Elder, had a full escort of power armor with her. She gave Commander Owri full honors on the spot, and said she'd promote her to Squall Commander as soon as this mess is done with."

That was good. The Empire needed as many good officers as it could get, and Commander Vahl'owri definitely was one.

"Sounds like it was fun."

"It was." She agreed. "We didn't get to be involved in anything else though. Kind of a shame, but at least we got some excitement in. Did your Agent friend tell you how things are going everywhere else?"

"A little. Keres are being unnamed, and all of the Human-dominant units are being disarmed pending investigations." I shrugged. "I think the Noroth and the Storm General are also going to be investigated for trying to handle things themselves instead of reporting it up the proper channels."

"You think anything will come of that?"

"Dunno." I admitted. "The Noroth might get nudged a little, and the SG will probably be transferred for not forcing a proper mingling of the species. Don't think they'll give her any real demerits since she cracked down so quickly though."

Fyth hummed, "Sounds about right. Well, hopefully that happens after Commander Owri gets her promotion. Maybe we'll get transferred with her to a better planet."

"Maybe." I felt my good cheer fade as she started to rise, stretching out her arms with a little groan. "Leaving?"

"Another amateur race today." She replied. "They had to move it to a dirt track outside of the city, which should be fun."

I stood up as well, and started to take a step forwards to hug her.

She stepped back before I could, adding another cut to my heart.

"I'm..." Fyth closed her eyes, exhaled, and shook her head. "Not yet, Ashe. This was fun, but I'm still furious with you."

"I... understand. Can... I still message you?"

"...sure, just... give me a few months to calm down, maybe."

I nodded. "I will. Bye, Fyth. Thank you for everything. Rest in safe harbors."

"Sail on calm waters, Ashe." She started to bring a hand up, froze, then sighed and walked away.

I watched her go, knowing I probably looked like a typically pathetic Human to the customers and staff. Staring down at my feet, I gave her a bit of a head start before heading to the exit as well.

If I stayed I wasn't leaving sober, and Rerth would have my head if I showed up hungover tomorrow.

Stepping outside, I had no warning before a hand grabbed my shoulder.

I spun around, jabbing a fist up to punch whoever had just grabbed me, only for Fyth to catch my wrist. I had enough time to see her glaring at me before she hauled me up against her and shoved our mouths together.

It was the most aggressive kiss I think we ever shared, and the bite she gave my lip before pulling back was definitely more angry than playful.

"Grow your fur out more." She said the moment we broke apart; me staring blankly, her tarah quivering. "It makes you look more exotic."

"I-"

She spun around without another word, and stalked off back towards the base.

I could only stare, and bring a hand up to check my lips for blood.

That was... not at all what I'd expected.

But somehow, as I started walking to yet another transfer station...

I still felt better.

Epilogue

I tossed my kit bag at the base of the stool before collapsing onto the seat. The bartender twitched his tarah in amusement, green eyes annoyingly bright and alive. "I'm not an expert on savannas, but you look like a mess. What do you need?"

"...Homeworld Hurricane."

Both tarah rose. "That bad huh? What flavor?"

"Khanna'tic." I lowered my head until it smacked onto the bar itself. The impact was too much for the tie I'd used this morning, and my still growing dark fur fell in a curtain around my eyes. "With an extra ration, please."

"You got it. Rank chit or currency?"

Grumbling, I fumbled in my uniform's pockets. Patting down a few of them let me find my rank on my lift hip, and I smacked the disc down next to my head without raising it. "There."

Fingers gently pulled it out from under my own. I heard him scan it before he pushed the thing back under my palm. "Be ready in a wave or two."

I mumbled something that a charitable man might have considered a thank you. His footsteps moved away, leaving me with nothing to listen to but the quiet chatter from the trio of sailors down at the far end. Plus the quiet muttering of the Naulian officers sitting together in the corner booth.

In a few hours this place would probably be too busy for me to tolerate, but for now it wasn't all bad.

So long as...

The stool to my left dragged on the floor, warning me that I had company even before I heard someone sit down. I had a pretty good guess as to who even before a young man spoke. "You're real fast when you want to be, you know that?"

...so long as my latest squad-mates didn't find me.

I didn't bother lifting my head, or replying at all. Not that my attitude stopped Mak from going on. "This is a nice place you found. Have you been on this station before? You sailed right for it without checking a map at all."

That's because I had been here before. Several times over the past six months in fact.

"Come on Ashe, don't leave us like this. Come talk to everyone one more time." Despite my best efforts to magically become a Vekki so I could telepathically make him go away, Mak just kept talking. "I mean, I understand why everyone's angry with you, you're like... a true, living avatar of Khahsh. You bring misfortune everywhere you go."

I wouldn't doubt it at this point.

Words kept flowing out of his mouth without any signs of slowing down. "Where did you pick up that kind of investigative training? Are you secretly an Imperial Intelligence operative? Is that why you keep getting moved from pack to pack? Ahlu says it's because you're an ungrateful alien, but I like my theory better."

By the blessed Aspects... "Mak?"

"Yeah?"

I enunciated each word to make my point clear. "Shut. Up."

The hunter sighed, a lot of the amiability dropping out of his tones. "I'm just trying to help you, Ashe. I've read your Index. You go through packs like other people go through bottles of ale. You keep this up and even the Empire is going to run out of places to put you."

Rather than respond to that, I pushed myself back to a seated position before looking to the bartender.

For once Khahsh was blessing me with good fortune rather than bad; the man was walking over with my order in his hands.

"A Khanna'tic Hurricane," He put a bright orange glass in front of me, ice cracking merrily as it began to melt. A moment later he casually poured a thin tube of neon-blue liquid into it, leaving a nice swirl in the center. "With an extra ration."

"Thanks." Taking the drink meant not talking to Mak. Sipping it meant trying to breathe through the utterly ridiculous amount of alcohol now burning through my head.

The bartender's tarah rose when I didn't choke at the first taste. "I'm not serving you another one, just so you know. I don't need your doctors or your packmates coming after me. What do you need, soldier?"

Mak stirred, "Just water. One of us should be sober."

He nodded and drifted away, leaving me to take another mouthful in the hope of actually tasting the various fruits. I did, sort of, but mostly I just had to suffer through Mak giving me a disappointed stare.

"What?" I demanded when I'd finished, finally turning to face him.

The only member of the squad who usually talked to me was a fairly handsome little man. About a foot shorter than me, wiry, with long tarah and striking emerald eyes. He drew a lot of attention when the others went out.

He'd have probably drawn some from me, if my life wasn't currently a rolling storm with no end in sight.

"I'm worried about you." He said, gray hands coming up defensively. "You're my packmate."

I scoffed. "No I'm not."

"Ashe-"

"I have no idea what's going on with my career considering how many times I've been put onto, and then pulled from units over the past few months, but I've been assigned to your unit for less than a week." I countered. "The HSL made it clear I'm not welcome, and considering I'm *already* being transferred again, I don't blame them."

His tarah lowered, expression pained. "How are you so casual about that?"

"Because-"

A woman, whose voice I'd really been hoping not to hear until I'd finished my drink, interrupted me, "Because the Empire has failed her, and as a result she is bitter, adrift, and in pain."

My jaw clenched, one leg kicking to turn my stool around. Mak followed suit after a beat, letting us both see the new arrival. Agent Rerth'riah was standing just behind us, tarah raised up.

"Did I strike true with that harpoon?" She asked, casually drifting a few steps closer.

I glared at her. "Rerth. I'm not any happier to see you."

Sky blue eyes narrowed dangerously, voice rising to a snap. "Your tone, Rifle-Experienced Lori."

Anger warred several other feelings. Sliding off my stool, I brought myself up to my full height. My best salute came with her actual rank, "Apologies, Agent Rerth'riah."

Rerth's piercing stare was ruined by Mak muttering, "Knew it."

The young man flinched when her focus locked on to him. Her right tarah flexing outwards was probably enough, but she added the verbal order.

"Rifleman Mak'col. Return to your packmates and inform them that Ashe'lori has completed her transfer. Half-Squad Leader Ahlu'col should receive the appropriate files within the day."

Getting to his own feet, Mak gave a silent salute of his own, followed it up with a pitying look in my direction... and then slipped out of the bar.

I was about to turn back to my drink when Rerth beckoned, "Leave it. With me, so we can discuss what you're doing here. *Sober,* this time as well."

Her words drew a flinch from me. I could feel the eyes of everyone in the place staring at my back as I picked up my bag, and then followed us as I walked out after her.

Trailing after the Agent, I kept a few yards back as she led me through the station. It didn't take us very long to get to an unmarked doorway on the main run. She opened it with a wave of her wrist-comp, entering into the small office on the other side.

Following her in, I found myself in a pretty typical Imperial Intelligence office. A plain desk with no fewer than three holographic displays, two chairs, and nearly every inch of the walls was covered in screens.

Another wave of her arm shut them all down before I could see anything classified, with motion number three telling me to sit.

"How did I do?" I asked, far more polite than I'd been at the bar.

She dropped the angry expression as she sat as well. "About as well as I could have expected."

I sighed and dropped my bag beside me. "That bad?"

"No, you're actually improving at both following orders and acting the part. The near disobedience in the bar was a nice touch." Rerth gave me a rare smile before it quickly faded. "It's more irritating that no one has attempted to grasp the bait yet. Your involvement in Oshflara's events is well known, I've made sure of it. Someone should have confronted you on at least one of your assignments."

"You're sure that those colonies were where the Keres were smuggling things to?"

She gave me a flat look. "Ashe."

I grimaced. "Right, sorry. An Imperial Agent is certain of nothing until it is factually proven."

"At least you can remember that much." My latest *real* packmate sighed.

I hadn't been surprised to find out that she'd rigged the transfer board on Oshflara to do exactly what she wanted with me.

I *had* been completely stunned when that turned out to be assigning me to her personal unit. When she'd told me that if I was going to pretend to be a spy, she would at least make an honest effort to train me up enough that an Academy would accept me.

Until then, I was her pack's decoy, thug, servant, or whatever else they needed for their mission.

It wasn't as nice as ending up on Huvu's squad... but it was better than anything I'd dared hope for. It gave me a real chance to do exactly what I wanted with my life.

Even knowing that I was one severe demerit away from a punishment discharge didn't stop me from doing my best.

"This is becoming aggravating all the same. Smuggling rings are usually not this adept at avoiding detection, or so self-controlled as to resist finding out why their source ceased operations." Her head shook, some of the irritation coming back. "And the others still have no leads on your burned priestess in disguise."

Which was why I'd been bouncing wildly between different units over the past few months. Why I'd made sure to go around blatantly looking for trouble on each colony I ended up on.

After all, the stupidly confident, alone Human was such a stereotypical look that no one noticed the Agent trailing after me the entire time.

Well, everyone except my latest squad.

"I don't know how often we can do this again." I said. "Mak figured it out, and he's not the smartest fish in the sea. If you assign me to another squad on a short little run it's going to get even more obvious."

Rerth grimaced. "True enough, unfortunately. We've probably been too aggressive with how many units I've rotated you through. We'll have to change our approach."

"What's the plan?"

"I think it's time you finally met the rest of my pack." She grinned when I perked up. I knew she, well, we, had two other packmates, but I hadn't been able to meet them in person yet.

"After that... there's a certain murderer I think we need to meet with.

Hopefully she'll talk to us instead of killing us."

"A..." My mouth opened, then closed. "What?"

"A murderer." She repeated, clearly enjoying my stunned confusion. "Welcome to Imperial Intelligence, Ashe'lori. You have no idea what you have signed up for."

I probably didn't. No, I definitely didn't.

But that didn't stop me from being excited all the same.

- *Zulflara* – The Homeworld
  - **Home Region**
  - **Population**: 5.8 billion
  - **Rating**: A0
  - The cultural and societal heart of the Empire of the Homeworld, Zulflara has never-the-less been largely surpassed by other worlds in terms of population and economy. As much as they revere the world they came from, few admit to enjoying its climate or limited spaces.

- *Gathahn*
  - **Capital Region**
  - **Population**: 11 billion
  - **Rating**: Ah0
  - The modern capital of the Empire, Gathahn is a considered a paradise world for the fact that most of its landmass sits comfortably in temperate zones, the ease at which crops could be introduced, and a relative lack of hostile wildlife compared to the homeworld. Both the Torlah and Imperial Circle reside on its surface, and all of the Imperial-wide Delne'lir ensure they have offices there.

- *Altair*
  - **Spinward Region**
  - **Population**: 9 billion Trahcon
  - **Rating**: Ah0
  - Not quite as universally beautiful as Gathan or Abantia, yet not as unwelcoming as Icar or Zulflara, Altair is a fairly typical garden world with scattered continents, variable climates, and plenty of raw materials. Most known for being the 'dumping ground' for a great many aliens absorbed into the Empire, with sizable Human, Naulian, and Meshicon minorities.

- *Iklahviah*
  - **Rimward Region**
  - **Population**: 7.8 billion
  - **Rating**: Ah1

- An oceanic world slightly too warm for Trahcon tastes, but still habitable and ideal for the farming of various seafoods. Notable for having a species of whale-like beings believed to sapient, they pathologically avoid the Trahcon colonists who in turn do not do more than passively observe them.

- *Icar*
  - **Storm Region**
  - **Population**: 8 billion
  - **Rating**: A0
  - One of the more 'homeland' style garden worlds that the Trahcon have colonized, Icar shares Zulflara's vicious weather but forgoes the equally nasty wildlife. The end result is a series of heavily battered arcologies and cities to go along with sheltered valleys and numerous undersea fish farms.

- *Shaidan*
  - **Near Reach Territories**
  - **Population**: 5.2 billion Naule, 1.1 billion Trahcon
  - **Rating**: A2
  - The homeworld of the Naulian people, conquered by the Empire several centuries ago. Despite now being a fairly quiet and loyal world, the stigma of the old kingdom's brutal religion and the actions of individual Naule in the Reaches in general continues to cast a shadow over the system. Despite several waves of forced emigration, in the modern times the population has recovered to pre-invasion levels with the addition of numerous Trahcon colonists.

- *Earth*
  - **Near Reach Territories**
  - **Population**: 4.9 billion Human, 200 million Trahcon
  - **Rating**: Y5
  - Humanity's homeworld is in poor ecological, economical, and cultural shape. Whatever recovery that began after the arrival of the Xenthan Ark Fleet was obliterated by the Imperial invasion. Much of the planet remains in low-level rebellion or in outright anarchy, those parts of it that are fit for habitation at least. Continued forced-emigration programs are at work, with the resentful population in steady decline.

Appendix B: The Imperial Military

The Imperial Armed Forces are massive, fueled by the universal conscription of every Trahcon within the Empire on sixty year stints, and aliens shorter terms proportional to their lifespans.

While the great majority of this force is dedicated to the logistical and support work required to operate mass fleets and armies at the interstellar level, or are stuck on garrison duty on various colonial worlds, there still leaves hundreds of millions free to fight on the front lines.

It this that focus on supplies and logistics that makes the Imperials an enduring foe against their rivals. More than any other state they can deploy, supply, and maintain far reaching operations well beyond their borders. This is a military organization that routinely deals with numbers that would stagger smaller powers, and even their more equivalent rivals.

While the supporting structure and army receive the bulk of the manpower, the navy receives the bulk of the budget in order to maintain the second largest fleet among the Compact Nations; only the Federation field more ships, though the Imperials almost universally field larger individual vessels.

Conscripts

The vast majority of the Imperial Armed Forces are made up of conscripts. Despite this, only a tiny fraction of these individuals ever actually see combat. The vast majority of these are those lucky enough to be drafted into the Imperial Navy, where as most Army conscripts handle garrison and support work.

Wind Formations

The 'professional' Army units are designated as Wind Formations. Made up of those who have completed their terms of conscription and elected to remain within the military, it is not uncommon to find units with decades to centuries of combat experience.

Unit Organizations

- **Sword Pack**: 16 Trahcon, led by a Sword Leader or Veteran. Usually composed of 10 'riflemen', two light or heavy machine guns, and then one anti-vehicle team. Often divided into two 'Half-Sword' teams.
- **Demi-Pack**: Two Sword Packs, commanded by a Dual-Commander, with at least one medical support pack attached.
- **Arsenal Formation:** Eight Sword Packs, commanded by Arsenal Commanders, with anywhere from two to four additional Sword-Packs attached in supporting roles (Artillery, Reconnaissance, etc).
- **Squall Formation:** Eight Arsenals, with up to four additional units attached in supporting roles.
- **Storm Formation**: The rough Imperial equivalent to a 'Division', a Storm Formation will consist of eight to twelve Squall Formations.
- **Army:** Any force of multiple Storm Formations will be referred to as an Army, with the only cap being that there should not be more than sixteen Storms attached.
- **Army Formation:** Multiple armies under a single, unified command. This is generally held as the highest 'official' collection of forces intended to operate together tactically, and will rarely exceed four Armies.

Army Rotation

Imperial Army units operate on a four-tier rotation during peace-time to vary the duties of any given unit. The size of the units on each 'cycle' differ depending upon the numbers and composition assigned to a world, as well as the requirements of the colony in question

- **Ah Cycle:** Units will be assigned to active training operations, long-range patrols, or colonial exploration missions.
- **Ae Cycle:** Assigned to direct protection of colonial settlements. Often operating from fortifications, while conducting patrols within and around cities/villages/settlements.
- **Bey Cycle:** Formations assigned in combat reserve, and for rear-area defense. These units occupy sentry duties, military police, and other back-line but armed roles.
- **Del Cycle:** The logistical and support cycle, as well as the rest and refit one. Formations will move supplies, repair equipment, and assist in entrenchment when called upon.

About the Author

Zach Watson is a fairly hopeless nerd who spends too much time painting little miniatures and studying history. He lives in an old house in Wisconsin with his wife, their loyal dog, and a feline who knows that she is royalty.